THE COLLECTOR'S LAST CANVAS

CHRIS CORBETT

Grove Publishing
Bleulerstrasse 7
Zürich 8008
Switzerland

www.grove-publishing.com

Copyright © Chris Corbett 2025

All rights reserved. No part of this publication may be reproduced, stored in a retrieval system, or transmitted in any form or by any means electronic, mechanical, photocopying, recording, or otherwise, without the prior permission of both the copyright owner and the publisher of this book.
This book is a work of fiction. The names, characters, and incidents are drawn from the authors imagination. Any resemblance to actual events or persons, living or dead, is entirely coincidental.

ONE

Getting into the private club was a challenge, more difficult than a foreigner breaking into the notoriously close-knit society in Zürich or one of their banks. It was all a matter of how much Vitamin B you had: *beziehungen* – connections. John Miller smoothed his jacket lapels and shot his cuffs to look respectable and worthy of admission. He was standing with his work colleague, a lawyer named David, outside the entrance of an elite disco called the Diagonal. He hoped being in the presence of an obvious player from the banking crowd would be his ticket to getting in. The members-only club was where a lot of the high rollers, models, yuppies and the idle rich from the Gold Coast went to be among their own. The 'Digi' was attached to one of the most exclusive hotels in Zürich, the Baur Au Lac, that had hosted kings and kaisers along with Sophia Loren and Brigitte Bardot. Now the guests were oligarchs and sheiks from the Middle East, chauffeured in discrete black Mercedes.

Watching the infrequent groups of stylish people coming and going John said, "What a scene. I wonder if any of these people are famous?"

"Legends in their own minds."

"I hope we get in tonight. I have a client who'll pay me for taking a photo of a V.I.P. who's inside. I need the money for my alimony payments," John said.

"Been there, done that. All my exes live in Texas."

"Getting a good shot will help build my rep as a commercial photographer. With the big re-org at our bank, you never know when you'll need a Plan B."

"I've already got a Plan C and D."

"I'm still on Plan A. For your information, my patron tonight is Diana Reichenberg, the infamous Princess Dianamite. Wild socialite turned philanthropist."

"Now you're talking. She's a total bombshell. This makes you a gigolo charity case."

"A photo pimp. She's been generous for work I've done for her environmental foundation. This job has something to do with supporting her brother. He was Germany's answer to Greta Thunberg, but died too young in the line of duty."

"I heard about that guy."

"It also never hurts to keep an important patron happy, especially when they're a millionaire many times over. She's got something most of the others lack – a moral conscience."

"I'll believe it when I see it."

"Don't worry, you'll be the first to find out when she does her next green campaign."

"I'm still not buying a Tesla."

"Anyway, it's a change from my usual freelance jobs at low level weddings."

"I'll be sure to call you when I get hitched."

"This paparazzi stuff is only temporary. I'm trying to build an on-line following with my stylized urban imagery to help get commercial gigs."

"You're better off being a photographer for some big name influencer."

. . .

The two young men waited by the entrance in front of an old villa, standing behind a fat red velvet rope strung between polished brass pillars to keep the eventual masses in line. They watched the crowd for any possible chance to get in. John felt conspicuous with his sports coat and cotton twill pants, contrasting the somber gray suit of his colleague and trendy evening wear of the club goers who passed by. Being a Friday, he was in 'business casual' because working in the marketing department of a large bank meant he was a creative type who didn't have to dress like a banker or wear a tie.

"I thought you were a member so you could entertain all your bigshot clients," John said.

"That was when I worked at the hedge fund. Now times are tough and memberships are a luxury." David made another trip to the young woman guarding the door, trying to talk his way in, and was again unsuccessful. Rules were rules, especially in Switzerland. The club's attitude was those who deserved to be inside, were inside. As he re-emerged, he looked past John with a big grin.

"All right," David said like he was welcoming home a war hero. "My main man." A perfectly groomed Asian in a cream-colored silk suit was approaching. He obviously had a membership. David said, "Let's go. The first round is on me."

The two of them breezed through the reception attached to the young man who promptly disappeared into a side room without inviting them.

Surveying the half empty club David said, "I guess we're early."

"That, and it's still school holiday time. A lot of people are gone for the summer," John said.

"Look, there's the crew," David said, pointing to some other suits. He headed off to where the group were sitting in an enclosed area with smoky glass walls separating it from the dance floor. At the sight of David, the men cheered, asking if he was going to buy the first bottle of vodka.

John joined them and looking around said, "Nice view." He was grinning at the spectacle of a number of ever-hopeful pretty young ladies, standing around in groups of two or three talking to each other.

"Unbelievable," David said, also scanning the guests. Some of them were Russians in garish Versace and dazzling bling, each skinny as a model with varying shades of blonde hair and endless legs. "All these babes and no one asking them to dance. My wife would kill me if I even looked at something like that."

"Tell me those aren't five hundred francs an hour professionals we're looking at."

"They're not. Mostly career women or daughters of the well to do looking to mingle with people from their own class. The rest are posers."

"They want to be mistaken for the best friend of one of the Kardashians."

"Those skinny *blondinos* from Eastern Europe knocking down the vodka tonics by the DJ are the ones you pay for. That's if they're not some dictator's daughter trying to get a second passport from some gullible schmuck like you."

John said, "Think I'll wander around and take some shots. Maybe I can sell them to *Zürich Life*. They're always interested in pictures of the rich and famous."

"Good luck. None of them left now that Tina's not around anymore."

"So sad. I always wanted to hear her sing 'Steamy Windows'."

. . .

The electronic dance music hammered out a steady beat that filled every corner of the club but only a few couples were dancing. Someone a few drinks along would sporadically call out for a song by Beyoncé or one of the older crowd requesting Earth, Wind and Fire. John bought an overpriced local beer at the bar that was the same cost as a 12-pack at the supermarket. He took a few minutes to patrol the club, checking if he could find the intended subject of his assignment. He spotted his target in a secluded booth with large framed photographs of old Hollywood stars like Clark Gable decorating the walls behind it. John didn't recognize the face or know the man's name, as he had only been supplied a description. John's strategy was to gradually work his way towards the man without him suspecting John's intention. He took the last swallow of beer and put the empty bottle on the bar. John approached a group of poor little rich kids posing by the disk jockey.

"Can you all say cheese, please? Swiss cheese. That's right, let's see some teeth." The flash popped, freezing some smiles, misdirected looks and unhappy stares. The group was young and unsure how to react to him. Maybe they'd be lucky and he was a nightlife photographer putting their picture on a party website they could share on Instagram.

After a few more shots along the dance floor, John approached the man he was after who was seated in the middle of a group at a low table. John kept his camera hidden under his arm to avoid scaring his intended prey away. There were three men in their early fifties and two young blonde women wearing little outfits that cost a big amount of money. Probably some private bank scene, he thought. The man who exactly matched the description he'd been given was wearing an elegant dark suit and maroon tie. The two others were Middle Eastern with colorful suits, bright shirts in loud tropical hues and no ties. The flamboyant men had a stone-cold demeanor and wouldn't have blinked if someone were killed on the dance floor. The women looked like professional escorts and started laughing at something the man in the suit was saying, putting on charming expressions.

John had been hesitant to take a picture earlier because the initial look the intended subject gave John when he first spotted him had a dispassionate sub-zero chill. It had made John think twice about taking a photo. Something in the icy stare that was backed-up by two companions who looked like violence and slow death were their favorite activities, compounded the effect. Noticing they had finished their drinks and no refills in sight made John think they would leave soon. There was a silver champagne bucket in the middle of the table with an empty, upturned magnum of Cristal in it that John knew from the bar card cost a shade under 6,000 francs. He took a deep breath and decided to take the picture, approaching from the side so as not to startle them. As he passed slowly in front of the group, John turned the lens to face them, the camera at his side. He had preset the focus and the flash went off as he paused for a split second and pressed the shutter release. The man in the suit froze in mid-sentence and turned to look at John. One of the other men sprang up from his chair and came towards John with a menacing look.

"Hey, sorry. I didn't know it was loaded. What're you doing?" John said as the colorfully dressed man grabbed his upper arm. He tried pulling his arm back but the grip was too tight. John was close enough that he could smell cheap cologne mixed with acrid sweat.

"Who do you work for?" the seated man asked bluntly and leaned forward, putting his elbows on the table to add weight to his words. His rumbling voice found its way through the disco music. It resonated in a way that made John feel like he had another hand on him, squeezing his throat like Darth Vader finding an intruder on the Death Star. John was surprised to hear a mild Brooklyn accent. The man had the rough good looks of a Robert De Niro but with a hard, world weary edge. He had what people called character but his tone and expression were compassionless and ice-cold.

"Can you please tell your friend to let go?"

"OK," the man said, nodding at the tropical suit, who released his grip and sat back down, without taking his eyes off John.

"Thanks. I ugh, work for the *Blick*." John paused to catch his breath which was constricted from the momentary burst of adrenaline. After taking a deep breath, he continued. "You know, the colorful daily with the nice page three girls."

"Very funny Mr. Photographer. Why don't you just let my friend delete the photo? Or better yet, hand over the memory card in case there are others and then we can all get back to enjoying ourselves."

"Don't worry, it's probably out of focus anyway. I'll take a look and if it's any good, I'd be glad to send you some prints at no cost."

David was next to him now, having seen the commotion and wanting in on any possible action. "What seems to be the problem?" he asked in an authoritative fake British accent, his bulk giving emphasis to his words.

"Your young friend has taken a photograph of me, a private person in a private club, without my permission. And I want the memory card with any possible pictures." The man spoke with a flat tone to indicate there would be no discussion about his request. The looks of his two colleagues echoed the words with an expression that said 'not open to debate'.

"As his legal counsel, I have to advise my client against such action. It would not be in his best interest to comply with your unreasonable request." David was visibly drunk, so his radar wasn't picking up the warning signals. He was leaning alternately left and right, steadying himself on the edge of the DJ booth. The young man with spiky hair spinning tunes gave him the evil eye to signal David not to make his record skip.

The American man cut him off. "Great," he said. "A couple of morons. One guy thinks he's Richard Fucking Avedon and the other idiot wishes he was F. Lee Bailey."

"Look, sir, that kind of slanderous language comparing my client to a, a..." David faltered, raised his voice an octave, and then continued with emphasis "a cheap opportunist is grounds for a lawsuit. Need I—" The speech might have continued all night if the club's manager hadn't stepped in, interrupting it. The middle-aged man was dressed in a black tuxedo, radiating elegance. He acted with calm authority, intervening before anyone knew he was there.

"Gentlemen, may I be of assistance?" His tone was the perfect balance between a professional bouncer and a diplomat.

"This clown took a photo of me without my permission. I just want the pictures." The businessman stared at the manager with an unblinking gaze that said 'deal with it'.

The manager turned to look John over, sizing up his casual jacket and slacks. He spoke with a noticeable Swiss-German accent. "I'm sorry, but the gentleman is correct. The club policy states that there is strictly no photo taking allowed without prior management permission."

David stepped in and looked the manager squarely in the face. "There's no posted notices advising against photographs being taken, and we signed no binding agreement to that effect when we entered. There were no stated terms and conditions on our entrance and use of the facilities. This is indeed a private institution but—"

The man in the suit cut him off with his New York flavored English. "All right, wise guy, here's two hundred francs for the photos. Go buy a round for your pals." He reached into a pocket inside his jacket, extracting a fat wad of folded money two fingers thick, with a thousand-franc bill on the outside. He started to peel a couple of hundreds from the center of the stack.

"I'm sorry but my client can't be bought."

"I heard enough." The man put his pile of money away and was standing now, his words signaling the end of the discussion. He was shorter than John had imagined. "I see it's going to take a Supreme Court ruling to clear this shit up, so forget the whole thing." He paused for a second to look at John with a look that threatened to suck the oxygen out of his lungs. "Come on, girls," the man said in a businesslike tone as he turned, offering a hand. After they carefully stood on their high heels trying not to expose any more than their short skirts already revealed, the man turned to David.

"Fine speech, professor, you must be thirsty." He stuffed two one hundred-franc notes into the handkerchief pocket of David's coat as he walked around him, the women close behind. The two swarthy associates started to follow, and the one that had grabbed John scanned him, memorizing his face.

"Real nice guy," David said, proud of his victory as the group made their way to the exit.

John said, "Yeah, you're probably right about that but let's not spoil the party." He reached over and extracted the bills from David's pocket, handing them to the surprised manager. "How about another round for my friends – and keep the change." The man's face hardened and he folded the money and walked stiffly to the bar. "What you got to do to have a little excitement, eh?" John said in mock boredom, as they both started to laugh.

. . .

John excused himself early, while the merrymaking in the private club was in full swing. He was sure if he was still there in an hour he'd have to buy a round for the bankers he'd been sitting with. He still needed to make it through the weekend with his limited finances. Zürich routinely ranked in the top five of the world's most expensive cities, which made life costly for expats like himself, hired with a local salary and paying tax in two countries. He climbed the stairs from the basement of the villa with a satisfied grin – his mission was accomplished. John stepped into the still warm summer night, walking past a long line of revelers in their party finery waiting to get inside. Between 2am and 3am were the best times to be in the club. The party people were chatting among themselves in small groups, scrutinizing anyone exiting to see if they were cooler. None of the people paid John much attention. A couple of young model types ahead of him in tall heels and glittery short skirts were also leaving, making a show for the line of guests, sashaying along. He remembered the party rule: all the best-looking girls leave first to go to the next party. The two ladies laughed at some private joke, falling on each other as they made their way to a waiting taxi.

John strolled along the walkway that traversed the side of the parking lot, leading to the street where he'd parked. The scent of honeysuckle on a light breeze coming from the villa's garden distracted him from the traffic noise on the Quaibrücke, where it crossed the river on the other side of a tall hedge. He heard a shoe scrape on the sidewalk behind him and started to turn. He thought it was some other guests wanting to pass him, but strong hands clamped his upper arms. Before he could shout for help he was pushed sideways, stumbling headfirst into the thick coniferous hedge, instinctively raising one arm to protect his face. Branches scratched his hand and caught in his clothes and hair. John gasped and sucked in dust and the smell of decaying vegetation while someone held his shoulders as his camera bag was pulled away. Then he was wrenched upwards by his jacket collar, his head held in place from the fabric bunched around it, so he couldn't turn and see the attacker. Before John could react, he was punched squarely in the side of the head and heaved deep into the bushes, as brittle twigs pulled on his hair and cracked in his ears.

John backed out of the foliage after a moment, sensing the attack was over. As he pulled himself free from the branches that snagged his jacket, he heard the squeal of tires from a side street and the growl of a powerful engine fading around a corner. John leaned on a nearby parked car to catch his breath. He rubbed the side of his head where a bump was forming. John felt like a victim and was angry his camera had been snatched away. The mixed emotions gave way to a sense of being abused and feeling sorry for himself. He was bitter for being another example of the poor getting poorer while the rich got richer. John was sure it was the businessman in the club behind the mugging because he still had his wallet and phone. It made John hate the powerful moneyed establishment that took what they wanted, when they wanted. His mind spun with visions of revenge as the last threads of adrenaline tickled his fight or flight instincts. But remembering the subject's companions, made the fight option soon forgotten as a goal. He could only muster an angry swear word in exasperation, spitting it out on the ground.

John dug out his mobile phone from an inside jacket pocket to call the police so he could at least have a report for the insurance company. He fumbled with the keypad with shaking hands that signaled the shock and adrenaline rush from the attack. He shook his head ruefully, wondering how a simple photo assignment had turned into a nightmare, intensely curious why his patron wanted a photo of this particular individual. While he waited for the police, John searched his jacket pulling out the various business cards he'd picked up during an earlier cocktail party where he'd been taking photos. John was surprised when he found the camera's original memory card he'd replaced in the club when it was full at the end of the night. Maybe he could get paid after all.

TWO

The news of her brother's death had been relayed to Diana Reichenberg a few months earlier by the German embassy in Zimberia. She was sure the cause wasn't an accident as reported and immediately flew to Africa to find out the exact circumstances. She knew from the initiatives her ecological foundation sponsored, how treacherous the work was for environmental activists. Every other day, one was killed somewhere around the world, with their deaths mostly going unpunished because of the big money in commodities. It didn't help that her brother had a bad habit of easily annoying any polluters he was investigating. Because of her family's background in steel production, she could arrange a meeting with the minister of the interior on the day after her arrival. The middle-aged African man with a touch of gray on his temples wore a perfectly ironed white shirt with a regimental tie. He personified a typical bureaucrat – self-important and greasy as an oil spill. Misogyny was his middle name. He had an impressive office for an impoverished country and sat behind his massive oak desk, calmly sipping a tea while listening to Diana's story. He hadn't offered her any refreshment in spite of the heat and lack of air conditioning.

"As I informed you in my email, we did a most thorough investigation. It was evident your brother was a bit of an adventurer, going off the trail like he did. All the young people today want to have the perfect picture for social media and some take one step too many. It's tragic."

"My brother wasn't the risk-taking type. He also was not a poser."

"I'm sorry. I don't know what to tell you. He was at a popular lookout point and it can be a very treacherous location. There were no witnesses to his fall, so we can only conclude it was a misadventure."

"He wasn't here on a vacation. He was documenting the mining activities that are destroying your pristine jungle."

"I know nothing about that. All commercial activities of which you imply are highly regulated and strictly observe our environmental regulations."

"I'm not here to debate how money influences your decision making. I just want to know the truth about my brother." Diana knew she was running in circles talking to the stuffed shirt. She'd met enough hucksters and schemers to know an intelligent conversation would never happen.

"I have told you what I know. Now if you'll excuse me, I have some urgent issues I must address."

"Yes, I can see that lowering your golf handicap certainly counts as a priority for your country." Diana stood up to leave. "Thank you for your time."

The man had already turned to his computer screen and waved a curt goodbye over his shoulder. Diana restrained herself from reaching over the desk and throwing the cup of tea on his head. She left for her next meeting with a local representative of a small conservation group that'd been documenting the mining activities her brother was looking to publicize.

Diana wanted to move incognito and couldn't help but

notice that she was being followed. A bored looking young man in a worn-out polo shirt had been waiting in the lobby of her hotel that morning and now he was reading a newspaper on a bus bench outside the government offices. He'd periodically look up from his reading, hoping his oversized sunglasses would mask his interest in her. She chose the direct approach. Diana took out her mobile phone and opened the camera while she walked towards the man. He was paralyzed by her bold approach and tried to hide behind the paper.

She stood squarely in front of him. "Hey, you." The man ignored her so she grabbed the top of the paper and pulled it away, throwing it on the ground. Her stalker was momentarily confused and, standing up, began to walk away. But not before Diana had taken a reasonably good photo of his face. She hiked a few blocks to avoid any other tails and found a taxi to take her to the rendezvous. Diana paid the driver and got out a few streets away from her destination and walked the remaining distance, sure now she wasn't being followed.

The young African woman her brother had been working with was sitting at a small table in the back of a local café, in a quiet neighborhood on the outskirts of the downtown area. She was dressed like a business woman in crisp blue blouse and neatly creased slacks in spite of the location having a target audience of working-class locals. Diana knew from an earlier call that the lady worked as a secretary in a large bank, which explained her outfit.

"Hi, are you Arya?" Diana said.

"Yes, I am. And you must be Diana. Please have a seat. Can I get you a drink?"

"A tea would be lovely." Diana pulled out a plastic chair from the ancient wooden table that looked like it was on its last legs and sat down. Arya returned from the serving counter with a mug of hot water and a tea bag floating in it.

"Thanks so much. And thank you for meeting with me. I know after my brother's death it must be an uncertain time for you."

"I'm so sorry about what happened. You have my sincerest condolences."

"You're most kind. A lot of people besides his family miss him."

"He was a good man and treated everyone fairly."

"Thank you. If you can, could you please tell me what he was doing here?"

"Yes, of course. Most of the time he was trying to gather information about one particular mining company called Ora Monte. He not only took photos of their operations but went digging in official records. My team were able to direct him where to search. The more he investigated, the greater his anger."

"What made him so mad?"

"I think it was the scale of the destruction without any regard for the environment. Then he uncovered what looked like illegal payments or what you call bribes. It was paid to government officials to look the other way."

"I think I met one of those today. The interior minister."

"Yes, he has blood on his hands."

"Why do you say that? Is he responsible for my brother's death?"

"I'm not sure about that. But I do know several local tribesmen who tried to challenge their acreage being bulldozed were brutally murdered. The other natives saw it as a warning and kept silent while the land where they hunted and grew crops was destroyed. No amount of requests for government help could get any support."

"Who do you think was behind this?"

"We're fairly certain it was the mining company's goons

behind the killings. They made threats earlier when we were protesting in front of their main mine."

"Sounds like standard operating procedure for these outfits. Do you think it's possible to visit the place where he died?"

"I will take you there but you'll need sturdy shoes. It's a bit of a trek."

"Can we stop at a sporting goods shop on the way?"

"I know just the one."

An hour and half later they were at the entrance to a national park and paid an entry fee to a man wearing a khaki shirt sitting in a small wooden hut along the road. Arya parked her car in a dirt parking lot one mile from the gate. It was surrounded by lush green forest, with signs indicating a trail going up into the mountains. There were no other cars parked there, only a beat-up aluminum camping trailer hitched up to an ancient Toyota 4x4. They parked on the other side of the lot to not disturb any possible tenants or else running the risk of being bothered by them. The two women looked overdressed for hikers, with each wearing a pair of slacks over their hiking boots. Diana had also purchased T-shirts for them that they swapped for their blouses behind the car as it was humid and hot in the afternoon sun. Arya led the way up a winding trail that followed a small stream and the hillside grew steeper the higher they went. After about forty-five minutes they reached a scenic viewpoint on a high promontory. It was a large, flat dirt area surrounded by a low wooden fence with an unobstructed 360-degree view of the surrounding countryside that looked like a field of mountain tops.

"What an amazing view," Diana said.

"Yes, we're so lucky to live on such a magnificent planet."

"Do you know where this so-called accident happened?"

Arya walked over to one of the low fences that had about ten feet of open space on the other side, before it fell steeply away over a rocky cliff. "This is the area directly above where they found the body."

Diana fought back tears as the reality of her brother's death became more final. "They actually believe he climbed over the fence to take a photo from the edge of the cliff? He's not stupid or daring. There's no way it could've been an accident."

After sitting on a low flat rock in a respectful silence for a few minutes, the two women started their descent. When they arrived back at the parking lot there was a pick-up truck parked on one side of the dirt field with two men in it. Arya pointed out a faded logo on the side spelling out Ora Monte, the mining company she'd been investigating. The men got out of the truck and started to walk towards the women, cutting them off from reaching their car. Diana recognized one of them as the man that'd been following her.

"Do you have your phone with you? We need to call for some help," Diana said.

"There's a very weak signal but I'll try," Arya said, pulling out her phone.

Before she could dial, the door of the broken-down trailer in the corner of the parking area swung open, banging against the outside wall. A tall black man with a large afro stepped out, dressed in only a pair of faded blue cotton shorts. He was carrying a pump action shotgun in one hand with his finger already inside the trigger guard. The two men from the truck paused to look at him, sizing up the threat.

"You best leave the same way you come," the trailer man shouted. He swung the shotgun up, leveling it at the men. They responded with a cold-eyed stare and slowly turned around, getting in their truck and driving off.

"Oh my god," Diana said, catching her breath, shook up from the threat of impending violence.

"How are you, sister?" the man called to Arya as he came a little closer.

Arya let out the air she had been holding in and exhaled. "I'm OK now. You're my guardian angel."

The man had lowered his gun as the dust from the departing truck had settled. Diana thought with his round cheeks and fuzzy hair he looked like a cuddly Ewok from a *Star Wars* movie. "Sorry to scare you like that. My name is Henry."

"Thanks, Henry, I really thought we were in trouble. I'm Arya and this is Diana."

"What are two well-dressed ladies doing out here in the bush? Even without those criminals around, this is a dangerous place."

"I'm here investigating the death of my brother. His body was found at the bottom of the lookout point."

"That was a tragedy to be sure. I'm so sorry for you. I heard he'd been doing some good work."

"Why'd you call those men criminals," Diana said.

"I was camping here and saw the two of them with a young man the day the body was discovered. I could see they weren't the hiking type and the other man looked like he was being forced to go with them."

"I don't believe this. Why didn't you tell the police?"

"Oh, believe me I did, ma'am. It didn't look right at all. Three go up and only two come back. I was the one who found the body. When I told the police about the men in the truck, they said I must've been hallucinating. Said I'd been drinking too much and was looking to make trouble."

"Were you drinking?" Arya said. Now that Henry was closer, the women could see his eyes were seriously bloodshot and the pupils a faint yellow, indicating a heavy drinker. It wouldn't be a surprise if he was drunk the day of the death.

"I must confess I was. It's how I find relief. I know what I saw and I always speak the truth as I see it."

"We're not judging you," Diana said.

"You're most kind."

"I think we better leave while it's still light," Arya said.

"I wish I could offer you more information," Henry said.

"You've been more than helpful. I'm going to look a little deeper into this mining company."

"They're dirty. Was they that forced me off my land."

"That's outrageous. If I can help in any way, please let me know." Diana got out her wallet and started to extract some money. "I'd like to thank you."

"Please put that away. This is not about money." Diana looked him in the eye for a second and put the purse back in her shoulder bag.

"If you find out anything more, I'd be happy to hear from you. You can contact me even if you have no further information." She dug out a business card and handed it to the man.

"Much obliged." He looked at the card a second. "Earth Goddess Foundation. You two are like little angels."

"You're generous with your compliments," Diana said.

"And here's how to reach me. I'm based here so you can easily find me," Arya said as she handed the man one of her cards.

They said their goodbyes and the women drove off. After a minute Diana said, "Do you think the man is believable? How do we know he didn't rob my brother and kill him to cover the crime?"

"I didn't feel he was that type. He's just one more of our displaced population."

"He did save us from those men from the mining company."

"That was very strange. How did they find us?"

"Most likely the ranger informed them after we entered the park. Or maybe they knew I was meeting you and had you followed. We're talking about someone with major resources."

Diana spent the next day at the public records office but had little success in finding any incriminating details. There were shell companies inside of other offshore companies with anonymous owners behind the mining company. A trip to the local newspaper was equally fruitless so she prepared to head back to Switzerland. As she was answering some emails from her hotel room she got a text message from Arya to call her.

"Henry's dead."

"What?"

"They found his off roader at the bottom of a ravine. Police blamed it on drunk driving."

There was stunned silence as Diana processed the news. "Oh my god, I can't believe this is happening. It's like the worst nightmare imaginable." Her grief came in the form of some tears and a feeling of anger wasn't far behind. "These bastards have to pay. I can't hear about another crime again."

There was another moment's silence before Arya spoke. She was afraid and sad to deliver the next message. "The other members of my little team voted we take a timeout in our activities. Some of them have families and are worried after the two killings."

"I completely understand. We don't want anyone else getting harmed. I'll keep pursuing this when I get home. Your help and kindness have been most appreciated."

"I'm sorry, I wish I could've helped more."

"You've already done so much. I'll stay in touch."

"Please do, and safe journey."

. . .

Diana did some more research when she got home from Zimberia but the trail had gone cold, and it hadn't even been warm to start with. She'd almost given up, when one day a month later, Diana was looking at the financial details of a company that'd bought a large number of shares in her family's steel business. She'd asked one of her financial team to do some research to make sure there were no criminals or sanctioned people buying into her company. The standard due diligence report revealed a large network of interconnected companies with various off-shore registrations. It wasn't an unusual structure in today's business world. The list was long and she was almost at the end when she stopped scanning the document. Her heart skipped a beat when she saw the name of the African mining company her brother had been investigating. Diana went back to the top of the report and the details of the parent company. The owner was an American named Stan Buck, a financial fugitive legally hiding in Switzerland, in a tax haven thirty minutes away from where she lived. Diana stabbed the report with her two-hundred-dollar fountain pen, breaking the gold nib and splashing ink on the paper. "Gotcha, you bastard."

THREE

John drove across the Quaibrücke at the end of the lake where the Limmat River started. Scattered along the wide sidewalks of the four-lane bridge were the occasional small groups of young people heading to a party or couples taking in the sights on their way home. The view down the Limmat as it rolled through the city was a colorful three-dimensional image of lit-up church spires on either side mixed with the peaked red roofs of the ancient guild houses by the old town area, attesting to the city's early trading roots. He caught a green light where Bellerivestrasse started and made the turn to follow the lake along the big square at Bellevueplatz, passing the opera house lit up like a Hollywood opening night with giant winged angels pointing heavenward on either corner of the domed roof.

Eventually he was driving along the lakeshore, leaving the city behind as he headed to his apartment a few miles away. He wasn't rushing, just enjoying the warm night air and the slightly exotic vacation feeling that a summer night created. The wind was blowing through the car and he had the radio tuned to a local rock station that was playing seventies and eighties dance tracks to try and clear away the recent memories. Whatever fire and excitement he might have felt earlier was gone now, lost in silent defeat.

The parking lot of a lakeside *terrasse* a couple of miles from the city had some vacant spaces, so he pulled in. It was one of the seasonal restaurants that were only open in the summer, offering a grill with sausages and burgers alongside a small bar with scattered tables on the lakeshore. It was a little before two and a last beer wouldn't be bad to help wash away the memory of the robbery. A few of the round metal tables circling an ancient cypress whose long leafy tentacles swayed in the breeze were occupied with people who wanted to extend the summer experience one more night. One was the waitress fan club with four teenagers in surfer T-shirts and baggy shorts joking around with the two girls in midriff baring tops and short-shorts that worked there. John bought a beer at the bar and found a white plastic lawn chair near a low stone wall at the water's edge. He stared at the water contemplating a swim, as it was still warm, the temperature of a bath. Looking back towards Zürich, past the small boats bobbing along the dock, he studied the next-door restaurant with its wide deck extending over the water. It was brightly lit by hanging lanterns, full of the local Bentley and Mercedes crowd. The well-dressed clientele was living large and loud in their secular celebration as a drum and bass soundtrack rolled out over the dark choppy water where a few small speedboats with red and green running lights crawled by. This was Zürich's Gold Coast, named partially because of its southern exposure, getting more sun than its opposite counterpart. Mostly the title addressed the lifestyle of the money people who could afford a lake view where the taxes were low and only a ten-minute drive from the center of town. A standard joke said that it was easier to find a bank CEO there than a cleaning lady. The critics commented that it was full of villas with a pool and well-dressed unhappy people. Even though John also lived along this stretch of the lake, he wasn't one of the glitterati. He had a one-room apartment in an ancient former farmhouse where the countryside began in the hills above the bar.

John sipped on his drink, replaying the scene in the club. One part of him wanted to punch someone and his mind raced with all the possible revenge scenarios. He was also angry with his client who hadn't warned him of any possible violence. Maybe he could also bill them for the insurance deductible. The anger gradually dissipated as the sound of the celebrating guests and the rainbow of lights from distant buildings on the far shore dancing on the water had a calming effect.

After he finished the beer, John noticed the restaurant across the street was still open so he wandered over to see if anyone he knew was there. A couple of motorcycles were parked out front. One was a customized Harley with an extended fork and a helmet hanging from the handle bars with streaking flames painted on it. He walked through the dining room with walls covered with colorful beach scenes designed to resemble a tropical hut. Only two young couples were sitting quietly among the scattered empty tables. Following the muffled sound of music, he descended a short flight of stairs that led down to a narrow back room known as the Warhol Bar. It was a questionably legal afterhours bar and the last party before the suburbs and farmland started. There were about thirty people with the usual ratio of eight men for every woman packed in around the bar and standing on the stairs. The young girls were trying to look old while the older women were trying to look young. Bertie, the chubby Australian bartender wearing a heavy metal T-shirt, was serving a non-stop stream of drinks, turning up the music on the rock anthems she liked. AC/DC was pounding out a thumping beat.

Without asking she put a bottle of German beer down in front of John with a cheery "G'day" while she clipped the receipt to the inside of the counter. "How ya doin', mate?"

John replied with a shrug and weak smile. "I've had better days but who am I to complain? It's Friday."

Bertie took a quick glance at the swollen bump on his head and discretely moved on to another customer. John briefly studied a nearly depleted bowl of potato chips and decided against trying some as it looked like too many fingers had been pawing through them already.

To keep the neighbors from complaining about the noise, the windows were closed, adding humidity to the already stuffy room, thick with a fog of cigarette smoke. He scanned the room, recognizing a few regulars. Sitting on the stairs was the ever-present ageless biker in leather pants with a narrow weather-worn face and his partner who could have been a seventies rock and roll groupie with her halo of bleached blonde hair and black denim outfit. At the end of the bar a half bald man looking like an off-duty accountant in a designer label polo shirt bounced on his barstool to every tune, trying to look part of the scene. John tried to read some of the graffiti on the ceiling and walls that looked like haphazard wallpaper. Some scrawls commented on memorable nights and others were just crude amateur drawings. Debbie Harry's eyes looked at him seductively from a poster of Warhol's pop-art portrait hanging behind the bar.

"John, I thought you were busy tonight," came a voice out of the crowd. He turned, spotting Tanya Beyer standing next to him with a naughty grin on her face. She'd been part of the last surge of people sweeping into the narrow room. Her dark blonde hair was pulled back in a braid, accentuating the high cheeks and bright blue eyes, oval-shaped like a cat. Her round face tapered into a small chin, with full lips that seemed to be perpetually pouting. The black leotard top clung to the soft, youthful curves of her body and flat tummy, disappearing into faded designer jeans that were correctly ripped by each knee. It was reasonably good camouflage for the daughter of a private banker. John smiled at her, happy to see his girlfriend.

"I was, but I was able to untangle myself earlier—" He was interrupted.

"Hey, what happened to your face? It's all scratched up." She started to reach towards where he was bruised but restrained herself.

"I had a wrestling match with a hedge and lost. It's a long story." They found a reasonably quite corner while her two girlfriends checked their phones and ignored the looks from hungry eyes. John recounted his evening's activities as Tanya listened intently, clutching her small bottle of Evian as if it were trying to run away.

"It wasn't so much about losing the camera but feeling like a helpless victim. The police took half an hour to show up and, in the end, they blamed the theft on junkies from behind the main train station."

"Well, there is a lot of crime now..." Tanya offered before taking a gulp from her water.

"Maybe. But this wasn't random. I'm sure it was somebody with the guy I was sent to photograph. Even though I told the cops about the argument in the club, they rationalized that nobody would steal a camera they could easily buy. They ignored the fact that my wallet and phone weren't stolen."

Tanya considered this for a moment and said, "Just be happy you didn't get seriously hurt. These days more and more people are getting stabbed."

They were both leaning on the bar with their heads together. John said, "In the eyes of the police I'm a foreigner. A typical loud American prone to theatrics compared to the serious Swiss. They probably thought it was just an insurance scam."

John explained the photo taking was a last-minute assignment he received that morning. The request came from Tanya's stepmother, Diana, who'd hired him on other occasions, mostly for the fundraisers of her environmental foundation. Tanya had originally recommended him to Diana based on his freelance work but hadn't indicated there was any personal connection as it had been at the beginning of their dating days.

Diana Reichenberg was one of the last members of an old, titled German family synonymous with the country's proud history and heavy industry, being the largest steel producer in Germany. In her twenties she'd dropped out of the finishing school she and the other debutantes of her privileged corner of society were meant to attend on the journey to a safe inter-family marriage with similar moneyed class or other minor royalty. Diana exploded in the late naughty-nineties hosting wild all-night parties with socialites and dancing on nightclub tables that quickly earned her the name Princess Dianamite in the press.

Her life was all about jet setting between St. Moritz and New York as an 'It girl'. She was well known for her outrageous styling, with crazy hair and makeup paired with designer outfits she would borrow from her famous designer friends in Paris. She loved partying with rock stars like Mick Jagger or staying out in clubs all night with Prince while posing in a Paco Rabanne chain mail minidress with her hair sculpted into a blue mohawk.

On a midsummer night a party was firing on all cylinders at one of the family's palatial mansions in the southern German countryside. A girlfriend of Diana's who was flying high and lit up like a Christmas tree, found her doing tequila shots and snorting cocaine with a grungy Berlin filmmaker and informed her there was an important phone call from her mother – an emergency. When Diana found her way to the phone her mother was sobbing and choked up with grief. Diana's parents were vacationing at their lakeside villa in southern Switzerland on the Italian border. Her father had gone out in a vintage speedboat, doing runs up and down Lago Maggiore. An intense summer storm typical for the region had raced by churning up the water, with intense wind and heavy rain. It blew over quickly but not before dumping him from his boat and he had drowned. It took her a few moments to grasp the weight of the message through the alcohol and drug haze. The impact of the news cut through the fog like an intense beam from a lighthouse and Diana found herself crying with her mother like a small child, wailing and moaning in misery. And now without the father she had routinely rebelled against, she realized she'd been deeply attached to him and felt like a little girl who'd never grown up. The party was over and as one naturally prone to extremes, she cast off her excessive lifestyle and did a 180-degree turn. Three years later with a newly printed MBA, Diana controlled the family business with an iron fist that would have made her father proud. She implemented the sale of some money losing units, squeezed costs and strengthened the balance sheet to keep the company shares from sliding.

A few years later with the steel business on even keel, she sold twenty percent of the shares to an investment group to support the company's stock market value. Diana stepped back from the day-to-day operations and took over as chairman of the board, handing over the business reins to a newly appointed CEO, the former finance chief of the company. She moved to Zürich to create some distance with her past identity and to found a non-profit organization committed to helping the environment. Her main motivation to move was the quiet style of living and the promise of anonymity where nobody cared if you were Tina Turner or Phil Collins – a couple of former Swiss residents who had enjoyed their privacy and the ability to live a normal life without getting mobbed in the streets.

Zürich was Switzerland's biggest city and Diana's German mother tongue served her well. An active social life eventually brought her into contact with a private banker, Hans-Peter Beyer, at a party. He was the connection to her old-world values while she was comfortable in private discos and exotic resorts where old money mingled with the nouveau rich. With her background it would have been easy to maintain a jet-set lifestyle but her new husband tempered this extreme with his moderate Swiss manner and they found a middle ground that could include both ends of the spectrum. Her experience of participating in the revival of the family business allowed them to discuss investment issues that Hans-Peter could never have done with his first wife.

Diana was only eight years older than his daughter Tanya, so she became more like a big sister than a mother. Sometimes she would forget this special connection and try and offer motherly advice which didn't always sit well with an equally independent Tanya. They were bound together on another level as Diana was an avid collector of modern art and Tanya had her own art gallery. Diana's favorite artist was Keith Haring who she'd met on one of her New York wild weekends back in the party days and later been a houseguest at the family castle. Some of his works decorated the halls of the main residence as it became a private art gallery, rivaling many large museums. Besides chasing new art to enhance her collection, Diana used her free time and family money to establish an ecological organization called the Earth Goddess Foundation. It helped native cultures and lands under threat, after discovering that a lot of the family mining activities were destroying animal habitats and indigenous tribes in the Third World. When John first heard about the foundation, he thought it must be grand to be rich and able to wash away your guilt with rivers of money that came from the very sources you were trying to pay penance for. Even so, he gladly accepted the infrequent photo assignments she'd hire him for.

Diana's younger brother, Klaus, had been inspired by her efforts and become a social media hero for exposing polluters as he travelled the world. The German press often cited his activities in their reports on climate change and he became a big hit on college campuses, lecturing on the environment. He was elevated to the status of a saint after his untimely demise while investigating mining operations in Africa.

"Diana sent me an email this morning saying I should make every effort to visit the Diagonal because there was an important person she wanted to have a picture of. I'd make 500 francs if I was successful. That was all the motivation I needed. I didn't ask any questions other than a good description of the subject. The only other information was that it would somehow support the memory of her deceased brother."

"I don't know anything about it. The answer will have to wait. Diana left this afternoon to visit her family for a couple of days in the Bavarian Alps outside of Munich. She usually does a digital detox when she's there, so won't be reachable."

"Not a bad life."

"I think Diana is still too identified with her high-flying background and hasn't really settled down."

"Maybe the closeminded Swiss culture has created a rebellious reaction Diana needs to express, which I totally understand."

"As much as I like her, I wonder at times if her supporting the environment is an attempt to look politically correct like so many other well to do people, afraid to be criticized for their extravagant lifestyle."

John listened without showing too much support, knowing that Tanya took every opportunity she could to complain about the one-percenters, which is how she had categorized Diana. It was part of Tanya's defiant attitude to reject her influential family that represented a materialistic culture while she pursued the life of an artist and small businesswoman, making her own way in the world.

Like a lot of other kids from her social circle, in her teenage years Tanya had made the rounds of the private clubs with the sons and daughters of the ultra-wealthy who had shipped them to private Swiss finishing schools like the Lyceum Alpinum in Zuoz to get their international Baccalaureate. The spoiled kids could flash daddy's black Amex Centurion card, capable of buying a yacht or house while ordering ten-thousand-franc, six-liter bottles of champagne. The parties extended to Mykonos and Ibiza when the season was right. This was not on the same level of Diana's globetrotting escapades, being mostly in the closed inner circles of Zürich where there were no A-list celebrities, only self-important people with money, perpetuating their own myth. The superficial nature of the endless parties and focus on showing off their wealth finally got to Tanya and she stepped back from the scene and began focusing on her painting and art history studies. She aspired to establish a separate identity from her family background by expressing her creative side, not unlike Diana did leaving the party scene after her father's death. And also, like Diana, tried to compensate the world's wrongs by championing unknown artists in her gallery in the red-light district, while dabbling in her own art. But while Diana still liked her forays to Monaco, Tanya preferred places like the Warhol Bar, which endeared her to John.

"Nice to see you anyway." Tanya was smiling, squeezing his arm. She couldn't kiss him as she wished. John was in the middle of a contentious divorce proceeding and needed to be discrete until it was final to avoid being punished extra hard financially for being the guilty party who went astray. The bar was close to his apartment and, after all, Switzerland was like a small neighborhood. Tanya pulled out a packet of cigarettes. "Can you handle me the ashtray?"

"I'd like to handle you too."

"What?" she replied, looking quizzical.

John had known Tanya the entire time he had been in Switzerland. It had started as a friendship as a result of buying photo paper for his printer at Metamorph, her combination gallery and art supplies shop. This had led to a relationship they both had avoided at first, trying be 'correct' even though there was a sense of inevitability to their getting together. Tanya knew he was married and wasn't the type to disrupt an existing relationship so was content to have him as another friend in the creative universe. Their natural closeness evolved after six months to where they jokingly started calling each other brother and sister – so near and yet so far. 'Isn't it a shame you are my brother?' It was their coded language to acknowledge John being married.

At that time John and his wife hadn't slept together for three months and he was about to move out and file for legal separation. He and his wife had finally concluded after two years of trying to fit a square peg into a round hole with the resulting increase in the number of arguments, triggered by cultural differences, that it was for the best to end their marriage.

The lingering attachment from his wife made the legal process contentious as she stretched out the divorce proceedings to keep him tied to her as a form of punishment for initiating the breakup of their marriage. The additional pain she inflicted was financial in the form of alimony, starting with initial payments until the case was finalized. The amount could increase significantly if it wasn't seen by the judge to be a no-fault divorce. John being married had been the only barrier to knowing Tanya better. The situation changed when he had helped her remodel her gallery after he was newly single due to the recent separation from his wife. A few drinks, followed by a couple of movies and the eventual dinner at her place led to their ongoing but discrete relationship. She had to remind a too gentlemanly John that he didn't have to consider himself her brother anymore.

Seeing an opening in the conversation, Tanya's two friends joined them and the talk shifted to everyone's plans for the weekend and which parties looked good. Tanya left with her girlfriends about 3 a.m. and John ordered an Evian to give her a ten-minute head start before driving to her apartment that was a couple of villages away. Bertie knew everyone along the lake and John not wanting to advertise his relationship, made it appear that they left separately. John's thoughts went back to the man in the club and he couldn't let go of wanting to exact revenge. He also knew some of his business cards were in the stolen camera case so he could have a welcoming committee one day that would make the theft look like a playdate.

FOUR

John considered it too early on a Monday to answer the phone even though it was a little after nine and he already had a double espresso singing through his veins. He was at his desk scrolling through endless screens of emails, trying to prioritize which ones to respond to first. The office was slowly starting to wake up. He watched outside his open door an ever-increasing amount of foot traffic that finally slowed to a trickle as people retrieved their coffees and got down to business. An American colleague who was a newly arrived transfer shuffled by with a sports sack and shopping bag John new were both full of papers. The man had a compulsion to print every email and document and went from using a briefcase to carriers with more capacity to ferry all the paper back and forth from his home. His office had finally been declared an official fire hazard by the compliance department from the stacks of papers everywhere and he had been forced to reduce the volume of documents.

A few instant messages had already popped up from his teammates sharing rumors about the latest management moves to streamline the company that were reported in the weekend press. The newest gossip was that the company was trying to sell its Swedish business unit, which was not communicated to the employees. The vows of transparency and 'employees first' that the management had made were window dressing to avoid panic among the ranks as changes were quietly being implemented in a massive cost savings initiative. His phone rang with its insistent digital ring tone. Recognizing the extension on the display he hesitated a second but picked it up anyway, hearing a familiar voice.

"Yeah, yeah, we caught you. Spying on the secretaries again. Always at it, uh-huh. So, how's it going, you dirty old man?" It was Sean O'Conner, more Irish than a leprechaun, wound up as usual on mischief and caffeine.

"What'd you wake me up for, don't you respect my need to sleep? And what are you doing here so early, just getting home from a party?"

"Sure. That's more your department. Did the police find the camera yet? The message you left on my voicemail was correct – you got ripped off?"

"Yes, it's true and no, they didn't recover it. I'll tell you the whole story later."

"Are you around this week? Let's go for a pizza sometime."

"Anytime."

"In case you're wondering I've got the photos from Saturday. Real high-class deal. The bride even wore a veil. And I tell you, by the end of the night the bride's father was totally drunk and incoherent."

"I already heard about it. Word has it you tried to shove a piece of cake into the bride's mouth. And that was only the reception. What really got to the father was when you backed into the baptism font during the ceremony, nearly knocking it over."

"I can explain everything."

"Well get up here and start explaining. The client was a

good contact for work and I don't want to screw up this arrangement. If I wasn't so charitable, I would've done it myself."

"Bullshit. You just wanted to go to a party with that babe you're shagging." The phone clicked dead. Sean appeared in a few minutes. He was about the same age as John and his faded jeans coupled with a rumpled Hawaiian shirt contrasted John's attempt to look business like with a white shirt and striped tie in the company colors. A pile of shoulder length curly red hair looked like it hadn't seen a comb in a week.

"You can always tell who the computer guys are around here. The only thing missing is an earring." John nodded at the casual attire.

"OK, you little yuppie mannequin, who do you think you are, Giorgio Armani?" Sean's words had a spring in them with the last part of the sentence spoken higher than the rest. "Let's hear about this robbery. Tell me you're insured."

"We live in Switzerland, even my damn underwear is insured. The deductible will hurt but I'll put it on the bill. It went down like this. After the usual fun and games at the TGIF party for the International Club, a bunch of us ended up at the Diagonal."

"The Bore Au Lac hotel. How thrilling."

"Not my choice, I was there on an assignment. The highlight of the evening was an argument with a bigshot partying with a couple of bimbos who didn't like me taking his photo. There's a picture of him on this." John held up the memory card from the camera. "When I left the club, someone grabbed my camera bag."

"What?"

"I was punched on the side of my head and tossed in some bushes by the parking lot. I'm sure it was this rich joker. I didn't see who it was because they were behind me."

"What did the police say?"

"The cops said it was probably heroin addicts from Langstrasse. Lots of crime in the city nowadays, mostly unreported in the papers and so on."

"But the connection should be obvious," Sean said.

"That's an understatement. The bastards didn't even take my wallet or phone. What really pisses me off is that this guy thinks he can push me around and get away with it."

Sean jumped up from where he was slumped in a visitor's chair like he was going to punch someone and slapped the back of the chair. "We should make a 'nice' print with some computer aided enhancements to sell to a trashy magazine for their celebrity page. Make it look like he has his hand on one of the girl's tits. We've got to make him fry. How'd you like a photo credit in the *Blick*? They want all the 'in' people caught at the hot spots of Switzerland in a possible scandal."

"You still have contacts there?"

"I do indeed. I think this idiot should burn." Sean paused to catch his breath with a momentary quizzical expression. "Minor problem though, who the hell is he?"

"No clue. It was Tanya's wild and wonderful stepmother who hired me to take the picture but she's away until tomorrow. Who knows what she's up to. The lady is on a mission to save the planet and said something about the photo supporting her brother who died in Africa. It could also be just a rich pal passing through town but I think there's something else going on. There's a good shot of my new friend towards the end of the series. Can you make some prints for me to show around? I also need some prints of some other pictures from the TGIF for a couple of the older, less digitally inclined members. Here's a list." Sean took the data card and small piece of notepaper from John and studied it briefly before folding it and putting it with the card in his jeans pocket. He turned for the door with a quick salute and an "adios".

. . .

John returned from getting a coffee to the office he shared with two other people on the marketing team who were on vacation. He found Rita, the team secretary, tossing mail and some pink phone message notes into his in-basket. She was a petite brunette in her early twenties, could type and book flights but after that she was challenged. She was British and had just finished her usual breakfast of a Pepsi Max, chocolate covered granola bar and some spiced paprika chips, wiping her hands on her skirt to get rid of the chips' seasoning powder.

She smiled and spoke efficiently in her best London accent trying to sound metropolitan but betraying her roots in the East End as she mangled some words. "You've had three phone calls. One from your lawyer. He'll call back later or you can call him. Second, Steve wants to see you. Something to do with the quarterly executive meeting."

"Oh yeah, *that*." John knew it was where all the big chiefs sat around in a fancy hotel and bragged about their group's performance figures and their respective vacation villa remodeling. "Can you dig out that agenda proposal so I can show him?"

"OK but..." she paused for emphasis and struck a pose that was meant to signal an important message with her hip cocked to the side and her hand on it in an authoritative position. "Mr. Richard Johnson from Bank National called personally and would like you to call him as soon as you can. He said this number was his direct line. He sounded *most* important."

"He's the European President of a major American bank and a good friend of our bank's CEO. Probably wants to get together over a couple of beers and chat about football scores." John lowered his voice to a tone of confidentiality, "The truth is, I give him advice on how to run his bank."

"Well, all I know is, it sounded kind of urgent," she

answered in an unsure tone, not knowing if John was joking as she left his office.

"Thanks, Rita. Let's sit together at two and see where we're at for this week," he called after her.

John dug out the message slip and dialed Richard Johnson. John knew he usually couldn't get the time of day out of Johnson, but John had just taken some pictures of him at the monthly party for the International Club, a business group for expats. He must be looking for some copies. The phone was answered on the first ring.

"Mr. Johnson's office, may I help you?" answered an efficient sounding perky voice with a hint of an upper-class English accent. None of these switchboards that keep you on hold all afternoon, enduring endless clicks and pauses with Kenny G. music in between.

"Yes, this is Mr. Miller returning Mr. Johnson's call." John tried to sound casual and important at the same time, swinging his feet up on the desk to be in the correct position to show humility and respect. A second later he heard a commanding voice.

"Johnson."

"Hello, Richard, John Miller." John couldn't resist being familiar.

"Good to hear from you, John." His tone was affirmative, stressing the name. "You have a nice time Friday night?"

"Yes, big crowd and a lot of new people. I even have some shots of you."

"Great – that's what I was calling about. I'd really like to see all the pictures from that evening." John couldn't mistake the emphasis on the word 'all' and the implied meaning. John managed to interject a quick military like 'absolutely' before Richard carried on.

"As good citizens and club members we need to show

respect and discretion at club functions and other locations where our colleagues are present."

"That's right."

"And I'm sure I don't need to remind you that showing a lack of respect for the privacy of individuals in the business community could be seen as a tendency that would not be harmonious with the values of your place of work or future photo taking." John knew what getting mobbed by his boss was like but this conversation was on a whole other level.

"The memory card is with a photo lab to make some prints for the club members too old to know what Instagram is. I can get everything over to you by mid-week. Is that soon enough?"

"Fine, John. Just express everything over to the bank as soon as you can, including the memory card. And please be sure no pictures find their way onto any digital outlet or to the members until I have a chance to review them. See you at the next event. Goodbye." The phone line went dead.

"Bye, Dick." John stared at the handset in disbelief before slowly setting it back in the cradle.

It was sweltering, which made it easy to rationalize leaving the office early. Heatwaves were becoming a norm for the Alpine country and the wing of the ancient bank building where John's office was located didn't include air-conditioning. The small fans the company provided could only push the hot air around. He was in the part of the building originally built in the late 1800's and didn't seem to have had modernized since then as global warming with hotter summers and colder winters was just now getting people's attention.

John had no trouble finding a table in the old town area as it was still school holiday time. The locals had abandoned the city, making parking places and empty tables easier to find before the tourist crowd showed up. John never understood why the natives would leave when it was the only few weeks of good weather a year that one could hope for. But as rain was an ever-present spoiler of the summer mood, families hedged their bets and headed south for certain sunshine.

All the restaurants were setting up for the evening meal, waiters putting paper place mats and table settings in front of every seat, discouraging the people who only wanted a drink. Slouching low in the chair, John faced directly down the Niederdorfstrasse, a slim canyon running the length of the old town area. It was formed by three-hundred-year-old buildings in a variety of faded pastel colors, about five or six floors tall. Most had shops, restaurants or bars with tables outside, underneath the apartments and offices. There was a constant cacophony of voices in conversation that rose and fell like a chattering mountain stream as small groups of strolling people dodged each other. Their shouted conversations were enhanced by a jumbled soundtrack provided by the neighboring kebab stand's Middle Eastern music and street musicians wailing along with their out of tune guitars.

The walkway where he faced opened onto a small plaza. A few young vendors had blankets on the ground with imported ethnic jewelry from South America, reproductions of famous photographs like Marilyn Monroe and Che Guevara plus a selection of fake Gucci purses. A group of three Jamaicans in colorful shirts and old jeans stood in a half circle, one with a conga drum, another with a guitar. As they performed some reggae songs the transiting sun hit them squarely from between two buildings like a spotlight, reflecting off the mirrored sequins on the drummer's pillbox hat. A few familiar faces flashed by in the stream of people. The crowds wouldn't let up for another two hours.

John spotted Sean bounding down the walkway, dodging

the oncoming traffic. He was half an hour late and that meant he was fifteen minutes earlier than John expected.

"There you are. Thought you got lost tying up your bicycle."

"Nah, came by tram. God, am I dying of thirst." Sean waved his arm high in the air before sitting down but the waiter at the serving station two tables away faded inside. "Damn service hasn't improved around here." The waiter reappeared with two plates of food. He nodded an acknowledgment at their shouted order for a couple of beers.

"OK, let's have another look at the shot of my 'friend' in all his glory." John pulled his iPad out of his shoulder bag and they looked through the photos and the last few that were from inside the Diagonal.

"There's the one you're after," Sean said pointing to the group picture with a fair composition of the mystery man and his guests. "It came out really sharp. Look, you can even see the diamond tiepin the guy's wearing."

"The money shot." John related the veiled threat that Richard Johnson had made that morning to sound Sean out on how much he should be concerned. "I think Johnson's request is too coincidental. The stolen camera case had some of my company business cards inside so it'd be easy to track me down. What worries me, is the thieves can also find out where I live."

"Can't change anything now. If they want to visit you, it's not your choice." John nodded, not sure if he was ready for another encounter. "The Johnson guy's blowing hot air. He can't influence any potential clients and besides, the magazines judge you on your work, not what some stuffed shirt might say."

"That's true, but he also implied bad behavior could influence my job situation. He does know our CEO."

"Any bookie in Las Vegas would give you less than fifty percent odds of surviving the latest reorganization, so it doesn't matter anyway if there was a complaint."

"I'd like to believe I have better odds. I already don't trust my boss to keep me safe. If I can do something to increase my chances for survival, I'll do it. I need to survive another six months to reach the two-year mark. Anything short of that and I won't qualify for unemployment. That would be a financial disaster given the usual long lead time to find a job. I was working freelance during my first year in Switzerland and getting paid under the table so the time didn't count towards my employment benefits."

"Patience, my friend. You're a key player on a high-profile project that will see you through 'til the end of the year. That'll keep you safe."

John nodded in agreement. "I propose we give him a memory card with only half the photos copied onto it and tell him that's all there were. Say the rest were in the stolen camera. It's my way of pushing back. He can have the TGIF snaps and the rest I can do with as I please. Besides, I want my client to pay me."

"Now you're talking. I can help arrange that, no problem." The waiter had just deposited some fresh cold beers so they raised their glasses in a salute.

"I'm really sure now that my encounter in the club had to do with the camera getting grabbed. More I think about it, the angrier I get." John scrutinized the photos again. The man and his group weren't perfectly framed but still recognizable.

Sean said, "You think he's married and not wishing to advertise he wasn't with the client he was supposed to be seeing? Or is he a genuine, privacy loving individual?"

"I'm guessing there's some business angle given where the request came from. Or maybe he's in the same boat as me, trying to keep one step ahead of his wife's attorney."

"I suggest we use IRA terrorism tactics to embarrass the man. Like planting a chunk of plastic explosives with his business card on it in a train so the police nab him for an attempted bombing."

"Great idea. It has a lot of merit." They both laughed. John knew about Sean's childhood in Northern Ireland and being exposed to random extreme violence like schoolyard bombings. Added to his traumatic childhood was the bitterness and anger of a broken family when his stewardess wife he met on his travels to Switzerland left him for a pilot and took the two kids.

"While I'm waiting for Diana to get back, I'm going to check around and see if I can ID this guy. If I ever want to know something about this country, or anything else for that matter, I consult that perennial source of information, Harry, the human Wikipedia."

"Good luck. If he's not drunk, he's full of B.S. but you can try. If your friend turns out to be someone important, we can get it in the paper as a last laugh."

"I hope you don't mean last as in goodbye cruel world…?"

"No, let's just do it. We'll stick the picture in the paper with some bogus name and he'll be so insulted he'll have his lawyer call and you can ask for your camera back. These clowns all have such big egos. Should be soon if it's going to be news."

"How quick can you get it in there?"

"I can stop by my friend's office tomorrow morning which means it could be in the Wednesday paper."

"First let me see what I can find out. I need to check with the lovely lady who requested the photo before creating a scene. One that could also get me tossed out of the bank, sooner rather than later."

"Suit yourself. I don't necessarily agree."

"You don't have to." John was starting to get angry and decided to change the subject after taking a generous gulp of beer. "How's your love life? Tanya says Susan really likes you but you never call her."

"Hey, I'm busy and have other options." Sean stole a slice of bread from the small metal basket the neighboring diners had abandoned and was eating it mechanically.

"Like what? Still got that Italian number chasing you?"

"She left me. We broke it off, tried to get it back together but it didn't work. Guess I was too pushy. She was interesting, but not interested. Anyway, I think there's a better way to meet girls. I'm going to put an ad in the rendezvous section of the paper next time I make eye contact with a real beauty."

"Old school approach from a digerati. I love it. I bet you read it every week to see if some babe spotted you, right?"

"Of course. Don't you?"

"I used to, but now I think I'm committed."

"Think? You either are or you're not. It's like bacon and eggs. The chicken is a participant but the pig is committed. Don't turn into some corporate-speak clone with shit like 'customer loyalty' and 'shareholder value'. Do you love her?"

"Yes, of course. I guess I said that because I want to be sure that me wishing for a good partner or being on the rebound isn't coloring my wanting to be with her."

"I know you well enough to see that you're not a player. This is the real deal. You guys are a good match. Don't get into your head about it."

"Now you're suddenly an expert on this?"

"Dude, I was so in love with my wife and kids and the pain of having it all ripped away went way deep. Try having your children disappear into the arms of a stranger and then tell me what real love is."

"Sorry, I get your point."

"Love isn't a mental exercise. You can't create it. Either it's there or it's not."

"It's definitely there."

"Then enjoy it."

"The thing is, we've been going out for most of a year and we're super close but I'm really afraid after my marriage failing that I'll screw up a good thing."

"Stop analyzing everything. Ambiguity is natural when you're that far along getting to know someone, especially if you're looking for a new partner."

"I just don't want to lose her because of my problems."

"Don't worry. If she really cares, she'll work with you through this tough time. You should dive into love without any doubts. Just don't turn into a bourgeois on me."

"What are you talking about?"

"Hanging out on the Gold Coast with a private banker's daughter..."

"I live a simple life in a one room hovel."

"No, I live in the ghetto by Langstrasse with all the hookers. You live by the lake with the chic crowd."

John picked up on the theme. "Sometimes I feel intimidated by her background. I'm not sure if it'll get in the way because I'm not from the same social class as her family. I know from my time in this wonderful country that gaining acceptance is hard for foreigners. Just look at my current in-laws."

"With a woman like Diana in the family, you look bloody conservative."

"True. I also feel embarrassed sometimes by my limited resources that are compromised by my alimony. I can't offer nice gifts like flying Tanya away to Paris for a weekend."

"Why don't you start with a small trip to the south of Switzerland where the palm trees meet the mountains? It's a perfectly acceptable romantic getaway you could afford."

"Great idea, thanks. I also feel uncomfortable when Tanya pays the dinner bill. I guess I'm operating from the age-old mindset of the man paying for everything. I know Tanya isn't attached to this gender-based rule but it reinforces my feelings of not being able to be an eventual provider."

"I totally get it. Why don't you see it as a form of generosity that one day will be repaid?"

A cell phone rang at the adjoining table and Sean turned to give the owner a wilting stare. He looked away a second, studying the crowd and shifted to a more serious tone. "Look, my friend, I didn't want to mention this until I was sure it was happening but now the word has come through." He took a large swallow from his beer.

"Get to the point, you drunk peat farmer."

"Yah see, I've got this partner in Paris who I sometimes go there to work with. You know the one I mean, right? Worked with him on a fashion shoot a couple months ago."

"Yeah, go on. Have another drink, you're starting to repeat yourself."

"Shut your face and listen. He's real established there and has some backers with a lot of money who want him to set up an agency. You always told me you wanted to be your own boss and work in a small outfit as a partner, right?"

"Tell me more."

"The plan is he'd have an office in Paris for the fashion work. I'd run an office here in Zürich for the German speaking customers and there'd be a third office in Miami. A lot of the fashion work from here is moving to Florida. The weather is more predictable, there's nice scenery and it's a lot cheaper to hire models and everything else. We're looking for someone to run that office. I immediately thought of you."

"I appreciate it. I'm just not sure if I have enough experience to go off on my own."

"You're a good photographer. And if you had a chance to pursue it as a career, I know you'd do very well. No doubts. You're also managing monster creative projects in the corporate world without breaking. If you can survive at Swiss Credit Bank, you can work anywhere. And as an American, you won't need a work permit. I know it's a difficult time for you to look ahead, especially with your divorce, but this could help you have a nice landing."

"And what about Tanya?"

"She could set up another gallery somewhere in South Beach and do really well for herself. European culture, Art Basel insider and all that." He paused thoughtfully. "You have to realize your days at the bank are numbered. It's not a matter of 'if' it's only a matter of 'when' they axe you. It's better you start to prepare. Imagine all those models you'd have to handle."

"Come on. Is this for real?" John asked with a questioning look. "I know you're drunk but it sounds too good to be true."

"One hundred percent, my friend. My partner is putting together the business plan. You'd get a decent salary paid in Swiss francs so there's no need to scramble for work all the time. Also, a lot of travel in-between all the offices so you could still visit here a couple of times a year."

"Keep talking. I suppose you've got Rosie Huntington lined up for a Victoria's Secret underwear ad."

"You never know." Sean smiled like the devil making an offer that was only the beginning of a descent into wickedness.

"What can I say, I'm overwhelmed. Hey, thanks, man." John reached over the table and slapped Sean on the shoulder. "Given the condition I'm in right now, it sure sounds good. I'd like to talk about it more when we're both a little more sober."

"Sure. We wouldn't be setting up anything for at least six months. It'll take that long to get the financing in place. No rush. I think it'd be something that suits you more than what you're doing now."

John knew he would jump at the chance if it was legitimate and could try and sell it to Tanya. But first he had to sort out his

Swiss citizenship and there were still many legal hurdles to overcome first. To add to the complexity of living abroad was the issue of whether to retain his U.S. citizenship or not. He didn't want to give it up but he was starting to think he had to. The States wanted him to pay income tax as did the Swiss and he couldn't afford both on top of alimony. The agency salary would have to be amazing if he had all these bills to pay.

"Hey, check this out, the guy's totally *overchicked*," Sean said breaking John's reverie. They both looked sideways at a passing couple in the middle of the stream of people. The man was short and round in a color coordinated lavender polyester leisure suit with matching shirt. His companion with mile long legs had her hair bleached almost white, matching a satin top that was held up by spaghetti straps over a micro miniskirt. They held hands like teenagers. A couple of people they knew stopped to chat and they bought a beer for a British singer Sean knew from a local blues band.

After the singer moved along Sean picked a fight with the young Italian waiter when he kept ignoring their signal that they wanted some more bread to go with their pasta. Sean addressed him in Italian, somehow insulting him. There was a shouting match, with the waiter in long white apron, black vest and white shirt waving an empty tray cursing madly in Italian. For Sean it was just the opening he needed to begin a tirade against the poor service that was typical in Swiss establishments. The workers were salaried and generally didn't get big tips as that was already included in a service charge. There was no motivation to provide customer service and guests were served with well-rehearsed arrogance. The bread never came.

"I think we should do a runner on this guy," Sean proposed.

"What, are you crazy?"

"No look, it'd be easy. We could get up and disappear into

the crowd going separate directions and that idiot would never find us."

"No way. I like this place and want to come back again this year."

"They'll never remember us. That guy is a seasonal worker."

"After what you said to him I doubt if he'll ever forget you. Besides, there's not too many people around here wearing a red mop on their head."

By ten o'clock the crowd had thinned to a trickle and it looked like the show was over. After a final espresso and grappa, they shoved their chairs back, stood up and said their goodbyes. As Sean turned and headed off through the old town towards the main station, John strolled in the opposite direction. The waiters swooped down and started to fold the chairs now that the last two customers had left.

John turned and headed towards the Limmat River, walking down a narrow, cobbled side street tilted at an angle, framed by ancient buildings. He followed the slow moving river towards the lake, weaving between the small groups of people on the Limmatstrasse. Some bars under the cover of the guild houses with their arched white stone facades were still open with an assortment of guests drinking at the tables. He passed under the base of the massive twin-domed towers of the Grossmünster Church that were lit up like a film set by big spotlights. Crossing the street, he looked in at the outdoor bar of the Terrasse restaurant. There were low tables scattered around a small garden that was the living room for the *jeunesse dorée*, the fashionable, wealthy young people of Zürich. It was a former strip bar that had moved upmarket when the whole area was revitalized in the eighties from a rundown part of town. John studied the crowd over the low hedge to see if any local stars were having a late drink. The *'cervelat promi's'* or 'sausage celebrities' were only famous in their region of Switzerland and their antics always enamored the Swiss natives who followed them in the press and on social media. He had a small camera in his shoulder bag so was ready if an opportunity presented itself. Not recognizing anyone in the crowd, he crossed the street again, keeping an eye out for trams and taxis piloted by lost immigrants. Dodging animated people spilling over tables in front of the Odeon Café, John heard someone calling his name.

FIVE

Mata Hari had danced upstairs in search of secrets while the waiters in the café sold morphine to war junkies. James Joyce, Einstein, Lenin and Mussolini had each sat at the Odeon Café's marble tables at different times while formulating their ideas for another reality in a locale modeled on a Viennese coffeehouse. The Dadaists, who originated there with their quirky art, would have felt at home today as ultra-styled young men French kissed behind Greek style pillars while transvestites straddled bar stools in elaborate drag in front of mirrored walls.

"Hello, John!" Tanya called from one of the tables jammed together along the sidewalk, virtually unrecognizable in a floppy hat. John turned to see who was calling his name. "Don't be afraid, we won't bite." Tanya was sharing a table with a dark-haired girlfriend in a sleeveless silk blouse and black satin vest.

John squeezed through the crowd passing in either direction to join them. "It's not you I'm afraid of, it's the boys. Hi, Susan." John quickly kissed each woman on both cheeks before borrowing a chair from the next table.

"When you're a cute guy wearing tight jeans in the gay

capital of Europe, you're asking for trouble." They all laughed. "Susan was just going but if you like, we could have a drink," Tanya said.

"Don't leave on my account. The more the merrier I always say," John said.

Susan said, "I noticed that at the party on Saturday. You drank nearly all the beer without any help, and were quite merry." They all laughed. "Let's see your Elvis impersonation again. The people here would like such a performance. Come on, Mr. King, let's hear 'Hound Dog'."

"I need some inspiration first. What are you ladies drinking?"

Susan said, "Sorry, but I really have to go. I'm working on a brochure design for a big client and I need some sleep."

"Come on, one little glass more won't hurt. We're celebrating," Tanya said in a slightly drunk but happy voice.

Susan nodded and smiled slyly. They ordered a half-liter of Chianti and after the small carafe arrived, toasted. Susan lit another cigarette, pursed her lips and drew in reflectively. She reached over her shoulder to scratch the back of her head exposing a tuft of light brown hair sprouting under her arm.

"We were at this totally wild private art exhibition this evening," Susan said. "It was in a partially demolished Art Deco movie theater just down the way on Seefeldstrasse. The building is getting a major renovation but you can still see these beautiful neoclassical friezes and frescoed ceilings that they're going to preserve. They looked so weird with all the destroyed walls looking like a bomb hit them."

Tanya joined in. "The developer's allowed it to be a pop-up cultural center for a couple of months. He wants to make friends with the local natives who were complaining about losing another landmark. It's on its way to becoming yet another upscale restaurant in the Seefeld district."

"Guess he wants them all to buy expensive dinners when it's finished," John said.

"The host of the exhibition was a local painter who goes by the name Miror. I've known him since we were teenagers," Tanya said. "He does Surrealist and Magical Realism flavored artwork inspired by the Spanish painter Miró who he stole his name from. The name Miror also refers to his skill at being able to copy a famous painting and make it virtually indistinguishable from the original. He had his hand slapped by the Swiss courts after he and a gallery owner were caught trying to sell a fake Picasso that he'd painted when he was a young artist showing off. They were both fined and the gallery was shut down. Miror was tossed out of art school and warned never to indulge in forgeries again, under the threat of going to jail. Because he was underage, he avoided more serious consequences."

The free-flowing wine was for celebrating Tanya being given a commission to sell a couple of Basquiats. She had received the request from one of the slumming rich kids they had bumped into at the party, a friend of a friend who was part of the local scene. They all raised their glasses again in a celebratory toast. John was amazed at the windfall and was beaming with pride at Tanya's coup. Each painting could be sold for double digit millions and the sale would be an internationally recognized event. Tanya's gallery was set to join the big leagues or at the very least establish a solid credibility that would attract other good works and artists seeking a home. She was happy to prove to her father she didn't need his help to become successful and could also pay off the loan she used to open her gallery.

Tanya and Susan broke off frequently into Swiss-German where every fifth or sixth word was produced with a rough hacking from the back of the throat as though clearing some particularly stubborn phlegm. The sound was meant to identify them as locals but it never failed to amaze John that from such delicate mouths such coarse sounds could emerge in conversation. It was a spoken dialect, unlike the clearly enunciated 'High German' that was used in Germany. The Germans took offense to the local language and used subtitles on news broadcasts originating from Switzerland, as it was as foreign sounding as Swahili to them.

"Where's Sean tonight?" Susan said.

"You just missed him. If he knew you were here, he wouldn't have gone home so soon."

"I'm flattered."

"Call him some time, he likes emancipated women who take initiative."

"That's a surprise. I thought he was only in love with himself," Tanya said.

"Ooh, get out the claws." John made a motion with his hand like a cat scratching in defense. John also knew that Tanya sometimes disapproved of Sean, seeing him as a bad influence on John as he tried to navigate the no man's land of getting divorced. She was afraid Sean's bachelor ways might give John ideas about wanting to play the field.

"Look. I've got to go." Susan quickly finished her glass of wine and took turns pressing her cheek against John's and Tanya's, kissing the air. She got up and wound her way through the tables, disappearing down the sidewalk with the top of the tribal tattoo across her lower back visible above the low-cut jeans.

John said, "They spent one night together and she expects him to move in or what?"

"No, just to show a little respect. He's so wrapped up in his work and whatever other 'projects' he has going that he doesn't think of anything or anyone else."

"Where have I heard that before?" John mused aloud. Without waiting for an answer he asked, "So how's Tanya?" as he lifted his wine glass.

She pointedly ignored the first question unsure where that discussion might lead and not wanting to spoil the celebration. "Not too bad. I didn't expect to see you tonight." She smiled and reached over, whispering, "Did I tell you today that I love you?" His smile returned the same sentiment as he slowly withdrew his hand. "Don't worry. None of your wife's friends would come here."

"It's more her students. You know how young people like to hang out and look decadent."

"All right, I'll restrain myself."

"So really, how are you?"

"Fine. Wish I could kiss you."

"I wish you could too. I want to kiss you, what do you think? But please," John begged, "not here. All I need is one word to get back to my wife and I'm dead. I've spent three years waiting for my permanent residence permit so I can get citizenship and I don't want to blow it now. But more important, is you and me."

"Thank you." She paused to inhale from her cigarette and then let the smoke slowly escape to emphasize the sarcasm of her words. She switched to a more neutral tone. "I know all about your story, you keep reminding me. But why don't you just tell your wife to grow up and get on with her life. She shouldn't try and punish you because she's equally to blame for it not working out.'

"In her eyes, the break-up's all my fault and the court battle's her form of retribution for wrecking a wonderful marriage. But she's at least letting me apply for citizenship if I don't scandalize her. She thinks if I still live here the door to reconciliation is open. I just need to be cool for a little longer until the legal story is over. Then it'll be the right time to have that discussion."

"I don't know how long I can wait. You get the best of both worlds – an uncommitted bachelor life and a girlfriend on call. I only get the leftovers. Every time we're together we have to sneak around and act like strangers. It's not normal. I want a relationship without these kinds of obstacles and games. When your wife's back from her vacation can you try and work out an arrangement? Promised?"

"The word is promise," John smiled as he corrected her.

She slapped his arm. "You never correct my English and when you do, you make fun of me. It's not fair."

"Sorry. I think it's cute the way you speak."

She angrily stubbed out her cigarette in an ashtray. "I don't care what you think. Do you agree to talk to her or not?"

"All right, I'll speak with her."

On one hand, John didn't want to rush things with Tanya to be sure it was love, not need, that was driving his side of the relationship. But he also saw that maybe his reluctance for a confrontation with his wife was just the over-cautious tendency he had developed after three years in a country where restraint and caution ruled. His doubting mind would kick in at times, making him temporarily forget the preciousness of the close relationship that had developed with Tanya. And then the good thoughts of their shared moments of closeness would arise, keeping him moving closer to Tanya and overcoming his doubts. He knew she also shared this feeling because their relationship had first started as a friendship that gave a solid base to moving closer. They could talk together easily right from the start and shared a light humor when looking at the sometimes too serious world around them. He knew Tanya was right about being more assertive, as she often had good suggestions when it came to giving advice.

John eventually made the first indication to leave. He'd wanted to go to the Rundfunk party the following night and take some pictures for an events website, but rest was required. The gathering was an annual tradition where a local pop-up radio broadcast live from an antique circus tent in the courtyard of a castle. Even though this was the summer with a seasonally light workload at the office, he did have certain physical limitations, so Tanya drove him home and made sure he got into bed without any delays.

The next day Tanya was at her desk reviewing framing orders in her combination shop and art gallery. Her two assistants work had to be examined so the wrong size picture frames weren't made up. The intensity of the midday sun warmed her through the tall windows looking out on the small courtyard. The gallery was tucked into the inner square of aged buildings along a tired street of timeworn small shops with faded lettering. It was hiding in a quiet corner of Kreis 4, the fourth district, known in the local dialect as *Chreis Cheib*, home to Zürich's suddenly trendy red-light neighborhood.

The district was generally referred to as Langstrasse, which was the name of the 'long street' that crossed the neighborhood and the historical epicenter of activities both legal and illegal. The area was still home for the remaining members of small ethnic clans of Italians, Spaniards and Brazilians who hadn't been pushed out yet from the rising rents due to the creeping yuppie takeover. The area was slowly being redeveloped with modern apartment buildings replacing older ones as the location became more valuable than the structure. It was part of the relentless push of urban civility that was extending slowly southward from the small downtown center to link up with the newly upmarket industry zone, Zürich West, that had also been a haven for underground clubs and was now getting gentrified into a modern neighborhood.

The prostitutes that had also made the *kreis* their home held on as the scruffy feel of an authentic quarter with strip clubs, cheap bars and mom and pop restaurants slowly disappeared. The mix of old and new gave the neighborhood life even as some natives said it was '*kein dorf mehr*' - no more a neighborhood - with the main street becoming a supermarket of clubs, meaning no more places for the locals. Tanya could have located her gallery in the renovated beer brewery in 'Zuri-West' where a lot of young gallerists started out, mingling with some big-name established exhibitors that called the building home. She wanted to be independent of the official art scene and give her gallery a more edgy reputation. It was symbolic of breaking away from her family's influence to become her own person in the real world where people worked for their money, rather than coasting on a family's wealth.

Tanya had initially enjoyed the beneficial situation in her twenties of daddy's money that made life easy, travelling extensively after receiving a university degree in art history. She gradually came down to earth when she began teaching in a local Swiss high school after a year working in a gallery in Florence. At the same time, her free spirit found its home in painting as she tried to find her own language of expression with forms and colors. Tanya had initially taken the plunge to open her own art space to feature the work of her fellow art school students. The ease of getting a bank loan was no doubt influenced by her family name. She hadn't gone to her father for money to make the point that she was capable of making her own way in the world. She respected her family history and knew her father labored to keep the family bank going in challenging times but didn't understand the need to make more money than you could spend. At least Diana had started a foundation to do good works and hopefully some of her influence might inspire her father in a similar direction.

Tanya made her way from the office area to the art supply cabinets, checking on painting supplies to be close to a lady who was browsing through posters, in case there was some need for advice. The woman steadily flipped over the metal-framed prints hinged to the wall, studying each one briefly, the clack-clack-clack beating out a lazy rhythm as she advanced along the row. The pictures ranged from Hockney and Haring to Van Gogh and the ones teenagers adored of sad clowns and harlequins with teary eyes as big as plates, done in depressing colors.

It was close to noon when Diana stopped by to take her to lunch. She entered the shop as the last two customers were departing and they both scrutinized her closely while going out the door. The Swiss tend to do this as a matter of routine, scanning people from head to toe, assessing their position in society from their clothes and shoes to see if they were acceptable. They stared mostly due to Diana being tall and striking with her swept back ebony hair and dignified features that created a classic elegance. This was accentuated by a luxurious white silk blouse, electric orange linen skirt and deadly high heels with pointed toes. She had a regal bearing that said money and class. Tanya gave her a dismissive look with a humorous smile that said 'this is Langstrasse, not St. Tropez'. While Tanya knew her way around the fashion world, she preferred understated elegance versus the blatant Dolce Gabbana look of glitz and eyepopping colors that Diana occasionally sported. To her, this show of fashion and money was opposite to her wish to be a simpler person, identifying more with her artist side where creations mattered more than Louboutin high heels with red soles. She was also smart enough to know it was people with money who bought art so she needed to maintain the ties to her roots, enough to keep paying guests coming to her exhibits. She walked the fine line between the two worlds, hoping to use the sales of better-known artists to support the up and coming talents. She learned to camouflage herself in the appropriate outfit to suit the occasion, comfortable as a style shape shifter. Today's working outfit was a pair of slim legged jeans and a white V-neck T-shirt.

Tanya and Diana related to each other more like sisters, and that is perhaps why Diana sometimes showed an extra measure of interest in Tanya's male friends at parties. Sibling rivalry? Tanya had mixed reactions to Diana's showing off in front of men she dated before she was with John. She knew Diana was a social butterfly who loved to be the center of attention but occasionally wondered if she had really seriously settled down with her father. It was Diana's first marriage and after many high-profile partners that came and went, maybe now the more serious side had finally found its home. Also, their cultural backgrounds had similarities but also vast differences as the social norms of Germany and Switzerland were far apart. The Germans were more industrious and expansive in their thinking while the Swiss plodded along with a narrow focus, only changing when it was finally necessary. Then Tanya would think of John and herself and knew if there was a real connection based on openness, caring and trust, that any differences could be overcome. And people could change. She loved John and hoped she didn't appear too Swiss to him while he secretly had the opposite fear that he was too much a Yankee to match her style.

She also didn't make an issue of being upset when Diana seemed too overbearing when trying to be motherly. While their relationship was compatible and supportive, in the background Tanya was working through a bit of a love-hate attitude because in some ways she hadn't fully accepted Diana replacing her mother. She knew her father was happy with his new wife but it didn't fully compensate for the replacement of her mother. There was no reason to blame any wounded feelings on Diana but felt she couldn't fully replace someone who had known her from birth. She knew it could only get better with time.

Tanya's mother, Claudia, was her father's Trophy Wife number one and they had known each other since high school. Claudia spent some time as a local fashion model before they married and started a family at a young age. While raising the children, she'd been active in the fashion industry, which influenced Tanya to discover her own path in creative endeavors. Tanya blamed her father for the break-up by his not being attentive enough to Claudia's needs as she tried to express her freedom in a culture that hadn't yet embraced emancipated women. Replacing one free spirited woman with another may have been his way of trying to evolve into a more modern way of life from the one he was raised in. A couple of years at Stanford Business School in California after college had helped make him more flexible than his counterparts. Marrying Diana could also have been atonement for the behavior that lost his first wife which meant Tanya was having trouble to fully forgive him. To make matters worse, her mother had run off with another finance type. He was a former Union Bank Switzerland fund manager who had set-up his own large equities fund and was aiming to attract some of the new wealth in Asia by having it Singapore based. This meant Tanya only saw her mother on holidays, when one or the other would fly in for a mini-family reunion.

Tanya locked up the shop like many others in the neighborhood did, shutting down for two hours during midday. One of her assistants would show up at two to open up so she could have a leisurely lunch or as was often her routine, take an hour or two to work on her latest painting in a small detached workroom next to her gallery. Tanya suggested one of the small seasonal restaurants along the lake where they could escape the oppressive heat that felt like a stuffy sauna. Stepping outside they could feel the high temperature amplified by the cement floor of the courtyard that stored the warmth. Driving across town with a welcome breeze blowing through the open car, Tanya asked about John's photo assignment. Diana said she would explain everything over a glass of wine as she turned up the music that Tanya recognized as a Hotel Costes lounge music compilation. Diana concentrated on navigating through the intersection at the Bellevue plaza where the perpetually stalled traffic was routed in different directions like a heart desperately pumping away with too many clogged arteries. Half the drivers didn't know where they were going, creating temporary stoppages in the flow of cars. Diana wove her light metallic blue Porsche expertly through intermittent traffic on the lake road and passed a couple of slow-moving cars. More than one driver they passed couldn't help but stare at two attractive women in a high-performance convertible. As the car purred along the lakeside Tanya updated Diana on her latest success of having two Basquiats to sell. The news resulted in an immediate offer to buy both, which was politely refused.

They were lucky and found a table on the terrace of a lakeside restaurant under the shade of an ancient Linden tree. It was in full bloom with hundreds of tiny yellow flowers forming a delicately scented canopy, with the fallen petals making a royal carpet. There was a wooden pier next to them where a couple of small speedboats gently rocked against the dock. One had a weather-beaten sign hanging over the side advertising water-skiing lessons. The greenish blue water had a faint scent of the ocean from the drying algae along the shore.

"How's Dad?" Tanya asked after they each had selected

their meal and been served a glass of cold white wine mixed with sparkling mineral water.

"All right. Working more than ever now. With economic problems and recessions everywhere, people want their money safe and Swiss banks are still seen to be secure. Good old Switzerland." She laughed, raising her spritzer in a toast.

"I just worry that he'll overwork himself. You both have enough money to live an easy life. Why does he still keep at it?"

"It's his pride. He's the last in a line of Beyers and your little brother just runs around getting in trouble and not showing any interest in the family business, except to spend his inheritance. Your father wants to have something to hand down."

"Juerg will come around. Let him graduate from university. Dad always pushed him too hard. Sometimes that has an opposite effect. I'm sure Juerg will be more sensible once he's settled down and finds out he has to pay for his own windsurfing holidays somehow."

"Sooner then he may imagine." Diana gave a wise parental grin. "You know what your father's biggest worry is? Getting bought out. Losing control and being turned into a powerless puppet. Like the Bank Leu family bank being taken over by Swiss Credit Bank."

"Sorry, I don't follow the business news too much."

"It wasn't done in a very pleasant manner. Everyone had expected a foreign bank looking for a way into Switzerland to be the friendly purchaser."

"You would think the Swiss would be happy to stick together."

Showing off her MBA background, Diana gave a small lecture on the finance world. "All the Swiss private banks added together have only ten percent of the total money under management here so they don't have much leverage when it comes to a fight. And in private banks like your father's, it's their own personal money that's committed to cover any trading losses and anything else like fines. Beyer is a typical small private bank and only manages about three billion in deposits while the big Swiss banks all together are estimated to have two trillion in private banking assets. It's the Golden Rule: 'he who has the money makes the rules'. Also, the big banks have bigger IT departments to support research and increase their market share. The smaller banks are out gunned and gradually driven out of business or bought out."

"What would a takeover mean for him? They would use the name and he just sits there?"

"He would still meet with the old customers but most investment decisions would be made over his head. It would be a 'boutique bank' to attract clients who think tradition and personal service come with the fees they pay to safeguard their money."

"Isn't that better somehow? He should take the money and run."

"There are only five true private banks today down from sixty back in the fifties. Do you want to live in a world of only a couple of faceless corporations – MacMoney?"

"Of course not, it's bad enough already. I like that Dad is preserving a family tradition that's been going on for six generations." She remembered back to when she was a child visiting the original family villa from the 1800's with the Victorian drawing room that was used for meetings. Her only memory was that it was kind of creepy, like visiting a haunted house.

"New clients like to do business with the private banks with the oldest reputation. And now most private bankers are shifting to a share-based structure because without it, the family's own money is on the line. But with a structure based on investors, they're not personally liable."

"I really hope he can find a decent partner."

"It's nice you say that. I know you and your father haven't always seen eye to eye but don't make the same mistake I did with mine and fight him on every occasion. Life is too short."

"You're right. He's not such a bad man." They both laughed.

"Anyway, all that bank stuff is business as usual in the world of modern-day commerce and we will fight it out. Your dad's a smart man. There's a bigger problem which is why I asked John to take some pictures." Diana took a deep breath as if she was diving into something that required special courage. "I wasn't satisfied with the explanations regarding the death of Klaus."

Tanya knew her brother had gone to Africa in support of the family foundation's work to expose the challenges to the environment. It was his latest expedition after trips to the Amazon and Indonesia to expose the destruction of rainforests. Tanya nodded, not sure if what she was going to hear was going to make her feel better. She was afraid that the deep sadness she had felt after his death would resurface again after she'd worked hard to process the incident six months earlier. He'd been like a big brother who was always ready with a smile, warm hug and good advice. Her own little brother was too young to fulfil the same role, so Klaus's support and positive outlook were always welcome. They'd grown close and their mutual interest in protecting the planet created a shared sense of purpose. Tanya felt that Diana was in part to blame for his death by letting him go on the expedition without any security because Klaus had died while independently supporting the foundation's goals. She felt with more caution and research into possible dangers, Klaus might still be alive. This low-level anger had yet to be articulated but created a feeling of resentment under the surface of their relationship. Tanya wasn't sure which would take longer to heal – the grief or the anger. At the moment, the sadness guided her memories but meeting with Diana brought out the animosity that was mixed in the intensity of her feelings. She wondered at times if her anger was a reaction to deflect the sorrow, serving as a form of denial. She also knew that Klaus had an independent streak like his sister and would spontaneously pursue a project if he felt passionate about it. But blaming a dead person you loved for their taking one risk too many wasn't the appropriate reaction.

"You know I found the official version of his death hard to believe because Klaus was not the mountaineer type. He wouldn't have gone alone on a peak without a guide. His falling off a cliff seemed too improbable. Klaus had been documenting activities of a specific mining group and they weren't happy with his picture-taking so there had been a couple of physical confrontations. Anyone disruptive to their operations conveniently dies. Usually it's one of the natives whose land was being taken over or being polluted. You remember how I was rescued from the mine's creeps by a kind local man? He was displaced and apparently was also killed for helping me when the security men showed up. In the case of Klaus, it had to look like an accident because if he simply disappeared, a big investigation would've been organized."

"I still can't believe it."

"He's not the only one to die. In the last year alone, over three hundred environmental activists have been killed around the world. Close to one a day."

"That's totally messed up."

"So, guess who ultimately owns the mining company? An outlaw billionaire here in Switzerland named Stan Buck."

Tanya had started crying at the start of the story as the grief became alive again and had to dry her eyes with a napkin. At the mention of Buck's name, she did a double-take. She knew the name because he was also a well-known art collector. Diana reached over and put a hand on her arm.

"Fucking bastard," Tanya spit out in a chocked-up voice.

Her anger and renewed sorrow momentarily overrode her commenting on the art connection.

"I agree." Diana's eyes started to tear up but she held off crying and took a sip of her wine. "I don't want Klaus to become just another statistic. That's why I wanted to get some pictures of this Mr. Buck. He's a fugitive from the U.S. and living in Switzerland because the Swiss don't consider his tax evasion a crime. It's just an administrative issue to them. I have a friend who is an editor at one of the largest weekly magazines in Germany and would publish a high-profile article exposing all his bad deeds. I'm hoping a big blast of negative publicity will shame the Swiss to consider sending him back to the States to go to jail. I'm also thinking of hiring a lobbyist to put some pressure on the government."

"He really sounds evil. No wonder he had John roughed up to get the camera."

"What are you talking about?"

"One of Buck's bodyguards grabbed him as soon as he took a photo in the Diagonal. Buck demanded to have the memory card but a friend of John's jumped in and blocked the request. Buck and his people all left the club and a couple of hours later when John was walking to his car, somebody punched him and stole his camera."

Diana made a horrified expression. "I hadn't realized how ruthless he was. I never would've knowingly put John or anyone else in danger. It only intensifies my resolve to make sure Buck will go to jail."

The comment made Tanya wonder again if Diana's being a little reckless had allowed someone else dear to her to be in danger.

Tanya decided not to comment on this and moved on. "Now do you want to hear something really strange? I guess our ex-neighbor down the lake Carl Jung would call it synchronicity.

This morning I put up the announcement about the Basquiat show on a couple of the important art news websites all the collectors and museums follow. And within fifteen minutes, the art consultant of our new 'friend' Mr. Buck contacted me. His client is interested in the paintings because he's a big collector of modern art."

"That's indeed peculiar. Almost makes me think he's spying on the family." Diana's paranoid thought was triggered by an intuitive sixth sense she couldn't quite articulate. It was the feeling of a threatening presence lurking beneath the surface like a partially submerged log on a lake that could sink an unaware speeding boat. Maybe triggered from seeing Buck buying shares in her company. "I actually met him years ago in New York during my party days. He was part of the fund manager, real estate developer, mega-rich crowd. He didn't seem so bad, but then none of them did at the time. I bumped into him again a year ago scoping out art to buy at the Venice Biennale, so he knows I'm married to your father. It could mean you're also on his radar, if he's keeping tabs on me because he knows about my brother."

"He must really want those paintings badly. His consultant suggested what's called a 'third party guarantee'. It's a binding offer for a set price ahead of the sale that would be higher than any other offer."

"I hope you didn't agree anything. I'd tell him to go screw himself." Diana picked up her drink and took an angry swallow.

"I didn't accept the arrangement. Honestly, I don't know what to think. Klaus's death shouldn't go unpunished but Buck is a world-renowned collector and his endorsement would give my gallery a lot of credibility and make me a primary dealer. Besides, punishing him is like punishing the president of the United States because of an American soldier in Afghanistan who kills a civilian. It's the soldier who must face the judge."

"The paintings are your ticket to recognition, not him. I agree, he wasn't directly responsible but he provided the environment where such action could happen."

"Yes, in principle, all these people destroying the planet should be challenged. And yet, a sale of an important painting to a prestigious collector would help me to get an invitation one day to exhibition at Art Basel or other big shows."

"Hear me out," Diana begged gently. "Jung defined synchronicity as meaningful coincidences. Perhaps there is a way we can use Buck's interest in the paintings against him. It's like the martial arts, you use someone's own energy against them."

"I'm happy to help where I can but at the end of the day it's my gallery."

"Now I've heard of everything. The guy kills my brother, has your photographer friend beat up and you want to enrich his art collection."

"I detest this man as much as you do, maybe even more after the news of Klaus. But treating a symptom does not cure the disease. We need to have a solid plan to get rid of him once and for all. He needs to go to jail and I don't see how not selling him a painting will make this happen."

"Right again. Buck wants something you have and that gives us some power. Let's keep our cool and see if we can find an angle to play."

"I'll think about it," Tanya said picking up her glass and tossing back some of her wine.

"Thank you. And besides, they're just paintings."

"It's my business and I'll make my own decisions." Tanya looked at Diana with a serious expression. For all her professed interest in art and artists Tanya thought Diana was missing the point about the importance of finding a respectable home for significant artworks. Art was not another commodity, it was a personal expression of an individual that created an emotion in the audience. And certainly shouldn't be used as a bargaining chip or held as ransom to punish someone. At the same time, Diana wondered if Tanya's youthful idealism was an incorrect or immature response to a more dynamic world of a game played at a high level where a stack of chips on the roulette table in Monte Carlo could quadruple with a little luck, strategy and positive intent.

"I respect that. At the very least, if he buys the paintings you could use some of the profits to support the environmental foundation. Klaus would've wanted us to continue the fight." Tanya nodded in resigned agreement. "C'mon – solidarity!" Diana raised her glass and they toasted to their common cause to save the planet. Tanya made the gesture to keep the peace, not really convinced of Diana's intentions but braved a smile.

They were distracted from their conversation when a stylish retired couple in white linen outfits walked past them and the man helped his partner into their speedboat with a small cabin that was tied up to the neighboring dock. The woman in a flowing sundress and straw hat had almost fallen in the water during the transition. The two women both suppressed a laugh watching the show and it helped lighten the mood. The waitress arrived, serving their salads. As Tanya reached for some bread Diana asked, "And what about this mysterious boyfriend you keep hiding from me?"

Tanya paused and took a sip of her drink wondering how honest she could be but sisterhood won out. "It's no mystery, it's John."

Diana laughed out loud. "You've been keeping this a secret all these months? Maybe you should be a private banker."

Tanya smiled. "It wasn't easy."

"Two free spirits with men who work in a bank." Diana

lifted her wine and they clinked glasses again. "Why not bring him over for a drink and meet your father?"

"Don't think it would work just now. He's in the middle of getting a divorce."

"Oh, that does present a difficulty. Are you his mistress or is this just a casual relationship?"

"It's serious." Tanya retorted indignantly as if she had just been called a whore. "We love each and as soon as his divorce comes through in a few months we can be together without any public limitations."

"You really believe all that?"

"Yes, damn it!"

"Sorry, I don't mean to play devil's advocate."

"You know how these divorce proceedings can go. If I got named as the other woman, it would make him the guilty party and he'd be punished even more financially. Could also lose his chance to stay here. His wife is being encouraged to do everything to throw him out of the country by her lawyer sister."

"I see your point. Next time I see him, I promise not to ask how his wife is."

They turned to watch a small dinghy from a boat school with a sputtering outboard motor repeat docking maneuvers so the student driver, an older woman in cut-off jeans and a bikini top, could get experience for a license.

Diana turned back to Tanya, "Can you arrange for the three of us to meet in the next day or two? Very discrete of course. I owe John an apology as well as an explanation. And maybe some money if he managed to get a decent picture of the elusive Mr. Buck."

"OK. We're going out tonight so I'll see when he's free. I know he's dying to find out what this is all about. And you'll let me know if there is anything I can do to help with the bank?

Even if it's just to chat. You know you can give me a call anytime."

"That's sweet. I'll probably take you up on your offer and ask for some help emptying some champagne bottles when I drown my sorrows."

Ernst Schmidt was trying to find some files but somehow the legendary Swiss precision and exactness fell short when it came to filing documents in public departments and the Fremdenpolizei were no exception. They were notoriously slow to get anything done, but the public accepted this, as the role of the foreign police was important. And when requests did get processed, freedom seekers were nickeled and dimed to death for every bit of paper they needed to produce for their citizenship application. Besides being a regular money machine, the whole bloated, inefficient system was necessary for the maintenance of democracy. Schmidt knew this well and had had an easy career as a civil servant until now. For the first time in his life uncertainty loomed as the first feeble attempts at restructuring the department were underway.

Change, oh how frightening. Nothing scared the Swiss more, but the world marched on, and slowly dragged them along, kicking and screaming. Unemployment hovered at less than one percent for so long that when it hit three percent people started to notice that their rose garden was contaminated by blight. Gone were the days you could find the hundred unemployed people in Switzerland for a group picture, now they were slowly moving towards the EU average. Schmidt's job had shifted to reflect the basic changes in Europe. As recessions, inflation and immigrations all soared, some of the Swiss natives grew restless and their xenophobia took deeper roots. Foreigners were taking their jobs, eating their food, marrying their sons and daughters and soaking up social benefits.

Schmidt had accepted the changes in immigration trends but something had to be done now because the situation could get out of hand without some proper management. He had the power to help, he was a *Schweizermacher*. Schmidt had to appear to respect the foreigner's rights but also show some strength to his superiors, which is why he was sifting through files.

He shifted his bulk in the complaining chair. Puffing, he opened and closed the complaining ancient metal file cabinets, a cotton sleeveless T-shirt visible under his threadbare white shirt. The tie was a superfluous addition to command dignity, almost as wide as it was long with ancient food stains indistinguishable from the pattern. It angled over his stomach that hid the belt that now was secured at the last possible hole having made that gradual journey with increasing speed over the past couple of years. Balding, with the well-fed profile of a bureaucrat, he was the last line of defense between the invading hordes and mother Switzerland. Checking *Ausländers* who wanted to defile the Swiss *fraulines* with their soiled, barbaric hands. Schmidt was idealistic and believed that Swiss democracy was a model society for others to learn from. After all, hadn't South Africa, Russia and Lebanon sent representatives here to study their political culture and the Dalai Lama suggest it as a model for a free Tibet?

Foreigners were getting too smart and there were getting to be too many of them, time to put on the brakes. One flaw and toss their file out and them with it. Tough times required extreme responses. Following lunch, he would take a little drive to look into an applicant who had surmounted the paperwork hurdle. Under yesterday's newspaper he found the file he was looking for. He would make sure to find and exaggerate a fault somewhere so he could decline the application. Show the superiors he wasn't soft. It would help his job security in case they were looking to retire him early like some of his colleagues. And while the anger against the United States was at a fever pitch in conservative circles for their forcing open bank secrecy laws that were a heritage of the country, why not target an American? He smiled and picked up a folder, this one should be perfect. The white label had a ten-digit number followed by a name: Miller, John.

SIX

Tanya drove over to her family house on a hillside in Zollikon. It wasn't a mega mansion like some of the Russian neighbors, rather an unassuming building from the fifties unlike the old villa that originally housed the family bank. That had been leased out to allow a move into modern offices in the city, providing a more up-to-date image. Her visit was a diplomatic mission to make sure her father would invite some of his friends and clients to the exhibition. Diana had assured her he was proud of his daughter and would support her, so the visit was also an opportunity to say thanks.

She rang the doorbell to announce herself and walked right in. As she entered the front door, the Italian housekeeper with a sunny face and deep dark eyes appeared and greeted her with a big hug. The woman has been with the family since Tanya was a child and was beaming like a proud mother. They exchanged a few short pleasantries and the woman pointed to the back garden where Tanya could find her father.

Tanya walked through the house appreciating how the interior was contemporary compared to the boring exterior. The living room was built around black leather and chrome furniture with some tasteful modern art on the white brick walls. She found her father on the back patio behind the kitchen. The lawn behind it dropped off and a bird's eye view of a small boat harbor was framed between a couple of ancient apple trees just starting to produce fruit. Her father was reading the *Neue Zürcher Zeitung* and sipping a gin and tonic. He was wearing a pale blue polo shirt and white linen slacks, looking like he had just stepped off a yacht. The heat wave was still baking the city, amplified by the *Föhn*, the warm wind that blew over alpine regions from the Sahara, depositing a fine yellow sand, covering cars with a dusty grit. It made the natives restless and some people attributed the unsettling atmosphere to an increase in suicides. The shade of a large chestnut tree only gave the illusion of coolness.

"Hi Dad," Tanya said with a big smile.

Hans-Peter got up and gave Tanya a hug, greeting her with a warm look. He pulled out a chair from the table for her.

"You're looking wonderful, darling," Hans-Peter said. The housekeeper appeared and placed an iced tea in front of Tanya who nodded her thanks.

"Thank you, but I feel like I'm melting." They both laughed. She started to fan herself with a section of the newspaper she had picked up and folded to try and cool off.

"I hear you are becoming quite recognized in the art world these days."

"If only. I'm taking my first big step. I was lucky to get the offer to sell those paintings."

"Yes, but you've also worked hard to be recognized as a trusted partner."

"Thanks. They say luck is where preparation meets opportunity. I was in the right place with the right people who supported me and made the introduction to the seller. It's a significant artist but I don't want to be a one hit wonder, forgotten after the exhibition. It's really important for me to cultivate a clientele that not only buys art but more importantly, find clients wanting me to represent selling their collections. These days a lot of significant paintings are finding their way to auction houses and galleries because of the three D's: divorces, deaths and debts. There are many opportunities for recognized galleries because of a fifty-percent divorce rate in countries like the US and also in quiet, conservative Switzerland."

"I can assure you I will keep my ears open for any such marital troubles. I believe Diana would be more helpful as she is better attuned to the social situation."

"And as you know, the rich are increasingly diversifying their assets to include art."

"I can't really advise any of my clients to go to your gallery because my bank's focus of financial advising is mainly limited to shares and bonds. But if a client should ask, I would certainly point them your way." It was as if he anticipated the question.

After Tanya prompted him, he agreed to invite his friends to the art show, a lot of whom knew her already. Next came the tricky part of the conversation. Tanya wanted to get her father's opinion on wanting to sell the paintings to Buck. She always trusted his levelheaded advice and was looking for confirmation. She knew Diana had told Hans-Peter about the involvement of Buck in her brother's death.

"Another part of my selling the Basquiats is finding a high-profile collector who loves his work. The publicity and recognition will support my vision of becoming a world-class gallery."

His response surprised her as she was expecting a neutral answer, leaning to support. It was obvious Diana had briefed him. "I'm sorry, but your selling the paintings to a wanted criminal would be on questionable moral grounds. In today's world, the public is giving critical scrutiny to unlawful acts as well as environmental concerns. And supporting a fugitive, even in as innocent an act as selling some art, could make the public perceive you to be an accomplice to his crimes. It's called 'reputational damage' and 'guilt by association'."

"It sounds like you're the one coming from a place of guilt based on the many scandals of secret bank accounts for dictators and drug barons. That's on top of the Jewish account scandal where the banks had remained silent and had made no effort to find legitimate heirs to the accounts abandoned in World War Two."

The usually pleasant demeanor of her father suddenly shifted to a strong defensive tone, having taken the comments personally. "Because of the few, the many shouldn't be punished and impugn the integrity of my bank and the reputation it's built on."

Tanya wound back the conversation, reiterating her reasoning to sell to Buck. "Some other collectors have also expressed interest, but Buck's has been the best offer. He'll surely mention to his other billionaire friends what an amazing talent I am."

It was clear her words might as well have been spoken to a chunk of granite from the Alps. Hans-Peter took a big gulp to finish his drink and put his glass down to signify the conversation was over. He gave her a stare that said there was nothing more to say. Tanya read the signs and said she had to go. With each braving a reserved smile, they stood up and shared a brief hug and said a quick goodbye before she left.

Harry Jenkins' range of contacts stretched in every imaginable direction. He'd been working in Switzerland for fifteen years, first as an auditor for an American accounting company, which had taken him into the headquarters of all the major financial institutions, insurance, and manufacturing companies. Using his network, he went off on his own, doing business graphics for the same clients he had helped earlier with spreadsheets.

John sat in the back office of Harry's studio over his lunch hour, sampling last year's Beaujolais after the girls who did the graphics had gone out for food. The logic for drinking was that Harry needed to make space for the new vintage. Harry gave a little speech about the wine's annual variations in anticipation of November's new unveiling. John spread out the photos from Friday night in the club that he had taken from his shoulder bag. Sean had dropped them off that morning.

Harry picked up the one with the group sitting at a table and pointed at the American businessman. "Looks like you hit the jackpot on this one. That's Stan Buck."

"What? You know him? Who the hell is he?"

"Only one of the richest men on the planet. He's wanted by the U.S. government for tax evasion."

"Why's he here in Switzerland?"

"He's like Al Capone. The Feds couldn't prove a single crime related to his oil trading and commodities business so they had to resort to tax evasion. An offense that will get you a one-way ticket to prison. Buck took up residence in Switzerland, because the authorities wouldn't deport him for something they didn't consider a crime."

"Wow!"

"Not only that, his commodities trading company in Zug has an annual turnover in the double-digit billions. It's second only to Nestlé in annual revenues for a Swiss company. He's the largest taxpayer in Switzerland, even with Zug having the lowest rates."

"I see why they like him here. Why would he want to grab my camera?"

"Could be one of his friends is camera shy."

"Considering who hired me, it probably has to do with someone destroying the environment."

"Buck's got a long history of mixing with the wrong people. Years ago, when he was a young trader, he sold Iranian oil during an embargo. That's what triggered the largest outcry after he was already under investigation for tax evasion. They called it 'trading with the enemy'. Later, he went there swapping weapons for oil with the Supreme Leader, Khamenei. Some of the Iranian oil went to South Africa for uranium which Buck sold to Russia and so on and so forth."

"What a wheeler dealer."

"Nowadays it's said Iran's back at it. Buck could be hanging out with anybody these days. He likes to support dictators and get mineral concessions for financing their coups. His main business is copper. No one can buy the stuff without doing business with him. The guy is such a weasel he actually sold copper to the U.S. Treasury to make coins – while he's a wanted criminal."

"That's what you call an entrepreneur," John said in mock admiration.

"I can ask around but it's probably better you forget this story. Right now, Buck has dozens of lawyers trying to reach a negotiated settlement with the IRS. If you have a compromising picture, I'm sure he's not going to like the publicity. I wouldn't push too much. He's got friends all the way to the top of the Swiss government."

"Anyone paying billions a year in taxes is going to be liked in Bern."

"And getting a smack on the head is minor compared to what else he could do."

"I know what you mean. The guy who grabbed me in the club was sizing me up like he was measuring me for a coffin."

Harry finished his glass of wine, getting more excited. "See what I mean? This is serious shit. And forget about digging up any dirt on him and or his numbered bank accounts. The only numbers in Zug are in the phone book."

"What about the police?"

Harry raised an eyebrow. "The police chief and head prosecutor there are on the boards of his companies, so you'll be up against a stone wall." He raised his arms in a shrug of exasperation. "Also, the Swiss have a law that gives the police the right to arrest anyone involved in activities disruptive to the Swiss economy. They can hold them without formal charges or a chat with a lawyer for two weeks. Which in your case they would graciously roll out to a month or three. If you want to stay out of jail, I'd say don't get on the guy's bad side."

"Sounds like a healthy idea. Are you sure the U.S. government can't touch him?"

"They tried like mad when he first moved here twenty years ago but the Swiss being as stubborn as they are, stuck by their laws and there was no chance. Plus, a small payment of fifty million dollars by Buck for miscellaneous fees didn't hurt either. The American government did put a three million dollar reward out for his arrest and he's been on the FBI's ten most wanted list for twenty years."

"And he's still running around free. Unbelievable. If you could check out who his friends are, I would be curious to know."

"This guy has so many friends, you can take your pick."

"You don't think there's any use in pursuing this?"

"Can if you want, but I'm saying your chances for success aren't that great. He's staying squeaky clean here by doing all his deals according to Swiss law. Always appearing to be neutral when dealing with dictators. He's got the Department of Justice and local police tipping him off on any schemes to nab him.

Remember, he's also a target for bounty hunters, kidnappers, competitors and even terrorists looking for that three million reward. That's why his security chief is ex-Mossad. But if it will make you any happier I'll ask around."

John took a generous swallow of wine and pushed aside some printouts of pie charts spread on the desk to find a stable place for his glass. "I just can't accept that money rules. And now these greedy bastards are pushing me around just because of a photograph that probably links the creep to even more crimes. While you and I as humble citizens are being forced to give up our U.S. citizenship because of all the scrutiny over tax evasion triggered by rich people like Buck hiding their assets."

"That's why I gave up my passport." Harry got up from where he was stationed at his worktable and wandered over to the window, casually looking out and taking a generous sip from his magically refilled glass. "If it's any relief to you, Buck had to pay five hundred million in alimony, so you're getting off cheap." They both laughed.

Harry poured some wine into each of their glasses. "As far as your photo, I'll do a bit of snooping. Maybe I can find something out about Buck's friends."

"My friend Sean is asking at the *Blick* if they might want to use the photo. But first I want to make sure I don't get on someone's bad side. I'm still waiting to hear from the lady that hired me to take the photo."

"Wise idea." Harry paused a second and spun the conversation in a new direction. "Don't forget, next week it's the Country Western party. I'll need those snaps for the September International Club magazine. Didn't our president look good in those photos from the last cocktail party? If nothing else, he sure knows how to smile for the camera."

"Don't talk to me about him," John said slamming his hand on the table and making his glass rattle. "Monday morning *el presidente* called me. He asked for the photos from the Friday cocktail party and any other events that night, as well as the original files. Even threatened to black ball me at my job and for any freelance photo assignments if I didn't show 'discretion'."

"Son of a bitch."

"What the hell is he going to do with the electronic versions? He's never asked before. It's too much of a coincidence if you ask me."

"Maybe no coincidence. Buck has money stashed everywhere and is always working with different banks to finance projects. He just did a deal to buy Russian oil and with no way to move it, built his own pipeline out of there. We're talking serious money."

"See what I mean about getting it from all sides? Buck is even trying to push me around at the office. Let's take a closer look at the photos, maybe your trained eye will spot something."

They went to a computer along the wall with a large monitor. John gave Harry a memory stick and he opened the party file with a graphics program and found the club picture.

"Nice shot," Harry said. "Let's take a closer look at those babes." He clicked on the zoom feature focusing on one of the blondes, increasing the image by a hundred percent. "Not bad. My guess is thirty-eight double D's, most likely silicon. None of them are wearing wedding rings so it looks kosher."

"Zoom in on the tie pin on Buck's tie. It looks like some kind of insignia."

Harry increased the image by another hundred percent. "Could be a kind of bird or something holding the stone."

John said, "Boost it a little more."

"It's going to get too grainy but I'll try." Harry increased the image again but the image blurred into small squares. "Let me work on it a little more with some photo enhancement software I've got on a more powerful machine. I'll get back to you on it.

All right, it's a wrap. I'm already late for a meeting with a client in Seefeld."

"No problem. Next time, I will invite you to that dive next door and we'll close it down again like we did the other week."

Harry smiled. "It's a deal."

SEVEN

"The only constant in this company is change." John was speaking to Susanne, a young Dutch lady who handled the public relations for another commercial department. He was paraphrasing a Greek philosopher that had been quoted in a change management course he'd been on. At the time, he hadn't expected it would be his own change he would be communicating. They were in John's office catching up on the company news over an afternoon coffee. John hoped it would counteract the drowsy effect of the red wine at Harry's office.

Susanne sat on the guest chair sipping coffee from a plastic cup, dressed like she was still a preppie at an Ivy League college in a plaid pleated skirt, black pumps and a short-sleeved white shirt with a high collar. With her wholesome look, Susanne just as easily could have been knocking on doors selling Bibles.

Susanne said, "What I can't get used to is how us work units are always the last to know when our lives are being rearranged. Unless you've got some horsepower from a mentor in a high place you're at management's mercy."

"All this garbage about employees first and one big family,

blah, blah, blah is just a bunch of hot air. After all, we should know how to promote." They both started laughing.

"You're right. What I heard was we're all going to be outsourced. It's something called Project Amalfi. The name was inspired by the lemon growing region in southern Italy."

"Making lemonade out of lemons. Which genius thought that one up?" John said.

"The plan is that some coordinator would consolidate department requests and farm them out to agencies. You and I'd become extinct. Then when the company makes money again in a couple of years they'll hire a bunch more marketing people for the 'personal touch'. Only this time, young kids out of university at half the salary," Susanne said.

"Who'd you hear that from?"

"One of my usually reliable sources," Susanne said.

"I hope they're wrong for once."

"Did you hear about the German guy in Investment Management? It was the last week of the month and he gets his notice by mail. His boss didn't have the guts to tell him personally. Looks like the wave they keep hinting at has started."

"It's a good strategy to do it in the summer. Some people will go on a vacation that never ends."

"Let's see if we can make it to the end of the month. It's all you can do these days."

The phone rang. After listening a few seconds John swore, "Damn. I'm sorry. I'll be right there." He hung up the phone, tossing it into the cradle and looked at Susanne. "A five-hundred-franc agenda, an email calendar and a smartphone and I still can't remember a meeting. Nothing ever gets decided anyway – all talk and no action. Nobody wants to pull the trigger. Ready, aim, aim, aim, aim..." They both laughed. "By the way, did you hear the good news?"

"No."

"You have a new position."

"Tell me more."

"That was the good news. The bad news is, the job's with another company, and you have to find it."

Later that afternoon the provisional director of the commercial department's marketing group, Ralph Owens, stuck his head in John's office, requesting a meeting right away. John thought it was odd, as there were no outstanding items to discuss. His stomach contracted with a spasm in a reflex of fear, as the other times Ralph had addressed him that way nothing good had come of it.

The physical reaction was an echo of the more massive stress he'd endured a couple of months earlier when he'd learned his mid-year review ranking. According to the company protocol, the manager and employee would enter their comments individually in an online system and review them together to come up with a balanced assessment that would determine his bonus and potential for advancement (meaning a bigger salary). Ralph had blocked the employee review process by not freeing up his comments for viewing until the day after the system locked in the feedback. There was no chance for John to review and discuss or have a talk to find a common understanding – he had to accept what was entered. And what Ralph had put into the system were comments that had no bearing on the three objectives they had jointly agreed. When the summary was given verbally in the closing minutes of their weekly meeting, John was taken by surprise at the negative statements.

Ralph was newly installed in his temporary role of John's boss and wanted to put John in his place and exert absolute control over someone he imagined was operating too independently. John thought it reflected his insecurity from being underqualified for the role. In the review meeting, John tried to ignore the harshness of the criticism and attempted to offer some counter points to the discussion but was mowed over. Ralph had finished his short speech with some comments he intended to show he was all about employees. He told John he liked his work and wanted to keep him on the team but the choice was up to him, as if John were on probation and needed to prove himself. There was a clearly implied tone to the feedback that said Ralph could and would dismiss him at whim, so John had better toe the line. John recognized he had no chance to challenge the review. The point that riled John the most was that any impartial person looking at what he had done against the agreed measures would see he had more than accomplished his tasks. He had no recourse except to accept the lies and keep his head down. A low ranking would mean he would not get a bonus and that amount was usually what paid the years tax bill. He kept his cool remembering the expression he heard from some friends in the States: 'keeping your job is the new raise'.

John's heart pounded as he walked down the hall to the corner office looking out on Paradeplatz. The large square viewable through six tall windows was where the biggest Swiss banks had their headquarters. Definitely an executive position to have this view. Ralph had it decorated with wooden plaques commemorating successful promotional campaigns, trophies from golf tournaments and various photos of his family members. Ralph was holding down the position until a permanent marketing head was hired for the commercial department. As a foreign transferee he was enjoying the perks the role brought with it. The housing subsidies, private school for his kids and flights home on top of a wickedly high salary irritated John who had none of these benefits as a local hire. That, combined with maintaining an attitude towards John that said he could do nothing right in his eyes, made their relationship testy at the best of times and left John never knowing where he was standing.

Ralph put down the memo he was studying and motioned John to a chair. He got up and puffed around his desk in an angled waddle as though his bulk would fit better between the furniture if he moved sideways like a supertanker squeezing through the Suez Canal. Ralph's cheap suit, even though it was gray with pin stripes, contained so much polyester John imagined that static was making sparks and audible pops. Ralph closed the door and sat on the edge of his desk trying to keep his balance with only one foot touching the ground in a practiced pose of informality.

Ralph started some light conversation that already made John suspicious. "Why the hell are there so many speed cameras everywhere? I got my second speeding ticket today."

"I know what you mean. The Green Party wants everyone to ride a bicycle so they're trying to make every street thirty kilometers an hour."

"That's ridiculous. I can walk faster than that."

To try and keep the low intensity chat continuing on a friendly level, John asked about Ralph's car collection that was his pride and joy.

"Yes indeed! I'm buying another classic Mustang and it only cost about thirty thousand dollars. I also have another one on order."

The story didn't help as John hadn't gotten a raise this year and one classic car represented a significant chunk of his salary. John thought that Ralph must have missed the sensitivity module in the employee relation's class. It was just one more example of making a show of his disregard for John.

Now that Ralph felt the mood was friendly, he started in

on the real purpose of the meeting. "John, I don't know how to tell you this," Ralph said. King of the Communicators tongue-tied? "I know how you like working in the commercial department..."

John quietly took some deep breaths to still his nervousness as his stomach knotted up reflexively.

"...but we've had to re-think our strategy. There's some reorganization being talked about to consolidate jobs. Yours is one of them under consideration." John was quiet and alert, a cold shadow passing over his insides.

"I can't tell you anything for certain but I thought I'd give you some advance warning so there are no surprises. OK?"

John was momentarily stunned and hesitantly mouthed some words. "Thanks, I appreciate your concern. Do you have any idea when the reorganization will be announced?"

"We are hoping in the next two months we'll have a definite organizational plan. These global restructurings take some time. The plan is to have all moves in place by the end of the third quarter."

"Are you saying I'll be out of a job or just transferred?" John found the courage to attempt speaking although his stomach was in knots.

Ralph smiled reassuringly. "If I had my way, we'd keep you where you are."

"I think I'm making a good contribution to the output from the team." John was calmer now, centering himself.

"I'm not saying that you're out of a job but it might not be a bad idea to talk to the Human Resources department about what other career opportunities you could pursue. And if you have a headhunter, you might want to reconnect, if you haven't already."

The room was suddenly very quiet except for the muffled conversation of the secretary coming through the wall and hiss of the air conditioning. "I appreciate you telling me all this. At least it gives me an idea where I stand."

"Good. If I can give you a little personal advice..." Ralph said with an extra spoon of sugar on top, sweetening his tone.

"Yeah, sure."

"Take a little time and look at where you want to go with your career. Could be you won't find a fulfilling future here. Maybe journalism is more to your liking and lifestyle. Or you might consider something entirely different like opening an American style restaurant on a beach somewhere. If you're laid off, there would be a good severance package. Think about it."

"All right." John nodded affirmatively, not too convinced a payout would even cover a month's rent. He couldn't believe this idiot was saying he would make a better burger chef. Ralph hopped onto both feet to signal the end of the meeting.

The Earth Goddess Foundation had a small three-room office in a Victorian house that was remodeled from a residence to an office space. It was located in the Englischviertel neighborhood, a short distance from the downtown that was a mix of classic houses and small commercial buildings. The foundation's name was listed on a directory on a wall of the entrance along with a couple of lawyers and an auctioneer who sold antique stamps. One room was Diana's private office, the second was for her secretary and the third was a large open office with a couple of desks sectioned off with dividers and a meeting table. Her secretary and chief of staff was Megan, a perky American who was a one-woman army doing everything from answering correspondence to linking up with other organizations.

Diana was meeting with her lawyer and Megan to discuss setting up a scholarship for the future environmental activists of this world to encourage the younger generation to become active in saving the planet. The scholarship would be in her brother's name as a way to keep his brave spirit alive. They decided a budget and basic structure, agreeing to avoid details of Klaus' death to prevent any possible pushback from African governments or a specific commodities dealer. The scholarship could also have been one way of deflecting her guilt from still being a major stockholder in a steel business. During her time of being the CEO she had steered the company to aim for carbon neutrality and like most large industries, it was like trying to turn around a super tanker in a small harbor. It would take time, there were no instant cures for transitioning to a totally clean business.

With outside investors holding a significant portion of the shares, the focus was on profitability and annual shareholder dividends. Knowing the steel mills still belched out noxious fumes made her wonder if she shouldn't exit the family business entirely. Tanya had told her it seemed hypocritical to have a foot in both camps and was an on-going debate they had yet to reconcile. Diana was able to partially convince Tanya it wasn't all bad because she was in a position to change an industry from the inside out, which was an opportunity a lot of concerned people didn't have.

Diana would use Tanya's friend Susan to design a logo she envisioned for campaigns, capturing the benevolent aspect of Gaia – the motherly nurturing spirit of nature which could also display awesome power in the form of volcanic eruptions, deadly storms and relentless heat waves followed by torrential rain. Occasionally Diana doubted about continuing to promote environmental awareness after her brother's death. She still blamed herself for supporting him in exposing crimes to the planet. It was all very new to her, shifting gears from running a major industrial company with a focus on production, quality and meeting quarterly financial goals. But her business school education was useful and helped shape the foundation's structure and initiatives.

When her doubts surfaced, Diana would take a walk in the forest above the Beyer family home, where the thick green woods grounded her. She'd follow a small stream, listening to its gentle music, pausing to soak up the tranquility. The Japanese called this 'forest bathing' and recommended it for curing depression and stress. At the top of the ridge she had a favorite bench which offered a postcard view over the lake. Looking across the water to the far shore with small villages below the green ridges, she was reminded of the Japanese tourists who asked their host why people were allowed to build houses in the large park. To them, the cultivated greenery so close to the city could be nothing else, which was a compliment to how the Swiss maintained a lot of green zones. She'd found her corner of paradise and thought everyone else should be so lucky. But if the public didn't wake up to the urgency of climate change, even this little slice of heaven would turn brown with droughts and the trees toppled by heavy winds, while the water would become undrinkable and sparse.

Diana wondered what her younger brother would be doing now. Would he still be in Africa or doing what she had done and starting an organization to educate people on the environment. He hadn't followed her party girl lifestyle and had been a quiet academic who studied marine biology with the wish to be the next Jacques Cousteau. After graduation he worked on some oceangoing research vessels for a couple of years, witnessing how the fragile underwater environment and coral were slowly being compromised. When his big sister had started her foundation, Klaus was an enthusiastic supporter and taking her initiative as inspiration, started his own one-man campaign. Before long he was a social media darling with over two million followers on Instagram, that started with college kids and spread from there. Soon the German press noticed him, rolling him out as their poster child whenever environmental issues were in the news.

Klaus thought Diana's foundation was bureaucratic, focusing too much on education. After some work to help restore the Great Barrier Reef off of Australia, he had set his sights on Africa. He'd offered to investigate destructive mining practices for Diana's foundation to include in their public awareness campaigns. She never thought his trip would end with deadly consequences. She felt guilty for his death and tried to temper this emotion with remembering his confrontational style from other work he did. He'd been asked to leave Australia for his outspoken comments on the government's lethargic approach to helping preserve the coastline and indigenous culture.

His death had caused waves of grief in the groups of people intent on saving the planet. Initially his death had appeared to be a byproduct of his adventurous lifestyle and in a few short months the news cycle had moved on to the economy, wars and who was going to be Germany's Next Top Model. He was seen to be a martyr by a lot of young people but as his social media posts stopped, other causes picked up the slack.

Diana pulled a phone out of her shoulder bag and opened a folder of photos. She studied a picture of her brother laughing on a beach, trying to feel his spirit and warm character. Tears started to flow and she held him close in her heart. Diana remembered her mother's reaction to Klaus's death which spun her into being a near recluse after losing her husband ten years earlier. Parents always expected their children to outlive them, so seeing her golden grandson die had been numbing. Her mother had retreated to the family castle in Bavaria and was rarely seen in her social circles in the past year since Klaus had died. Even though she didn't blame Diana, she felt she had let her mother down. It was her own self-flagellation for not being more attentive. Hans-Peter had been supportive of the grieving process and been a caring set of ears as she voiced her doubts and self-blame. He also had a son and Klaus, while being older, still looked at Hans-Peter as a father figure the few times they'd met.

Diana looked back on her life and realized she could've met a similar fate as her brother from her earlier extreme lifestyle. Her indiscreet adventures could've led to any number of deadly scenarios from car accidents after a night of drinking or passing out from too many drugs and asphyxiating on her own vomit. Sometimes her feelings bordered on a case of Survivor Syndrome as Diana wondered why she was allowed to carry on with her work while her idealistic brother was a victim. Instead of battling the forces that pulled her into these dark spaces, she'd rally her energies to focus on the positive elements in her life. Choosing to find gratitude over self-rapprochement. It wasn't an easy process as sliding back into the feelings of despair was an ever-present option. Gradually the tide was turning and looking back, she felt an unseen protective hand had been guarding her and a wave of gratefulness washed over her. Life had a special sweetness as the sun warmed her and the birds called to each other from high in the trees. She remembered what someone had told her at Klaus's funeral – it was sad he was gone but a gift to have known him. She got up from the bench to head back to the house feeling a renewed spirit of wanting to honor Klaus with the actions of her foundation.

John drove through town after work to Tanya's shop, enjoying the sparse traffic. One day while slumming in the Kreis 4 he had gone in Metamorph to buy some photo paper and had remained a loyal customer ever since. Support your local artist had been his motto. He greeted her as any good Zürich person would: "*Hoi, du!*" He'd pushed the conversation he had earlier at the office to the back of his brain, trying to compartmentalize the issue. He tried to adopt a more positive tone so he didn't sound like a complainer. First it was the divorce story with the citizenship hassles and finally a camera theft to round out the picture. All that didn't leave room for yet one more episode from his slowly unwinding existence to make him look like a total loser in Tanya's eyes. John was also afraid that his identifying too much with a corporate life would emphasize the distance between him and someone who focused more on the creative world than commerce. He wasn't in the mood for sympathy, so he reminded himself not to look backwards because that wasn't the direction he was going. Being with Tanya always affirmed his artistic aspirations and made him feel part of the greater community of like-minded individuals. All of them looking to pursue an existence of creativity and expression though a chosen medium, free of the confines of corporate dictums.

Tanya laughed at his mangled German from behind the sales counter and returned the same greeting, in an over-done seriousness usually reserved for a three-year-old. He tried to pay for a marking pen, but his money was refused. The two teenaged girls who were her assistants pretended not to notice. It was a few minutes before closing time so Tanya told the youngsters they could leave. It was clear they were happy to have a few more precious minutes of summer and headed off to the lake for a swim. John and Tanya were going to the Rundfunk party but John wanted to change into something more casual, swapping his business attire for a T-shirt and jeans he'd brought along in his sports bag. Tanya had offered a couple of times to update his wardrobe and even bought him some clothes when he wouldn't go shopping with her. She preferred him in a freer look than the standard white shirt and black pants banker's outfit. Even the casual American style of dressing with chinos and a button-down shirt didn't match her vision of a European bohemian. She said if you want to develop your creative side, you have to look original and start dressing more like an artist.

While he started to change in her office, Tanya came in when he was unbuttoning his shirt and said, "Did I tell you today...?"

"No, but maybe you can show me."

She couldn't resist helping him off with his clothes and soon they were on the sofa in a delicious frenzy of kissing gymnastics and mutual undressing. They ended up with Tanya on top, angling for the closest possible position to ride herself to pleasure.

John and Tanya crossed a small plaza behind the main train station that was framed by waist-high neatly trimmed hedges and the imposing gray stone walls of the massive museum building. Small groups of people were scattered around on stone benches picnicking while others huddled in their own private party. They approached the entrance to the National Museum, which was an arched doorway in the base of a large square stone tower with a tiled roof and spire on top. The building was modeled on a French chateau and looked like the kind of place you would see Robin Hood swinging across, rescuing a fair damsel.

John wore a baseball cap and big sunglasses as a disguise so he could circulate with Tanya unobserved by any of his wife's friends. After a brief search of Tanya's purse by the security men, they passed through the thick walls and were in the inner courtyard where hundreds of people milled around while infectious drum and bass music penetrated every corner, trapped between the high ramparts. The DJ station and dance floor were located in an antique circus tent in the center of the courtyard with bright red fabric and wood panels around the sides but it was too hot and loud to be inside. They squeezed through the thick crowd made up of small groups of mainly young people in their twenties and thirties. Half were the so called 'alternative' types or hipsters in unique, trendy, stressed looking attire while the rest had come from work or had changed first but still had the yuppie look of designer polo shirts or expensive white linen outfits brought back from their last vacation in Greece. Tanya said hello to a couple of people she knew while John used his phone's camera to take some pictures of the castle walls where colored banners were blowing decoratively in the light breeze. They wound their way to the back of the courtyard where a kitchen covered with orange canvas awnings was set-up and each ordered a green Thai curry and some wine. Finding a place at a picnic table at the edge of the food area, they watched the parade of people circling the courtyard trolling for friends. The club music soundtrack stimulated the animation and combined with the crowd noise into one big wall of sound.

After a polite '*en gute*' to wish a good meal, John ate half his curry while he listened to Tanya's update from her meeting with Diana. She went into in greater detail than the brief update on the drive over. During their short journey he had told her that he'd discovered who the mystery man was. She'd cryptically said she also knew but the conversation was cut short as they focused on navigating the crazy summer traffic close to the main station and finding a parking place. After Tanya finished her story, they looked at each other like 'what now?'.

After a pause to let their information settle, John said, "I'd be happy to meet Diana sometime soon and see what next steps are possible. I agree with her that your idea of selling the paintings to Buck doesn't sound too supportive of the goal of bringing Buck to justice. I can't see any angle where that would help."

He stopped short of saying she shouldn't put money before family. He wasn't sure how closely Tanya identified with her role as a gallery owner and if any criticism would be taken personally. The fact that the real reason for the photo taking had to do with a death of a relative engaged in a worthy cause motivated him more than ever to want to do some kind of further action against Buck, in spite of Harry's cautioning him. Plus, thinking about the interference with his career from the same source solidified his anger, especially after today's conversation with his boss.

Tanya didn't respond to his comments about supporting Diana which was her way of avoiding a difficult discussion and sticking to her original view of selling the paintings. Finally, after a thoughtful couple of minutes while they each sipped their wine and studied the crowd, they agreed to disagree.

John had been reluctant all evening to share the bad news Ralph had so craftily presented him. He didn't want to bother Tanya with his office drama, but remembered they'd made a rule to keep their relationship on a solid base. No matter what, they would be one hundred percent honest with each other, independent of how difficult or how bad the news or emotion was to articulate. Besides, Tanya was very intuitive and always knew when something was up, so a secret couldn't remain hidden for long. John swallowed his pride and told her about the meeting.

Tanya was immediately sympathetic and offered her support, putting her hand on his. She knew the pressure John was under, both at the office and with his pending divorce. She'd given him his space and gentle support in the past which had worked wonders to help him over the issues. Just having a friendly and sympathetic ear to share his situation with was already a huge help to John as he replayed the latest conversation with Ralph. The act of retelling of the story helped take the edge off.

Tanya listened quietly and reminded him again that his real talents lay in photography. "Don't forget to keep that as a primary focus. You're in an unfortunate situation but it will change in time, as does everything else in the world. Because you're at such a low point, it can only change for the better. Try to be patient and keep focused on what you're meant to deliver so there's no more negative feedback. And as far as the reorganization, that's something out of your hands. And like the Stoics recommend, better to take life one day at a time. You've come this far for a reason and I believe in a merciful and benevolent universe that supports the weak and downtrodden."

John was all too familiar with feeling like a victim. While the advice was good and helped lift some of the weight off his shoulders, John would retreat out of habit at moments like this into his more rational male view of the world, that dealt in practicalities. Things like subscribing to a masculine definition of what it meant to be successful. It was all right for Tanya to talk about art and following one's dreams. She didn't have to worry about survival with a wealthy family background and no alimony to pay. John had a sense of pride and although he knew Tanya would do anything to help him, his more macho tendencies of wanting to be the self-supporting male made him rule out any considerations of asking for help should he stumble and be unemployed. His ego was already challenged by feeling uncomfortable for not being able to be in the typical role of provider for Tanya. At times it would create a feeling of inadequacy when she would pay for drinks over his objections.

John had one more topic he wanted to share that he'd been holding back and didn't know the best way to bring it up. Sean's offer could be either a blessing or a curse to his relationship. He dived in and explained the job possibility from all directions objectively as possible and how it could also benefit her. After she listened silently the look on her face said it was the wrong subject to bring up at the moment.

"Seriously? Were you guys smoking some funny tobacco or something? I don't know why you believe a word of this, considering the source."

"It's totally legitimate, I'm sure. You're always telling me I should pursue my art."

"Yes, but not across the ocean. It's difficult enough to have a somewhat normal relationship, even when we live in the same city. I don't know what your priorities are, but it doesn't sound like us being together is at the top of the list."

"Darling, we are my number one priority. Don't worry." He dipped his sunglasses and gave her a sincere look to substitute for holding her hand. She returned the look with a hint of a smile, like she wanted to believe him, but not appearing entirely convinced. "Anyway, it's still in the planning stages. I think it's a good thing to start thinking of other possibilities outside the bank." He flipped his sunglasses back up.

"Yes, but please, not outside the country. I think Sean is a nice guy but I don't think he's entirely reliable. Look at how he treated Susan. Couldn't even find time to call her or even send a text."

John decided not to start defending Sean because the last time they talked about him, Tanya expressed how hanging around a woman-hopping bachelor maybe wasn't providing the best influence for their relationship. "You're right, it's only a fantasy at the moment. I just wanted to share it with you so we can think about our future."

"For me to work in the States would mean having a Green Card. You're not even divorced and you want to get married again? Sometimes I don't think you're using your brain. And you found this out on Monday? Why did you only wait 'til now to tell me? I thought we agreed we would be honest with each other. If you hide things like this, why should I think I can trust you to not hide other things?"

"I think it's also a Sean fantasy which is why I didn't give it much importance." He was spinning the truth like he was paid to at the bank. He then shifted roles to being a real partner. "All I know is that I want to be with you. I've no doubts we'll find our way."

"I hope so." She gave a teasing smile like she was giving him a hard time.

Two animated ladies in swirling India print scarfs and multi-colored hippie dresses stopped to say hello to Tanya. They were both artists who not only were customers but part of her circle of friends. John left Tanya to chat with them and wandered the grounds looking for some more subjects to photograph. Having circled the courtyard, he was at the bottom of the wide stairs leading to the arched entrance when a couple he knew materialized through the small groups of people. They were both dressed in colorful loose clothes like they should be at a sundown celebration in Ibiza: the young man with shaggy hair was the party's organizer and his elegant, dark-skinned partner was a former model. They shared a round of hugs and the two superstars were happy to pose for a portrait. John would either sell it to a party website or else just post it on Facebook to do some free publicity for the event and get his name in front of their fans for finding any possible future photo assignments.

When he returned to Tanya, her two friends were saying their goodbyes and he offered to share a dessert. While dueling with forks over a piece of apricot tart, they discussed Diana again and Tanya said she would make sure they'd all meet as soon as possible.

There was no more direct sun shining inside the tall walls

which meant John would have to shed his sunglasses and risk bumping into people. Even worse, by wearing them in the dark, look like he was a slumming celebrity that everyone had to checkout. It was a 'school night', so after a few eventual extended goodbyes to a couple of Tanya's friends she met on the way out, they found their way to the exit where a long line of people were waiting to get in. As they crossed the small plaza, John noticed a rotund older man in an out of date suit and ugly fat tie sitting on a concrete bench who seemed to be studying them. The man wasn't eating anything or reading a paper, just staring blankly, mainly at him. John guessed he was probably a foreigner with no place else to go except hanging around by the main station to get out of his small overheated apartment and watch people. They found Tanya's car on a side street on the other side of the river and set off down the lake for their own private afterparty.

EIGHT

Susan wheeled her retro looking bicycle into the courtyard of Tanya's gallery and parked it in the bike rack in front of the entrance. It was half an hour before the shop opened but Tanya was already there.

The two of them sat outside at a small round metal café table and talked over a coffee. They debated how environmentally friendly the 'What else?' capsule system was that delivered their perfect espresso at the push of a button. They were meeting to discuss how Susan could provide some graphics support for a new referendum coming up for a vote. Tanya was a member of the organizing committee and had taken on the task to come up with some posters. The Swiss public were considering an initiative to clean up their drinking water that had been discovered to have surprisingly high levels of pesticides. The runoff from the farmers had found its way into the water supply and some concerned citizens were demanding action from the government. It meant going head to head with the large Swiss chemical manufacturers who sold most of the pesticides. An earlier government order had banned the use of one of the most toxic compounds but the manufacturer had thrown an army of lawyers into battle to reverse the decision. As they shared their Italian breakfast of espresso, cigarettes and biscuits, they debated the most effective imagery.

The Swiss far right had used shocking images in an earlier anti-foreigner vote. The picture of a white sheep kicking dark sheep out of a pen had drawn criticism from the United Nations for being racist and it was taken down. A more recent vote on banning cigarette ads had tobacco companies putting up posters saying if this advertising prohibition was passed, the next thing to go would be the beloved sausages the Swiss considered a national treasure.

The two women wanted a more positive image so skull and crossbones poison warnings were out. Images of innocent children happily drinking a tall glass of crystal-clear water in a natural setting seemed the more appropriate direction. Susan agreed to work up some concepts for review by the organizing committee. The next equally pressing topic was men. Tanya lit another cigarette and started the discussion.

"You won't believe what John told me last night at the Rundfunk. He said Sean offered him a job in a photo agency he's developing and John could run their office in Miami."

"Are you fucking serious?" Susan said in amazement, half laughing while making a wry expression. "Sounds like a total fantasy, given the source."

Tanya nodded with a big grin. "I think Sean is spending too much time partying to have a sense of reality. But what made me angry is that it took John three days before he mentioned it. I told him it made me think about how much I can trust him because we based our relationship on having no secrets. We talked it out and made our peace but there's still a small nagging doubt that pops up occasionally."

"It sure wasn't the best behavior on John's part. He was

probably being over protective of your relationship, trying to avoid disruptive events."

Tanya countered and said, "It could also be a measure of uncertainty."

"It's typical for a man to expect women to be mind readers and guess their commitment. They make a small gesture with their hand they think is articulating a range of emotion, while the woman needs to guess what the signal was meant to express. Sean is equally guilty of failing in the communications department." They laughed and shook their head at what strange creatures men were, echoing the same view men had of women. "I really like Sean. But I hope his bouncing around between projects will eventually slow down."

"It's probably his way of working out his anger and frustration of his wife leaving him." Susan nodded in agreement. "It's similar to John's situation."

"I wonder how long it will take each of them to move on from their history?"

Tanya said, "John is committing as best he can and I know that he'll eventually be a good partner." Tanya's two helpers arrived signaling it was time to open the shop, so the two women said their goodbyes and shared a hug.

....

The Dallas House was the name locals gave to Stan Buck's ten-story office building next to the train station in Zug. It looked like a giant blue glass Rubik's cube where someone had figured out how to align all the same colors on the side. The name was inspired by the eighties soap opera-style television drama called *Dallas* that featured the exploits of J.R. Ewing, a hard driving Texas oilman. Built about the same time by Buck, it was an obvious association, linking the charismatic American oilman in Texas to 'The King of Oil' in Switzerland. It'd been put up quickly and shocked the conservative Swiss with its futuristic design some called the peak of U.S. bad taste. The building had suburban myths attached to it, like hired guns stationed on the roof and a secret tunnel from Buck's offices so he could avoid detection when going for his daily meal at the restaurant down the street. Neither story was true. Any local worker going to lunch from the adjoining office buildings could see Stan most days at the pedestrian crossing waiting for the walk signal like any other office worker, with the added company of two massive bodyguards.

The local authorities protected their own. When U.S. marshalls showed up with an arrest warrant a couple of years after his relocation, it wasn't Buck the police brought to the airport, it was the marshals. As a token of thanks for their support for this discrete action, Buck opened his private dining room in the Dallas House that day for the local police, which set the tone for an on-going cooperation. The U.S. government had considered all possible means of bringing Buck to justice, even planning to land a SWAT team on the front lawn of his lakeside villa in a helicopter. But lack of local support and the presence of ex-Mossad agents in the security details prowling the garden made the elaborate plans to kidnap him futile. The older politicians thought what was good for Buck was good for Zug, especially with billions in tax revenue. When the U.S. government offered the mayor $700,000 to help capture Buck, he answered: 'I'm a politician, not a policeman'.

In spite of this arrangement of informal protection, the mood was gradually changing. Local support was declining in part due to the incessant attacks by the U.S. on Swiss bank secrecy which branded any American an enemy of the state. Adding to the stress of having to look over his shoulder more than usual, Buck was still reeling from his 500-million-dollar divorce settlement and his wife heading back to New York with their two daughters. He loved his girls dearly and this made the pain of separation harder to take than the depleted bank account that was on track to soon be replenished. The marriage had been long and stable with his wife's early support allowing Stan to build his business. She had dutifully followed him to Switzerland when times got tough but relocated back to America after the divorce, being exempt from the case against Buck. Stan's wife had a musical career to advance as a songwriter for performers like Celine Dion. New York City was more suitable to this pursuit than a former farm town in a remote area of a small provincial central European country.

Stan believed he was a decent man, saying he was a businessman not a politician. He therefore wasn't condoning or condemning any particular regime, rather serving the neutral government of Me, Inc. He liked bringing clients together who would officially have nothing to do with each other. His commodity traders were more discrete than even the Swiss banks in their various deals. Besides Iran, his customers over the years were a Who's Who of questionable governments including those in Cuba, Angola, Nicaragua, Libya, Romania, and Chile.

He also felt his moral bill was paid in full from helping his second adopted homeland of Israel (where passports were handed out to good Jewish people independent of tax evasion accusations). Which in turn meant he was helping the U.S. government in a roundabout way with their Middle East efforts. His extensive organization with offices in key cities worldwide, meant Buck's staff were well positioned to pick up unofficial news that would later become headlines. Or even initiate the actions behind the news if it meant they could profit from it. He'd been discretely turning over critical information to the

State Department over the years, giving them information their normal channels weren't privy to.

The Dallas House had now turned into a source of local indignation. As Buck needed to keep liquidity for his transactions after paying out some serious cash to his ex-wife, the blue cube had passed into the hands of a bank. The bank decided a more modern, taller building could be put up in its prime location. The city wouldn't give it a historical designation, paving the way for its destruction. Buck had no say in its future, so it was one more change he had to accept without the usual micro managing capability he liked to have over all areas of his life. A symbol of the glory years was soon to become only a memory. It made Buck question how much longer he wanted to play the game or could remain relevant and if he should rather cash in his chips and enjoy life. His secret fantasy was that the tax evasion charges would be dropped and he would be fully exonerated. This would then allow him to use some of his money to acquire an ambassadorship by some strategic donations to whatever president got elected the next time around. He could redeem himself and show what a patriot he really was. Buck already knew a variety of world leaders so he would be a natural choice. France wouldn't be bad, could spend his time between Paris and the Riviera. An acceptable Plan B would be Spain where he had citizenship and a villa on the Costa del Sol.

The tax evasion and subsequent 'trading with the enemy' hysteria that was the main argument for jailing Buck was stirred up by the career climbing U.S. Federal Prosecutor Rudolph Giuliani, intent on a bid for mayor of New York City, governor of the state and beyond. Buck's original case on tax evasion was also engineered beyond a reasonable reaction. And although a settlement would have been ideal, the over-zealous political animals had made the fines too high to ignore and a matter of principle not to pay. Buck had hired a number of expert witnesses, including a Harvard law professor, who all testified that he had in fact not broken any laws and the charges were a political witch-hunt. Using every legal resource he could muster, Buck was trying to break the impasse to agree a settlement.

The driving force besides getting the U.S. monkey off his back of possible jail time, was that one of his daughters had contracted leukemia. She was too sick to move to a hospital in Israel where Buck could've visited her. As she was in New York City, he couldn't risk a trip because he would've been apprehended upon arrival and locked up. So he waited, tortured by his desire to see his child but blocked by narrow-minded politicians intent on using his transgressions as a springboard to a better office. His acting as an unofficial diplomat in trouble spots, peacemaker in conflict zones, savior of failing countries and benefactor to museums was not what the press wanted the public to focus on, so it was an ongoing battle. Because of the chaos within the different government departments where he was favorably known for his help in their activities, any support from them for his cause was lost. He knew the clock was ticking with his daughter's health in decline, which made him desperately pursue every means possible to get the legal stranglehold released.

The press had been gradually ignoring him as time went by so he wanted to be sure no renewed interest would be awakened. That's why he didn't mind clamping down hard on the young photographer before anything would come of his picture taking, considering who Buck's company was. It could also complicate another project he was pursuing, the purchase of his own legitimate bank as a front to finance his various larger projects while preserving his own capital. And what could be better than a bank in the most non-political country of them all called Switzerland? He was working with some investors to buyout a smaller family bank in Zürich and were very close to completion of the deal. Unbeknownst to the bank's owners, a rogue family member was facilitating the sale. He had to laugh, knowing the banker's wife was one of the craziest jet set party girls he knew, from back in his New York days. They had similar business interests and he had even bought some shares in her family's steel business a year ago, making his new acquisition plans a sort of family affair. With a chess master's strategic plan to keep a couple of moves ahead of his opponent, he created a distracting smokescreen to obscure his maneuvers. Buck had told his broker to acquire another significant chunk of shares in the German steel company which he was sure would keep Ms. Hotpants and her fondue chomping husband focused elsewhere while he worked with the banker's cousin to quietly finalize the takeover of the bank.

John rang the doorbell outside Tanya's apartment building from the 1930's and admired its retro grandeur of curved balconies and tall bay windows. A buzzer released the locked door, and he climbed three flights of stairs, which didn't help his composure. He was already sweating as much from the smothering heat as from nervousness. Dynamic women who also happened to be beautiful intimidated him because he felt he could never say the right words to engage them and be accepted. He knew from his previous brief encounters with Diana for photo work that today would be no different. And the possibility of a difficult discussion had set his mind racing. He didn't want to lose a well-paying client over family differences, if he was persuaded to agree with Tanya about selling the paintings to Buck. He worked to overcome his jitters, as he wanted to get some details on Buck. Tanya greeted him at the door looking radiant in a colorful summer dress with her hair falling over her bare shoulders in gentle waves. After a courteous peck on each cheek, she ushered him in with a mischievous smile. He let her enter first, playing the gentleman.

"So nice of you to stop by, Mr. Miller. It's a real pleasure."

"Yeah, the feeling's mutual." He was hesitant whether to elaborate. "Nice hot day, too good for us workers. Here's a little something for your wine cellar." He handed her the bottle of wine he'd brought as the customary gift and Tanya glanced at the label before setting it down on a narrow table in the entranceway. John hoped it didn't look too cheap and wondered if the barcode had been put on the bottle '*en chateau*'.

Tanya turned and walked through the living room toward the balcony. The furnishings reflected her eclectic taste: African rugs, modern paintings and small sculptures filling in the space around a low sofa; cushions in an oriental lounge type of arrangement. A few tie-dyed velvet hangings and large candles in one corner gave a hippy ambiance, hinting at her more alternative leanings.

Diana was seated on a lounge chair facing the lake and stood and turned when she heard them approaching. Visions of beauty, images of paradise, John couldn't help to do a double take. She was tall, dark and lovely, in a bright blue sleeveless designer top with matching shorts. The sun setting over the distant hills behind her completed the waking dream. She looked like she was waiting for him, a sly grin on one corner of the carefully painted bright red mouth.

"Hello, John. Nice of you to join us," Diana said extending her hand which John gave a light shake. She spoke relaxed and precisely as a hint of heavenly perfume wafted over him. Her High German accent had a British lilt to it.

"Nice to see you again. I think the last time was at the

gallery when the African pictures were introduced to support your foundation."

"You're right. That exhibition was really moving."

"Yes, the artist captured the landscapes so well with the vibrant colors and passion."

Tanya interrupted. "Let's all have a seat." She motioned them to a round glass table, where there were some tapas of grilled vegetables, olives and pieces of cheese next to an aluminum ice bucket with the neck of a white wine bottle protruding. Tanya poured three glasses, sat down and lifted her glass in a toast, *"Prost"*, clinking glasses first with Diana then with John. John repeated the phrase, touching his glass with Diana's next. Eye contact was important in this country. Diana had the shy look of a blushing bride with a secret. Like a tiger, soft looking and yet deadly. Diana said her name out loud as they touched glasses, signaling that John could officially address her by her first name. This was a show of power, as the most important person had to initiate the move to the 'du' form. It could take months or years in the traditional Swiss business world to move to this informal stage but Diana was more direct and not a prisoner of convention. John repeated his name with a smile to accept her invitation.

They started in on the weather, moved on to the foundation's latest environmental projects that led to John's work, Tanya's business and eventually Diana's yoga class. The conversation came around to John's latest interest in taking time-lapse pictures of the lake boats. When he finished describing his project, Diana took the cue to answer the burning question she knew John was waiting to ask.

"I suppose you are very curious about the last photo assignment I commissioned from you."

"Tanya filled me in after you explained the situation to her. I think I understand what you're trying to do." John reached for a toothpick to spear one of the snacks while he waited for a response.

"Good," Diana said quickly smiling at Tanya. "First, I owe you an apology. I had no idea that you would be attacked for your photo taking. This puts Mr. Buck in a whole new light."

"Thanks, but I wasn't hurt too badly – just a knock to the head," John said modestly. "I was more angry about people with power taking what they want from an average person like me."

"I understand." John wondered if she really understood as she had casually asked him to snap a person well known for having tough bodyguards.

"I'd wanted to get as many pictures as I could of this Mister Buck. Preferably in a not so flattering light." Her demeanor had changed giving her voice a hard-edged tone. The anger of her brother's death was overriding any sadness of his passing and boiling up to the surface.

"That reminds me." John took his mobile phone out of his jacket pocket and after a couple of swipes had the club photo displayed on the screen. He handed it to Diana. "There he is with two of the most unfriendly men I've ever met. I have someone who is trying to identify them, which may or may not help your cause."

Diana studied the picture, stretching it delicately with her fingers to zoom in. "I don't know who the others are. I do know the blonde woman on the left, it's Buck's latest girlfriend."

"And you would know that because…?"

Tanya spoke up. "Mr. Buck is a major art collector and member of the Swiss Arts Council which sponsors important exhibits. Diana and my father go to some of the openings as they're also both big supporters of the arts."

"Hard to imagine Buck has any interests beyond money," John said.

"Everybody loves art," Tanya replied.

Diana jumped in as she sensed a potential conflict brewing. "Yes, I do know him socially. It's the business side that's most troubling." Diana handed John's phone back to him. "I'd like to get some more pictures but I don't want to put you in any danger. Oh, and don't forget to send me an invoice."

"I think I can take care of myself now that I know this guy likes to play by his own set of rules. What's more important to me is that we can find a way to punish him for your brother's death and also the man who helped you in Africa. It makes my bump on the head look like a mosquito bite. If you can tell me where I can find him, I'm happy to take some more pictures."

Diana nodded in affirmation. She took a sip from her wine and her neutral expression quickly turned serious. "One of my old friends in Paris who is a broker called me this morning. He heard a part of the shares of my family's steel company that were sold last year went to one of Mr. Buck's holding companies. I already knew that but now that same company is asking if any more are available. It supports his apparent aim to get control and perpetuate the bad deeds in Africa my father also managed to turn a blind eye to until I sorted them out."

"But Diana, anyone running a steel business would do the same, no?" Tanya asked.

"There are ways of extracting and processing raw materials that are more environmentally friendly but they require a large investment. And when you buy a company, you're interested in quickly covering the acquisition costs to maximize the profit for your shareholders. Clean business practices aren't the primary concern."

"It's criminal what these people are doing to the planet," Tanya said.

"Yes, and more frightening is that my friend also told me that Mr. Buck is in negotiations to seriously expand his operations in Africa. There's a new president in Gabon who put himself into power in a type of coup and is very receptive to exploiting, sorry, I mean developing his country's natural resources. Buck helped them out back in the nineties to get access to foreign banks and they owed him a favor."

"Helping his own bank account of course," John said interrupting.

"And, as Mr. Buck is already a player in the country, he's paving the way to make one of the largest strip mines in the world. Totally unregulated of course. There are rumors going around saying Buck actually funded the coup to get a sympathetic politician in place." John angrily stabbed an olive, popped it in his mouth and after a few quick chews washed it down with a large swallow of wine. Diana said, "I know Buck's actions are reprehensible, but he's in the business of making money. As bad as his actions sound, he was technically within the local regulations, so there weren't a lot of options to oppose him."

Tanya and John looked at each other, silently wondering why Diana was now defending him. Tanya was thinking that in the end maybe money was thicker than blood. And she could've also been defending her family history and its own continuing operations with coal fired factories.

Diana added, "His criminal charges in America were trumped up and he in fact has several philanthropical efforts that seem to have balanced his bad karma. I believe his feeling of persecution echoes his parents having to leave Nazi era Belgium because of their Jewish roots. It's a shadow that's hovered over him in his youth and made him want to accumulate wealth as it meant independence. The world is not black and white – there's a lot of gray in between."

"Yes, and the Swiss seem to live in the gray. And I don't mean just the weather. The gray zone is what the Swiss call neutrality – not taking sides. That's why I don't see a problem selling the paintings to Buck. I'm not his judge," Tanya said.

This comment was met by silence and John and Diana looked at each other not sure how to respond as it was clear Tanya was set on her position. And after Diana's last comments it looked like she could be softening her opinion.

"I'll only support the sale if it's a means of ultimately getting Buck in some kind of legal jeopardy as payback for my brother's death." Diana looked at Tanya to see if her point was made. "Come a little closer said the spider to the fly."

Diana paused and sipped her wine to let her point settle in. She changed the subject and related some of the similar pressures her husband's bank was under. It was partly to educate John while showing-off her *powerfrau* business side so he knew she just wasn't eye candy. It was also a roundabout way of reminding Tanya of the stress on her family and why rallying together was important. Tanya made a face like 'here we go again' and got up and went to the balcony, looking out at the lake.

Diana carried on. "Bank Beyer is basically trying to keep their head above water in these troubled times."

"Join the club. Sounds like where I work," John said.

"Right. Like the increased financial scrutiny from the various governments looking at bank secrecy. Then we have to meet the various solvency requirements, which means needing to shore up the bank's reserves either through cost cutting or selling assets."

"Cost cutting is the flavor of the month where I work."

"Neither of these are ideal choices. It's an increasingly competitive marketplace and especially difficult being a small bank. We're already running a tight ship so there's not a lot of employees to trim. And selling assets like major real estate properties of office buildings and apartment blocks means cutting short our long-term investment plan timeline."

"The small guys always get hit the hardest, don't they?"

"Then to add to our grief, there is an extra administrative overhead for responding to all the enquiries around secret accounts set up for tax evasion."

"I don't even have a secret account and I have to report every year to the IRS. And the banks really hate setting up accounts for Americans because of all the extra paperwork."

Diana wound up her lecture on Banking 101 by giving the example of two of Geneva's oldest private banks, Lombard Odier and Pictet, who had both

restructured from a limited liability partnership to corporate entity. "The good news is we've found another family bank we'd like to partner with to do the same."

"We really can't let the bank disappear," John said with a determined look.

"No way!" Tanya shouted from where she stood by the railing listening to the discussion. Diana and John laughed at her outburst. After the noise died down John brought the conversation back to focus on Buck again.

"I like your idea of a photo essay showing Buck with all the dirty players he runs around with and also some of the environmental disasters he's creating. Then the U.S. will never let him off with just a fine and we can hope that the Swiss won't want their country tainted with him living here."

"This is a chess game," Diana said. "Let's keep our cool and take some time to think of what would work best. We all need to think about a Plan B because the impact from a photo essay alone will probably fail to discredit Buck, sad to say. Given the public's short-term memory from an overload of news stories, each one drowning out the last, his story will be a small blip on the radar. But for now, let's keep trying this approach. Maybe we get lucky and hit a slow news day and he goes viral."

"I'm ready. You do know that if Buck were caught in another country like France or Germany where tax evasion was a crime, their extradition treaties with America would mean Buck being shipped home," John said.

"Very interesting," Tanya said slowly as she internalized the information, her mind already starting to consider scenarios.

John took the plunge back into the controversial subject they'd just touched on, going for a direct shot. He felt confident knowing Diana was on his side. "You just hinted that it'd be a good idea to let Buck buy the Basquiats beyond expanding his art collection. Do you really think it would somehow help bring him to justice?"

"I don't have a concrete plan at the moment but it could get us closer to him to find a point of weakness. I've seen his type before. They buy expensive paintings so they can show off publicly how much money they have. When a person lets their ego lead them, it provides an opening," Tanya said.

Diana said, "I still believe it's dishonoring Klaus. And unless there's a better reason than just some possible leverage, I still don't want him to have the paintings."

Tanya said, "I understand your concerns. All I'm asking is you both keep an open mind while we see how we can achieve our common goal." There was a silence.

"Can we at least agree to keep the dialogue going to find a way everyone is happy?" John said trying to be diplomatic and preserve their unity.

"That sounds fair," Diana said. "In the meantime, I'll see if I can find where his next public appearance is for Mr. Photographer here. Now I hate to be unsociable, but I have to get home. There's a dinner party by the lake I need to get prepared for." She edged her chair back and John stood up.

"It's been a pleasure." Diana extended her hand for John to shake, they exchanged goodbyes and then she walked to the door with Tanya.

. . .

The problem was finding the place. It was 10 p.m. and Tanya and John were totally lost, standing in the courtyard of a huge abandoned factory complex. They were surrounded by a ring of dark six-story buildings that had been gutted, leaving only a ghostly shell illuminated by some harsh yellow construction lights in a few doorways. They were in pursuit of a pop-up art show in an industrial area outside of Zürich. The invitation in the form of photocopy art that had been mailed to Tanya didn't provide many clues other than the name of the gallery and a nonexistent address in Google maps. They instinctively trailed some punk looking young people with worn out baggy black clothing and facial piercings through the maze of buildings, but quickly lost them. After a few false starts down echoing hallways and a long walk through an underground parking lot devoid of any vehicles, they detected a muffled beat. It led them up a short flight of rough concrete stairs, through a sliding panel doorway to a partly open massive steel door. They entered a huge, brightly lit hall overflowing with deafening music.

The noise originated from a trio: keyboards, guitarist and singer. The group was setup in one end of the cavernous room, surrounded by stacks of speakers and sound equipment. A small audience, maybe fifty in total, clustered in groups of three or four around the wall of sound gear. The vocals were buried deep under massive chords of feedback. The singer was wearing a bird-like mask with a long beak like at the Venice Carnival, topped with a stovepipe hat. The other two men wore elaborate makeup like Maori warriors on acid.

"Performance art," John shouted in Tanya's ear. Certainly wasn't danceable, whatever you called it. The lighting was industrial, a couple of large spots on temporary stands. Glancing around the crowd, John noticed a fourth person standing behind the group, unmoving. He was dressed completely in black, including a ski-mask with only the eyes, nose and mouth visible. He clutched a pump-action shotgun across his chest.

"Guess we have to like it," John shouted pointing out the figure. The noise was hurting their ears, so John and Tanya retreated to the back of the hall, where a bar area was set up. They looked around for Sean who John had forwarded the details to, but didn't see him anywhere. John surveyed the artwork on display, huge murals of paint splattered abstract images with political themes, or collages of circuit boards, spray can tops and assorted odds and ends, with Day-Glo paint highlights lit by black-light lamps. The titles covered everything from tanks, heroin and Aids to the current president of Switzerland. The prices started in the low thousands. The performance ended abruptly, generating wild cheers from the crowd.

Sean popped out of the crowd and bought them each a drink at the collapsible table littered with bottles of alcohol and mixers that served as a bar. With a drink in hand, they made the rounds, reviewing the compositions. A majority of the people studying the paintings were dressed in black and for contrast there were a couple of men in fashionable suits, hoping to unearth an undiscovered genius. Mostly it looked like students and starving artists in their party finery of import shop shirts, black denim and heavy silver. Sean promptly disappeared, deep in conversation with a young lady in an Indian print dress and a guy in a cowboy shirt. Tanya's artist friend Miror wandered by wearing an electric red T-shirt under a bright blue suit jacket and stopped to say hello. Tanya made the introductions and thanked him again for hosting the party where she found the Basquiats. John had imagined a tall, stately character from Tanya's earlier descriptions and was surprised to see he was short and slightly overweight. She enthusiastically described to John his original artistic style based on the surrealistic work of Miró and also his talents in being able to paint like any master he wanted. Miror seemed shy and a bit embarrassed by the praise. She repeated her standing offer to exhibit his paintings but he didn't respond and slowly excused himself to join another group of people.

Tanya should've been in her element, but she went off to sit at a small cafe table at the far edge of the bar area. She'd been moody tonight and John knew she was feeling conflicted about yesterday's meeting with Diana. She idly dragged on a cigarette watching the crowd, while John barged into Sean's conversation with the singer. The man in the cowboy shirt was continually sniffing and his eyes darted back and forth like a trapped rat. It was clear to John he was supporting Zürich's status as one of the top cities in Europe for cocaine consumption. It wasn't limited to musicians, as John knew a few of his work colleagues, primarily in the trading group, trying to have a competitive edge, were also dancing to the tune of Bolivian marching powder.

Eventually they all ended up at Tanya's table, joined by a graffiti artist and his girlfriend, an ex-lover of Sean. Sean then cornered Tanya in solo conversation to distract her from the funk she seemed to be wallowing in.

"This is going to sound weird and possibly inappropriate, but can I ask about Susan? I just want to know if I still have a chance given how much time has passed since our last date. Somehow the longer I wait to call her the harder it seems to summon the courage. And the more I hesitate, the worse I appear. It's like I'm not interested."

Tanya chided him. "You men all think too much. You over-analyze your way into a state of paralysis. Just pick up the phone. Even a two-minute chat would be a sign you haven't forgotten her. These small actions are what women appreciate. Nothing is insignificant."

Sean had a visible 'a-ha' moment where he actually shut-up for a second and let her words sink in.

"I'll let you in on a little secret and you didn't hear it from me. She also likes you."

He said "thanks" and leaned over and kissed her on the cheek. Sensing the chat was finished, he pulled out his phone to check for messages. Tanya looked over at John and asked to leave.

Noticing their intentions, Sean said, "Can I quickly tell John something? You want anything at the bar?" He got a headshake 'no' in response. John said he would have some water before driving. Tanya nodded to the suggestion, like it was a good idea. The two men each got a small bottle of water and stood at the end of the serving table.

Sean leaned heavily on John's shoulder. "So how about publishing this photo, eh? We'll get a check end of the week and then we can really have a celebration."

"I'd rather we just slow down a little on this. I'd like to get enough ammunition for a solid attack, working with Diana."

"Now what are you saying?" Sean looked intently at John's face, not quite focusing. "You mean to tell me that you get beat up, robbed and threatened at your job because of this bastard and you want to turn the other cheek. The only cheek you got left, buddy boy, are the ones you sit on. Are you saying you're going to let yourself get kicked in the ass again?"

"That's not what I had in mind—"

"All right then, let's get some more snaps of this clown and sell them to *People* magazine and the *National Inquirer*. Put him in with the 'Space Man Had My Baby' articles, Michael Jackson sightings and Madonna's latest husband. He ain't gonna do no more than he's done already. He knows who you are, so it's too late to back out now. Sorry, but you're just a flea to him anyway. Look, you tell me where to find Buck and I'll take the pictures. I can use the money and I'm not afraid of the big bad wolf."

"All right, all right. Here's the scoop but please keep it confidential. Tanya's stepmother asked me to take the photos to expose the guy 'cause he's responsible for her brother's death in a roundabout way. Plus, he wants to buy up a lot of shares in her company to start propagating more Third World environmental catastrophes."

"See. This guy is slime."

"She's going to tip me off where he's going to show up next. She has a big German glossy magazine lined up that will do a montage of real-life criminals in our midst."

"Awesome."

"We talked about it earlier today but it's not certain that even a big exposé will do the job."

"All the more reason to act now and get some extra exposure."

"Problem is, I don't think we're going to see him again in the local discos anytime soon. He's such an asshole."

Sean laughed and slapped John on the back. John still resented that Diana and Tanya seemed to be making their own plans where he was only a supporting player. Also, his ego was still bruised from the combination of the job news.

"Publishing the picture will help take your mind off of the Swiss Credit Bank circus for a while. I can get my journalist friend to make up some text and we'll see if his scandal sheet will pick it up."

"OK, why not. Keep me in the loop so I can see what's proposed and synchronize it with Diana."

"And if the shit hits the fan, don't forget about my agency deal."

"I'll believe it when I see it." Just then Tanya hooked her arm through John's in a move to leave.

. . .

John and Tanya had started the drive through town heading towards the lake, sharing some commentary on the art show that trailed into silence until Tanya spoke up. "John, what do you think about having kids?"

He was instantly sober, with every warning light, buzzer, alarm bell and foghorn signaling attention. "Well, it's a little hard for me to plan on these things, especially now. Given the right circumstances, might be all right. Honestly, I haven't given it much thought."

"Don't sound so defensed."

"You mean defensive."

Tanya shot him a glance that said 'take it easy'. "I'm not talking about right away. Maybe in a couple of years, when you've sorted out your problems."

John paused for a second, aware that his answer could be a relationship killer if it was wrong. "You're right, today it's out of the question. But the circumstances will change and then it could become a real possibility." He smiled to reinforce his comment. A part of him inside felt a warm glow at the thought of seriously settling down and having a family with someone he truly loved. "Why do you ask?" he said in a playful tone.

"Are you still drunk? I'm just wondering about us. If you want to have a family, we have to start planning now."

John was well aware of this critical window of opportunity in the female life cycle. He'd been expecting the topic to pop up. The idea was of course appealing but the inner voice of his conservative side rose up again. It told him he needed more time with Tanya to make sure this wasn't a relationship of mutual blind desire or dependency and need, rather than love. He knew a divorce had a funny way of creating reluctance in even the most solid committer when the next opportunity to step up presented itself.

The chemistry between them felt really good, much more

so than with his wife. There was a natural closeness and John could see Tanya had shed enough of her Swissness to be more open-minded than his ex. The responsibilities of running her own business had matured Tanya and once the professional side closed down, she turned into a spirited and fun companion to lead John through the authentic side of Zürich the tourists never saw. The spontaneity was exhilarating and opened doors inside him that John never knew existed or were even closed. The first time they had seduced each other was in the back seat of his car, on a small country lane like a couple of teenagers. They let the subject drop and fell into a silence that John filled by turning up a pop song on the radio with a lady singer rolling her words along above the electronic beat. Tanya looked out the window and John could see she wasn't entirely satisfied with the outcome of their short discussion. He sensed she had anticipated a more enthusiastic response and would've liked to have given her one. He reached over and took her hand, holding it for a second.

John effectively diverted the direction of the conversation by moving on to a hot topic. He'd sensed that during their discussion with Diana that Tanya's resolve to sell the paintings to Buck had possibly weakened. Her facial expressions had said it was coming under consideration. "Let me guess. This show you're having with your friend's Basquiats really will include a guest from Zug?"

"And what if Buck does show-up – it's a public exhibit. I can't keep him out. And I can get him to fund our efforts to improve the planet."

"It's dirty money. Did you already forget about what happened in Africa and what his plans are?"

"The Swiss bankers have a saying: money has no smell. I'm like them, completely neutral and will gladly take from whoever wants to share it. Switzerland is not the world's police force. Legal matters should be dealt with at the source."

"Wow, you really are a banker's daughter."

"And what's that supposed to mean?"

"Let's not discuss banks and dirty money, you know I think it's a moral issue." He looked at her quickly to make his point.

"Look, my dad had to change how the bank is structured. I'm not stuck on tradition. I feel sorry for him being boxed in by how the world is changing because it's not the same place it was, even twenty years ago. I don't like the way the planet is turning into large impersonal conglomerates for music, art, publishing and most of all, banking."

This somehow seemed like a concession on her part, and John reached over and tentatively took Tanya's hand again and was glad when she squeezed back.

They drove past lit-up restaurants, with colored light bulbs dangling in long strings over the outside tables still packed with people. John was steering with full concentration, the top-forty sound-track fading in and out on the radio.

"Let's stop and go for a midnight swim," Tanya suggested.

"It's way past midnight."

"The water's so warm now. It's really nice, warmer than the air temperature. I haven't done it yet this year. We can stop up ahead, there's a small *Strandbad*."

John swung the car into a narrow parking area between the Seestrasse and a wide lawn along the lake. There were only two other cars in the lot, and nobody in sight. John grabbed a couple of beach towels from the trunk and tossed one to Tanya. They spread the towels between some trees at the far end of the grass covered strand. John sat cross-legged on one and Tanya settled on his lap, locking her legs behind his back. The full moon was as bright as a searchlight, giving the scenery a dull glow and the deep blue water shimmered like hammered silver. Other than the occasional car zooming by, the only sound was the lapping of the water on the shore.

"Do you see that mountain there just below the moon?" Tanya asked.

John unburied his nose from the side of her neck and looked where she indicated. "That's the Albis. Legend has it that a Celtic sect of the white goddess originated there. Albis is like albino, you see."

"Mmm, and I think you are a descendant of that goddess or maybe it's just the moonlight." John started nibbling on an earlobe.

"When they knew they would have to convert to Christianity or die they released a white deer and followed it to where it rested by the Limmat and that's where they built the Fraumünster Church."

"Very interesting. I think we better sacrifice a virgin because it's the full moon." Tanya pushed herself back laughing. They shrugged their clothes off and climbed carefully over the large, flat stones bordering the lake into the tepid water. Tanya swam a few hundred yards out and returned. They floated around and did an exaggerated water ballet in neck deep water, dancing on the toes of one foot. John lifted Tanya like they were doing a performance of *Swan Lake* before heading back to shore. Lying on their towels not bothering to dry off, they let their passion rollover them as they pressed together in a slippery and warm embrace. Ten yards away a periodic stream of cars whistled by, unaware of the lovers hard at work.

NINE

John picked up his phone when he saw Harry's name accompanying the ringtone. Harry was gridlocked midtown in what had become a perpetual construction zone in the city center, struggling with an erratic signal on his static choked mobile phone. Through electronic scratches and pauses he managed to get across to John that he had some news about Buck. John squeezed the phone hard against his ear to make out the words. It was set to maximum volume with no result and he shouted his reply. His company had outsourced their phone service to the cheapest provider and was paying the price. The connection sounded like it was going via mainland China. John stretched out his leg and kicked the office door closed so he could have a private conversation and eliminate any extra noise.

John didn't get all the words that Harry was saying so he started his own conversation. He was still pumped up from the talk with Sean the night before and wanted to exert his own influence as much as he could in bringing Buck to justice. "We need to make Buck more famous than Al Capone. They got that bastard for tax evasion, and I want to see the same thing happen."

"It hasn't worked until now with the Swiss government on his side," came the scratchy reply.

"If he didn't have so many bodyguards, I'd grab him myself. With a three-million-dollar price on his head, he'd fund my retirement account. I could also make a press pack for those maniac mercenary publications like *Soldier of Fortune* and get some bounty hunters on his tail."

Harry hit an area where the signal was stronger and the static diminished. "Calm down and let me give you the news. I hate to spoil your party but I was able to enlarge your photo where Buck was wearing the tie pin. It's the logo for a Middle East oil trading firm. Then I heard back this morning from a contact who studied your picture and two and two added up to ten."

"And..."

"You know who Buck's guest was? Ready for this? It was the Iranian President Khamenei's favorite nephew, Ahmed. Runs an import-export business based in Geneva, mainly dealing in oil. Just before the last set of sanctions they moved him out of Iran after being too violent when he was the head of the secret police. They call him 'Nails'. Seems he likes to hammer nails into people's heads."

"Are you serious?"

"Got a lot of his training in the Eastern Bloc. He has diplomatic status in Switzerland and probably came here to work on deals to get around economic embargos and God knows what else."

"You're putting me on."

"Wish I was. That's why you should keep clear of Buck. If he can steal your camera without a problem, his friends can play carpenter on your brain. But now that you put that picture in the paper, I'd say you're in real serious shit."

"What are you talking about?"

"Didn't you see the morning *Blick*?"

"What? That idiot Sean must have put it in without telling me." John's stomach dropped through the floor. "Whose name appeared in the credits?"

"I don't remember. Some Irish dude. You guys better lie low now. Tell your hothead friend to keep his mouth shut. I know he loves to stir things up, but now this is getting serious."

"I have to check this out. Let me know if you find any more information and the name of a good plastic surgeon."

John called Sean but an answer machine started talking to him so he dialed the mobile number. It rang endlessly without the voicemail activating and he hung-up. He walked to an office down the hall and borrowed a copy of the *Blick* from a perpetually hungover South African speechwriter for the CEO who always hid behind a computer screen. The front page prominently displayed a gruesome murder and lottery winner. On the third page a provocatively posed teenager named Helga sprawled on a sofa with nothing on but black lace stockings that squeezed her upper thighs so they looked like a white Bavarian sausage. John found the party picture buried in the middle of the second section that featured society events.

The image wasn't bad, all the people were recognizable and Buck was named. The composition suited the sleazy tabloid's criteria for journalism: famous person in elite nightclub with other important looking individuals and sexy girls. If that wasn't Buck's latest girlfriend, it could start some name-calling which was the type of commotion the local scandal sheet liked to stir up.

The phone rang. It was Sean. "I know why you're calling. No need to thank me—"

"Are you out of your mind? You said you were only going to

see if your friend would publish it. And I told you I wanted to review the story first."

"If I had to wait for you to quit being such a nice guy all the time, life would be so boring. No money, no girls—"

John interrupted him again. "The mystery guest in the photo is the nephew of Iran's Supreme Leader and well known for torturing people. How does the name 'Nails' strike you? The guy is known to be real handy with a hammer and nails. You think your pierced ears are cool, by the end of the week it will be your whole ugly head."

"Hey, cool down. Didn't you see the credit? It's that perfect Irishman, Stephen Dedalus."

"I don't care whose name is on the credit, the fact is I took the picture and these clowns know it. Now not only do I risk getting crucified but they're also going to get the club president to start pushing the bank again so I get fired right away." Sean sighed, exasperated with his slow-witted friend. "Why the hell didn't you ask me first? You know I'm working with Diana. I told you clearly I need to align with her efforts to make the most impact."

"You know how it is. First, the papers aren't into old news and second, you're so conservative the photo would never have seen the light of day. If you're so hung-up, you can have the whole two hundred francs."

"You're too generous. I'll use it to hire some security."

"And what are you so worried about the job for? If they don't lay you off now, it will be in the next round. Did you really think you were going to retire from this company in another thirty years?"

"Believe it or not I like my work and I need the salary to pay off my lawyer and court costs. Trying to find a new job today with my limited language skills and only a U.S. passport will be impossible."

"Don't sweat it. It's out of your control anyway."

"Thanks for the pep talk," John said. "All I know is this guy has dangerous friends and now you've made things a whole lot worse. He's going to be seriously pissed off and now I'll have to watch my back so I don't get clobbered by a hammer."

John angrily clicked off without saying goodbye. He'd hoped Sean could be an ally. Now publishing the picture would jeopardize his taking further photos for Diana as Buck would be on the lookout and alert his bodyguards. John also had a pang of anxiety thinking how Buck could also easily track him down and exert some retribution to make him back off. Photo-taking with a broken arm would not be so simple.

The incident triggered a review of all the possibilities a rich and powerful enemy could instigate, all the way to John's own deportation. It wasn't just Buck to blame as John knew the pure white image of cleanliness and orderliness that Switzerland wanted to portray was only a façade. The politicians were as corrupt as in any other country. Bribes had only been made illegal in 2000 but not a lot had changed. Big businesses, like everywhere else in the world, told politicians what to do so the rich could get richer.

Stan Buck paced his living room, screaming into a cordless phone, weaving between his low slung modern Scandinavian furniture and ignoring the expensive art on every wall. There wasn't another other human on the planet as angry as he was. His rage knew no limitations and threatened to spill out into senseless, violent actions. He'd only finished breakfast an hour earlier and was already thinking about a drink. A bottle of red with lunch would go down fine.

Stan could normally keep his emotions under control to

coolly manage all the many deals he perpetually had in motion. He was known to be humorless and high-strung but now he was feeling more boxed in than ever and worse, increasingly helpless. In his early days of exile there were no limits and his empire grew to make his outfit the largest commodity company in the world. Everything and everyone can be bought and sold. Governments were irrelevant. In his prime, he had been called The King of Oil, dealing a million barrels a day. When Russia opened up he was their main oil trader, considered the Godfather to the Russian oligarchs. Other businessmen in the commodities industry had called him the Greatest Trader of the 20th Century. But that too was a slowly fading memory. The only consolation was he still belonged to that exclusive club of being able to loan one billion dollars for a transaction.

Buck liked empire building but the world was changing and his inability to be in control was being challenged from all sides. Commodity prices were falling, he'd made a couple of money losing deals from having some bad advisors and the Middle East mostly didn't need him anymore. Perhaps he was losing his touch from starting to drink too much.

He was particularly frustrated by his efforts to negotiate a settlement to get the U.S. government off his back which was starting to create distance between potential business partners who didn't want to get on the bad side of the Americans. He kept having setbacks because of the prosecutors' political ambitions. He couldn't buy them off like he could in some Third World countries. He thought he was being played in spite of having good intentions. Hadn't he secretly provided the State Department with information on key people in power in politically sensitive nations where he did business like Iran, Africa and Arab countries? That was patriotism.

There was a time his intelligence gathering network was the most sophisticated in the world and knew critical information before the CIA. In theory, this 'service' would have made him a hero, not a criminal. But the U.S. government was such a convoluted mess, this information hadn't found its way to the New York D.A.'s office in time to avert a judgement. And now, even if he could reach a settlement there was no guarantee afterward that a principled local cop wouldn't find some unpaid fine to start the whole mess all over again. It was a no-win situation. He wasn't bitter about the good deeds not having any influence on his case, angrier at being branded as a traitor.

He believed he'd also done other idealistic ventures (all in the name of money) like rescuing Jamaica from bankruptcy with an aluminum deal and helping Angola linkup with international banks when they were broke. His team could always find a financial solution, acting as an investment bank for developing countries, which in the process made them king makers. And even though he traded oil with South Africa during apartheid, he continued to do business with them under Mandela. Wasn't that noble of him?

The normal frustration of doing business was compounded by the feeling that he was bleeding in a bottomless ocean and sharks were circling, smelling blood. His divorce had been an emotionally draining public spectacle and created a lot of bitterness after a two-year battle that cost him a fortune. Now the sharks were circling closer and even his company was being looked at as a takeover target.

What was really killing him was his daughter's declining health. Buck had managed to get a video-conferencing set-up in his daughter's home to be able to talk with her while she underwent treatment. Her condition was worsening which made him deeply sad because even with all his wealth and power a deadly illness was beyond his ability to help. Worse yet, he couldn't be there to hold her hand and comfort her. It was like having part of yourself ripped away while you stood by watching helplessly.

He wondered how he'd fill the gap once she was gone. It was unimaginable, as they had been so close.

"Who the fuck do these bastards think they are? I'll send them all to hell. Break their backs and shit on them. Fucking unions think they can control everything. Goddamn them." Buck suddenly clicked the phone off and slapped it into the hand of his waiting assistant, Elmore, and told him to charge it. Elmore's sweating face was shining as much as his glasses' lenses.

"Stan," came the calm voice of reason from Elmore, "they are technically within their rights. We're lucky they don't put up a picket line at your office building here. We'll have to negotiate a settlement before it gets out of hand. We can't ignore this."

"Screw them. I've got friends in the government, and I'll have something arranged. They're nothing but a bunch of ignorant, greedy apes, and the only thing they understand is a kick in the balls." Buck was trembling with rage, gripping a glass paperweight with such force that his knuckles were white.

"I'll make some calls to see where we stand legally and find out what else is happening at the other locations. I'll let you know," Elmore said before he trotted out.

Buck picked up a mobile phone from a low glass table next to some bronze Giacometti sculptures and called his office to talk with his logistics wizard who gave him an update. The video image showed the typically shabbily dressed man who had earned the name 'the Admiral' for making all the ships full of commodities run on time. He explained that the unions in the States were making a lot of noise about layoffs at one of the big steel mills and had linked together with other metal workers unions, including some in Europe. They could block their planned purchase of some Czech steel mills that were going to be privatized.

"If I could get out of Switzerland to deal with the unions it'd be a whole lot better. But every time I try to land in a foreign country with extradition treaties, I have to divert on approach because of the reception committees," Buck said. He had generously paid contacts in the State Department to warn him of any attempts to arrest him on foreign soil but Buck felt like a caged lion at the zoo. He abruptly clicked off the call after the update.

He made another phone call but was interrupted by static. "Elmore. Hey, Elmore." The bellowing summons produced his puffing assistant, out of breath from running the length of the house. "Damn it, those workers are screwing up my phone connection again. Tell them to lay off. Goddamn foreigners never listen." He turned back to the phone. "Listen, Ahmed, I'll have to call you back when I've got more info. The Iranian president is keeping those U.N. guys guessing if he takes the next oil allotment or not. We can clean up again betting on the oil futures like the last couple of times. My traders are ready. It's like a license to print money. Don't worry, we'll be all right." Buck hung up the call and tossed the phone onto a plush sofa that faced out over the deep valley leading down to the lake, and walked across the split-level house to the kitchen.

Buck's girlfriend, Bridgitta Gubser, with her blonde hair fluffed out like cotton candy, was having a coffee at the kitchen counter and reading the latest *Paris Vogue*. The sweetly scented perfume she wore hung thick in the air as if an exterminator had just sprayed against malaria-infested mosquitos. She wasn't a stranger to magazine covers or fashion house runways in Milan. But Bridgitta's face wouldn't earn the usual five thousand dollars an hour at this moment with no makeup and the wrong lighting, even with her high cheekbones and sparkling eyes.

"*Jah, schätz,* something wrong?" Bridgitta asked as Buck wandered in.

"Just the usual bullshit with these clowns in Sweden. They know I can't follow up personally, so the bastards bleed me to death."

"Calm down, darling." The voice was breathless, and as sincere sounding as a six-year-old child. She presented the megawatt smile that kept her in demand as a top model. Bridgitta put the magazine down, and reached over to hold Buck's hand. Leaning forward, a delicate wedge of cleavage was exposed. Buck bent over and kissed her quickly on the cheek. He took a deep breath and exhaled audibly.

Buck said, "That's what they all say. But they don't know what's going on. Only I can see the whole picture." Bridgitta looked up with a pout on her face, as if she had been scolded. "Look, I don't mean to take it out on you. I have a meeting at the office in an hour, and thought I'd be better prepared." The dogs were barking wildly down in the kennel, and one of the guards went down to quiet them. Buck absentmindedly scratched his belly, watching the scene. He went to the refrigerator and retrieved a Diet Coke. "So, what are you doing today? Got any lunches or women's society teas in the works?"

"No, not today. Think I'll have lunch by the pool, and go into Zürich for some shopping. Need anything? Your tuxedo should be ready for the museum opening. I'll have Elmore pick it up while I do my errands. Why don't you take a day off tomorrow and go sailing? It's a wonderful escape and the weather's so nice. You always love it when you're on the water." Her heavy German accent slurred the words, but it gave them a quaint charm to his ears.

"Nah. I don't need anything. Remember, we're going on vacation in a month. I can do some sailing then."

"Do we really have to go to Spain again? It's the same routine every year."

"How many times do I have to tell you? Most other countries would toss me in jail and ship me back to the States if I showed up. There're not a whole lot of choices this side of Siberia." Bridgitta nodded in defeat. "Where's Elmore? I want the Rolls ready in an hour." Buck spotted Elmore down the hillside, talking with the guard. He flung open the kitchen window and bawled at him.

Half an hour later a shriek pierced the quiet cocoon of domesticated silence like the ripping of wood by a crosscut saw. The wail came from the living room where Bridgitta stood in a silk housedress hysterically waving around the morning edition of the *Blick*.

"*Oh mein Gott*! This is impossible! How could they do this?" Her screams got Stan Buck out of his study to investigate with the short, sweaty, dough ball called Elmore close on his heels.

"What's all this noise about? I'm trying to work," Buck said.

"Did you see the paper? Look what they've done," Bridgitta said.

"What are you talking about?"

She thrust the paper in his face. "Look, just look at this. They made me so unattractive. I want you to call your lawyers immediately. You can't let them do this to me. My agent will drop me if he sees this. I look like I'm eighty years old."

"Oh God, that's all I need," Buck said studying the article. "I'm trying to negotiate a settlement with the U.S. government to get them off my back and now here's a photo of me with the brother of all brothers."

Bridgitta, known for her tantrums in front of designers,

grabbed the newspaper and threw it across the room. "You've got to do something, Stan."

"All right, all right. Cool your heels. The damage is done but I'll find this bastard and have him torn in half. It's that punk from Swiss Credit Bank who took the photo. Elmore, I want you to see who we can squeeze there."

Elmore put the paper down. He had retrieved it and was looking at page three trying to remember if he knew the girl on the plastic sofa from somewhere. "I'll call that vice president we do business with," Elmore said.

Buck said, "I already spoke to the head of the International Club but that chump was useless. The files he retrieved didn't include this picture. That kid doesn't seem to respect authority, so now I'll really have to put the screws to him."

"We buy and sell a lot of oil with Swiss Credit Bank financing the transactions, Stan," Elmore said.

"I know. At least I can get this punk photographer tossed out onto the street. And if he tries to get work anywhere else on this planet, I'll sabotage him. He'll be living in a cardboard box on the sidewalk and eating out of garbage cans when I'm finished with him. And Nails would be really happy to teach that jerk a lesson with a hammer instead of a fist like last time."

TEN

Rumors; how everyone loves them. It was the fruit of the unofficial grapevine, nurturing the creative thinking of people. Usually truth was stranger than fiction, but in John's company the opposite was true. It showed a superior knowledge or insider link to be the first to toss out some controversial news. Offices, especially large ones, were fertile breeding grounds for the rumor culture. The usual question of 'what's new' was a back-handed attempt at eliciting any latest under-current of change. Transfers, redundancies, consolidations, affairs and screw-ups were the usual fare on the rumor mill buffet. And lately the whispering in hallways was echoing the management messaging that was seeping out to the general staff about jobs not going forward, downsized, discontinued, involuntarily severed, surplused. Special leaves, separations, re-balances, bumpings and cascade bumpings. Lunch was a good place to catch the latest buzz. And the day after the photo was published, John was eager for news from any source that could indicate his fate.

John was having a quick after-lunch coffee with a French work colleague named Jacques. They were sitting outside at the Café Leone on the Bahnhofstrasse, in the shade of the white domed ceilings supported by the massive pillars of the former Bank Leu building. Roaring lions' heads jutted out from the sides of the cathedral-like structure, proclaiming its position as Switzerland's oldest bank until a couple of scandals forced it to merge with one of the big banks. The café was packed with suited bankers swapping tips and rumors, as insider trading was considered a clever way of making money. A young trader type in a suit and vest was at one end of the bar puffing on a cigar and at the other end an elder banker with a van Dyke goatee held an even larger cigar, chatting with the waitresses who all knew him. A Bloomberg terminal was mounted on the wall in the back with the news and share prices rolling by in German. There was an occasional sprinkling of businesswomen and secretaries in summer outfits adding some color, alongside some desperate housewives in body hugging outfits and styled hair looking for an afternoon's entertainment from a possible playmate. Jacques liked to feel part of the banking scene as he was a contractor in the finance department. He wanted to be accepted as a player, which is why he was always immaculately dressed. Jacques was also the most notorious woman chaser John knew and watching the midday parade of well-dressed women on the city's main shopping street was another reason for frequenting the café.

"I hear you guys are reorganizing," Jacques said in his best U.S. English, talking fast and adjusting his tie while surveying the crowd to see if he was stylish enough.

John had a flash of panic, thinking that the finance department knew more about his future than he did. He tried to downplay it. "If there wasn't something changing, I'd worry." He tried to sound positive, masking whatever doubts might be floating not so far beneath the surface, while sounding like a company man.

"I heard the layoffs that happened this month in the States were completely random. They did it regardless of performance. What's bad is that lately a V.P. here said in a staff meeting we're thirty percent more expensive per employee than our competition. The company executives said at the last quarterly results announcement that they weren't meeting their cost savings targets. But why did they only figure this out in the last quarter? It's not a good indicator of competent management." John nodded and took a sip of his espresso. "So, to keep the employees happy after this joyous news they promote their People Power program that's meant to facilitate career mobility as employer of choice. And in true corporate fashion, it's really a means to see who to outsource once the profiles were filled in. Appease the shareholders who are clamoring for bigger dividends."

"Sounds like they're preparing the ground for some serious redundancies," John said in a neutral tone like it was the first time he heard of it. He was hoping to get a little more dirt.

"Could be. But I think their arithmetic is wrong. It's the interest rates that are killing us and with too many banks chasing too few customers, it's a buyer's market. I also heard some of your guys are also on the line. Five to be exact. Who do you think that could be?"

"Well, it's news to me, I haven't heard anything in particular." John wanted to avoid exposing his vulnerable position in case it became a new rumor ending up as a self-fulfilling prophecy and his gut tightened reflexively. "The guys I pity are in the accounting group. They have to work like maniacs to get a new computer system set up that's going to replace them in six months."

"Digging their own grave," Jacques said shaking his head pitifully.

John thought of his recent request to help create the change management communications which would include writing a friendly letter sugar coating the layoff news, that he'd also be a recipient of.

They paused a second to look at a couple of young women walking by. Judging from their svelte gym sculpted figures and casual designer clothes, they were trophy wives who didn't have to work for a living. They both wore oversized sunglasses and a small leather bag diagonally across their shoulder, covered with logos. Jacques scanned the ladies from top to bottom, mentally undressing them and gave an expectant look. When he couldn't catch their eye, he sighed and turning to John said, "The trouble is the big bosses with lots of shares like layoffs because Wall Street does. Share prices go up when a company demonstrates its efforts to streamline. It's a tough life, ain't it?"

"I guess we're all masochists in disguise, waiting for the bite of the whip while we try to climb the corporate ladder," John said tossing back the last of his espresso.

"How'd you know what our illustrious leaders are doing with their call girls on the weekend?" They both laughed as they knew fiction is often close to truth. "Oh, and I guess you heard about that story leaked to the Inside Paradeplatz website detailing the reorganization. Supposedly it came from an unhappy employee in one of the impacted departments, like marketing." He looked at John expectantly, waiting for either a confession or a name.

John made an innocent face that said 'I don't know what you're talking about' as he shook his head slowly from side to side. Actually, he was sure he knew where the blame would land.

John was back in his office fighting a state of drowsiness as the blood rushed from his brain to the stomach – the dreaded ALS – After Lunch Syndrome. Visions of friendly young families with freshly scrubbed kids frolicking in verdant fields, overlaid with a subtle pitch about family planning and pension plans swam before John's closed eyes in a waking dream. His friends' faces started to appear on some of the characters, including an image of Tanya in pigtails with a cute rug-rat in tow wearing dungarees, that startled him. The phone rang, disturbing his reverie. Harry's excited voice sounded close, like he'd found a better telephone exchange than Beijing.

"John, you're not going to believe who I just saw. Your old buddy, Stan Buck. He's right here in town, at the Storchen. Looks like he's having a late lunch."

"What? Are you sure?"

"Of course I'm sure. If you don't believe me, check it out with your own eyes. But don't wait too long. I'll be in the bar downstairs having a coffee. You coming?"

"OK. But you better be right. Or else you're going to owe me big. Ciao."

John pressed the call forward button to transfer calls from his office phone to his mobile, locked his desk, and was out the door. He knew Ralph was working from home so it wouldn't matter if he disappeared for a short time. As long as he kept the instant messaging app on his phone active to show he was available, he would be safe. He'd overcome his fear of any retribution from Buck as he rationalized any violent acts in a public place involving the same person would help John more in building a case. And in support of Diana's project to avenge her brother, decided if an opportunity presented itself, he would take it. He exited the building through the double sets of security doors and quickly crossed Paradeplatz, dodging the small groups of people waiting for trams and the Japanese tourists taking pictures. He crossed the Bahnhofstrasse, passing the Savoy Hotel and Gucci shop on his way to the Fraumünster Church with its Chagall windows. He crossed the open square and had to avoid cars navigating the open areas in search of a parking space. Two minutes later, after breaking every speed limit on the narrow sidewalks known to Swiss law, he arrived at the Storchen Hotel alongside the river. John thought it was an appropriate location for the world's biggest trader of materials to dubious regimes as the hotel had been totally transformed early in its history by the Swiss industrialist E.G. Bührle. He was once Switzerland's richest man, best known for selling armaments to both sides during the Second World War and amassing an impressive art collection. Some of the pieces were of questionable origins from 'helping' refugees trade their masterpieces for currency. John found Harry reading the paper at a corner table in the downstairs bar.

"Have they left yet?" John blurted out, throwing himself into a chair, sweating and breathless. He opened his shoulder bag and took out a camera, lens and separate flash that he started to attach to the top of the camera body.

"Calm down. They're probably on their third lobster each. They make it so fine, nobody can eat just one."

"Is that why you're here?"

"I just stopped in to have a cool drink after my last delivery of the morning and voilà." Harry made an expansive gesture like a magician conjuring an elephant out of thin air. "What are you going to do – get your face scrambled by a bodyguard again?" Harry laughed to wind John up, because he couldn't wait to see some action. "Looks like he's got half the Marines with him. Those two goons over there are in his group." He made a discreet nod towards a corner on the other side of the room.

John gave a casual glance to size them up and turned back to Harry. "Wonderful. The one on the left thinks he's King Kong. I'm sure he's one of the creeps who grabbed my camera." There was some motion at the other table. "Hey, check it out, Kong's leaving. The other ugly is on his cell phone."

"Probably calling Japan to see if the Nikkei index is down. If you're going to snap him in here, you'll need that flash. Otherwise, it's better outside."

"Damn it – there he goes," John said, starting to slide out from behind the table.

The Buck party had descended by the elevator, bypassing the stairs at the back of the room. Buck was out the door before John or Harry could move, with a trail of people including his girlfriend and another tall blonde who looked Russian. John rushed towards the exit with his old digital camera, pulling the lens cap off in the process. Harry hastily threw a ten-franc bill on the table and followed. The two bodyguards had split up, with the one bringing up the rear turning and studying the two approaching men with a menacing look that made them freeze. After giving a respectful pause before charging out the door, they noticed an enormous black Mercedes waiting with the driver in a chauffeur's outfit holding a back door open. For a second, they thought that was where Buck was heading as an exotic blonde from the group, turning tourists' eyes with a hot pink miniskirt was leading the charge towards the car. The two pursuers also made their way in that direction, going around the field of small tables full of the late lunch crowd that filled the patio in front of the entrance with animated waiters scurrying around like a pile of ants. Some small groups of Asian tourists posed for pictures on the periphery of the classic postcard scene.

Seeing some other activity in the opposite direction, John and Harry looked towards the river and were surprised to see Mr. Buck descending from a small dock into a waiting speedboat with the help of one of the bodyguards. Two blue and white striped poles marked the end of the dock, framing the blue green water and sleek boat while the captain held it close to the pier. In America they would have been barbershop poles, in Venice a gondola-parking zone. Here they were a nice decoration to frame the southside of Mr. Buck as he stood next to the captain looking towards the lake. John and Harry had stopped, not knowing which way to proceed. The rest of Buck's party was getting in the large Benz with blacked out windows, idling in the walkway in front of the hotel. John stared frozen in disbelief as the high-powered speedboat leisurely pulled into the river with Buck and his girlfriend under the watchful eye of a bodyguard. It headed for the lake, visible in the distance. The boat was already under the first of two low gray stone bridges along the river. The other boat with four wheels slowly crossed the Gemüsebrücke, sliding past some jewelry shops and the Dolce & Gabbana boutique, parting the small groups of tourists and shoppers who were looking at the vegetable and food stands setup along the sides of the wide bridge. John took a couple of shots getting the license plate number and Harry was by him then.

"Aha. The bird has flown the coop." He sounded philosophical. He understood John's obsession but didn't mind the lack of a confrontation. "Well, what are you waiting for, don't you feel like a swim?" He was laughing now as they watched the boat slowly disappear under the last of the bridges before the lake.

"Alright." John was abrupt. "Where's your car, wise guy?"

"Just around the corner." Harry turned to face John. "You sure you want to get more involved? I don't want to be visiting you in the hospital." He mopped his forehead with the back of his hand as the midday sun magnified the thick heat.

"I'm sure he would love to punch me out but let's see where he's going. Could be a clue to help set him up for a fall. Maybe even another photo. Looks like he's heading up the lake towards Rapperswil."

"My car doesn't have a propeller."

"Let's go."

They retrieved Harry's van from a nearby loading zone, and

were soon on the Seestrasse, racing along trying to see between gaps in houses and down side streets if their quarry was in sight. They were lucky and hit a favorable cycle with the traffic signals. As they came to the cross streets, the lights were just turning green as if someone was switching the signal just for them.

They had to wait until they had cleared the Chinese Garden park area at the edge of the city before there was an open space along the water. The road was separated from the lake by only an open metal railing for a couple hundred yards. They saw Buck's boat steadily moving along farther up the lake with only an occasional small sailboat drifting along in the weak wind. The road straightened and they were able to pass some slow-moving traffic before the two lanes merged into the single lane that continued for the entire length of the lake.

They had to brake madly where the two lanes converged as a convertible BMW with the driver on a mobile phone refused to make space thinking they were trying to race him. They slowed to a respectable eighty kilometers an hour, although the posted speed was sixty. The lake was hidden again behind several big villas. A few minutes later there was a long straight-away as they passed the Zollikon Strandbad that only had a low cement wall between the road and the lake and they could spot Buck again. The lake was narrow at this spot like a river. The blonde hair of his girlfriend was like a beacon, outlined against the far shore.

Five minutes later they pulled into a small parking lot further down the road and were relieved see their quarry hadn't disappeared and was still heading along the shore a few hundred yards out. There weren't too many other boats on the water besides some older speedboats and a large double-decker lake ship full of tourists chugging along on its lazy zig-zag route down the lake. Buck's cruiser was a high-powered race boat, better suited for Cannes or Portofino, but not an uncommon sight on this small lake, as what use was money if people didn't know you had it.

"Come on, he's getting away," John said pulling on Harry's arm. Back on the street a turbo Saab with spoiler, air dams and chrome wheels was barely doing the exact sixty-kilometer-per-hour speed limit and John was getting anxious he would miss his opportunity. "Pass these guys! Come on, come on."

They kept looking for a glimpse of the boat through the gaps between the big houses lining the lake, but were unsuccessful. John fumbled in his camera bag for a telephoto lens.

"Oh shit," Harry said. The traffic suddenly slowed to a crawl. A farmer returning from market with a tractor and wagon blocked the lane, and the conservative drivers were too afraid to pass. They maintained an attitude of dissatisfaction expressed through standard maneuvers generally exhibited at high speeds on the autobahn. The lead car would stay as far right as he could so that the slow car in front could see the long line of autos backing up.

"Fools," John grumbled as they picked up speed when the tractor finally turned down a side street.

"What are you going to do if he crosses the lake?" Harry gave a know-it-all look, appearing amused to watch as John thought a good photo would solve all his problems.

"Just drive. He would've done it by now if that's what he wanted."

They had just gotten up speed, approaching seventy kilometers an hour when a beat-up Volvo station wagon with a purple *'Baby am Bord'* sign waving with merriment in the back window suddenly pulled out in front of them from a side street without looking, causing them to brake.

"What the fuck is that, a license to drive like an idiot?"

"If I get a ticket you're paying," Harry said.

They couldn't see the lake as they were passing through the outskirts of yet another small village and the larger estates on the water not only had tall trees but also high walls. They passed the small gravel turnout where Italian men played *boule* Sunday mornings. Then there was a long descending curve and they were passing the Steinrad swimming area with a parking lot fronting a long green expanse of lawn the locals called a beach, but the boat was no more in sight.

"OK, pull over here." John motioned towards the small lakeside terrace he always frequented but never knew the name of because it changed each year. Harry parked close to the beach bar with colorful red and white beach umbrellas with the Coke logo. John jumped out of the car and ran down to the rickety wood dock. He scanned the lake but there were only a couple of recreational boaters who'd anchored in the middle of the lake to go for a swim. There was also one water skier being towed, and on the horizon an ancient passenger ship slowly making its way across the lake.

"Damn, damn, damn. We lost him. Shit." John turned in frustration. "That fucking farmer." He started back up the dilapidated dock when something caught his eye. The speedboat they'd been chasing was nicely tied up in the boathouse attached to the neighboring restaurant that catered to the Gold Coast elite. It was hidden from view unless you were close to the water looking back towards the shore.

"There it is. Look," John said. Harry had followed him onto the dock and was scrutinizing the boathouse built into the underside of the building.

"Are you sure? There're a lot of fancy boats on this lake, my friend."

"I'm sure of it. Come on." John started off, intent to spy on Buck and get a good picture. They held themselves back from running and were walking with quick steps across the parking lot. A short, round man in an ancient gray suit appeared from between the cars lined up in the parking places, and stepped in front of them. They tried to pass him, but the man held out his hand to block them.

"Excuse me," John said. The man didn't move. He didn't look like he was with Buck so John said, "Get out of my way or I'll call the police."

The man spoke slowly and deliberately in a deep voice. "That won't be necessary. I am the police. I'm sorry, you'll have to wait." His words were delivered in a heavily accented English. He held up a plastic covered card with POLIZEI in large letters across the top that he pulled out of his jacket pocket with one free hand. It looked like someone had made a bad photocopy of some text on an index card and then sat on it for five years.

"Now what?" John said turning to Harry.

"Told you it was going to cost you. I hope he doesn't pull my license."

They both stared at the man with a shining fringed dome for a head, underscored by a walrus moustache. John thought he recognized him from somewhere, like having a deja-vu.

"Mr. Miller, I believe. My name is Schmidt." He had put his arms down, so the way wasn't blocked, but the two Americans were dazed by his knowledge of John's name. "Can we talk for a minute? Your friend Mr. Buck won't be going anywhere for a while, so you can relax."

There was a pause due to the settling in of the fact that the man also knew about Buck. It was silent for a moment except for the cars racing by and music from the bar's sound system. John spoke up. "Just what do you want? I don't know you." He paused, starting to smile. "I get it, you're actually with a newspaper or magazine, and know me because of the photograph."

"Please, let's find a place to sit. I'll explain everything, but I'd rather not talk on this busy street."

The cars had been whizzing by in both directions, unnoticed by the three of them. But now it seemed a little ridiculous to be standing in a parking lot next to fast moving traffic with the chance of getting run over by a sun-dazed driver trying to land his two tons of steel in a four-foot-wide parking space. Herr Schmidt walked around them back towards the small lakeside terrace. John and Harry looked at each other, shrugged their shoulders and followed. They sat at a shaky round metal table close to the water. John took a chair where he could face the neighboring restaurant. The small summer bar was almost empty, as it was early afternoon on a weekday. The lunchtime crowd had gone, and a few retiree stragglers and a couple of German tourists were settling into a timeless afternoon.

John noticed that in spite of the heat, Schmidt was wearing a woolen suit jacket that looked like it was bought twenty years ago. Wide, high lapels accented it, with the fabric right off the seat cover of an imported Japanese car. He wasn't wearing a tie, and his patterned white shirt looked like it would dissolve in one more washing. The waitress arrived as soon as they were seated and took their order. They all agreed on local beer in tall bottles.

"So what publication do you work for?" John said.

Schmidt leaned close and spoke in a low tone that the men had to strain to hear. "I'm sorry, I'm not a journalist. I really do work for the Swiss government. I assure you the credentials I showed you are real." John and Harry looked at each other, as if to ask 'did you pay your taxes last year?'

The beer arrived, and they each poured themselves a glass. After a polite *'Prost'* they all took a big gulp of the cold brew. Even in the shade of a large willow tree that draped over them, the heat was stifling, bubbling the thermometer up to about 95 degrees. The man paused and looked out across the lake for a moment and when his gaze returned there was a look of anger mixed with shame. "I am not being completely truthful with you." He hesitated and took another generous swallow of beer, wiping the stray foam from his moustache with the back of his hand. "I work for the *Fremdenpolizei*, investigating those who apply for citizenship."

John interrupted him. "So, you spy on people to see if they walk correctly, and eat fondue the right way." He was softly sarcastic in tone, but stopped before reaching the offensive level. He suddenly realized with a pang of anxiety this could be about his request for a Swiss passport.

"Yes. You may think it funny, but until recently those things were not taken seriously. Now with so many immigrants seeking asylum, it's important to have some controls. My responsibilities also include helping with criminal investigations, and naturally, because of my background, those including foreigners." Herr Schmidt continued in his strained English. "I know about you, because first of all, as you may have heard, our government has extensive files on people. Not only foreigners but its own citizens for that matter. At first, I wanted to see you turned down for citizenship. Then I overheard you talking about your interest in bringing Mr. Buck to justice. An honorable ideal."

"What! You were tapping my phone? That's illegal. You just can't go around doing that. I'm not a criminal." John was angry now.

"Come on, John, calm down," Harry said. "The man can obviously do whatever he wants. You've got to understand this is a police state. That's why it's the land of law and order." Schmid nodded, staring into his beer, looking not too sure he liked the direction the conversation was going. "Don't you remember how the papers reported a couple of months ago that the government had hundreds of thousands of files on foreigners and Swiss? You didn't ask for a copy of yours?" Harry was trying to sound rational.

John poured the rest of the beer into his mug, and took a big swallow. He flashed back to a week earlier when he received a letter from a Swiss friend he knew from the local photographer mafia. It was a copy of the friend's police file and a lot of his reported activities were blacked out so the sources couldn't be identified. It included the address he had moved to two weeks earlier. He'd sent it to friends as a change of address card.

Herr Schmidt interrupted John's reverie. "Sorry, but can we talk about the real subject of interest here. You see, Mr. Miller, what you don't realize is you are touching on areas of national sensitivity and security by seeking to publicize Mr. Buck. I'm going to speak quite plainly because I trust that whatever I tell you will not go beyond this table. I can't afford to compromise myself further. I was recently given a warning at my job for also taking an interest in Mr. Buck. Giving away government secrets is serious. I would not only be dismissed but lose my pension I'm due to start collecting in another few months. And I could also be jailed. That's how serious this business is." He looked at them each straight in the eye for added emphasis. "If I get into more trouble, you go with me. We're on the same side, and share some mutual goals." He paused to see if they were listening and seeing he had their attention he continued. "Mr. Buck is starting to become an annoyance, no matter how much taxes he pays in Switzerland. The American government is getting impatient for his return as a symbol of tax evaders finding justice. We Swiss are getting tired of Americans in general, after being bullied into ending our bank secrecy, and especially the ones that would give our country a bad name. Buck has some politician friends in Bern, but there are a few people in the government who would like to see him gone. The federal interests that want him to leave are concerned in another area. About ten years ago there was an aborted terrorist bombing of a large hotel in Geneva. The terrorist is still in jail, and it's suspected that he and his fellow conspirators were funded in part by money from heroin sales, laundered in Switzerland. This is where Buck came into the picture. With his vast wealth and constant need for financing, he had interests in several money trading companies. Some of which were believed to be part of something called the Pizza Connection." Schmidt had paused, out of breath from his speech, to take a couple of swallows of beer.

"The what?" John asked.

"You're sure to have heard of this famous money laundering business that was in our Italian-speaking region. They also had offices here in Zürich. Some say," he paused, looking around and leaning almost flat on the table to whisper, "it reaches all the way to the Justice Department in Bern. To the very top." The last word was hissed out in contempt. "Our justice minister, Frau Kopfstein, was forced to leave office for telling her husband who worked for the illegitimate finance firm that he was being investigated."

"That was unbelievable. The first woman justice minister and she had to resign," Harry added sarcastically raising his beer in a mock toast.

Schmidt sat back gazing over the lake with a look of passing sentimentality. "Therefore, my work is hard and I didn't know who even in my own department I can trust."

"Yeah, alright. I get the picture." John's anger was dissipating as he sensed a possible ally in his photo project. "Maybe we do have a common interest." He kept the discussion personal as he didn't want to mention the Beyer family.

Schmidt looked at John with an expression that wasn't too amiable and started in again on his speech, getting to the point he'd been leading up to. "The photo of Buck that got published was actually counter-productive to my efforts. My superiors noted the photo was taken by you – a case that I'm managing. They asked me to rein you in. I suspect some of the Buck friendly politicians are behind the request. Now it's lose your job or corral a loose cannon in the form of a young American on a mission. The choice was clear." Schmidt looked at John to be sure the message got across. "You'll have to stop your photo taking and leave it to me and my fellow anti-Buck forces to find a way to bring justice. Now that I've been warned once, I can't afford any more scrutiny from my superiors. If you want to help, you can act as an extra set of eyes and ears to provide information on Buck's activities that might be helpful to my cause."

John couldn't mention the Beyer connection but he dutifully defended his right to picture taking. "This is a free country and there's no law against taking pictures in public as far as I know."

John was rebutted by the person who could easily and legally see that he got deported. "Maybe you weren't listening. I know my English is not perfect but you are interfering in an official action."

Harry had been sipping his beer, occasionally looking out across the lake, as if on a holiday with two squabbling old aunts. He breathed a sigh of exasperation and spoke slowly. "Look, I'm a former American citizen, and although tax evasion is viewed by some of my old countrymen as a criminal act, I don't worry about it. Where do you draw the line? Here it's tolerated as a national pastime, in the knowledge you'll pay up sooner or later. In the States, it's a preoccupation to shift attention from a mismanaged government. I'm not going to get into a debate about what's right and what's not. As for you two, I think you share a common goal of having the same enemy, and you'll both succeed if you work together."

"Your friend is right," Schmidt said. "Please let me finish." John nodded and took a sip of beer. "We have an advantage working together. I can help you, and you can help me. There're not too many people I can trust any more, and if I accomplish nothing else, I will be happy. This man is supporting crimes against my country, and I cannot let it go by. If Buck can be arrested or removed from this land, the past good intentions of myself and other patriots will be acknowledged and I can go back to work as usual."

"That is really crazy," John said. "We can work together but I don't have any more information than you do."

"I have friends who are willing to help – unofficially of course."

"OK, I'm in," John said after a brief pause, extending his hand. They shook hands across the table.

"Can you watch my chair?" Schmidt got up abruptly, and headed for the toilet.

John's gaze followed him out of the seating area, until he disappeared into the building behind the serving station. John had a momentary thoughtful stare into the lake water that was initiated by the kaleidoscope pattern of sunlight on the many small waves around the dock. The hypnotic effect was induced in part by the quick manner in which his beer had disappeared. He was lost in weighing the words of wisdom he'd just heard, but his scales that determined right from wrong needed some fine tuning.

"I think Schmidt is trying to sound honorable," John said. "He's got an authentic nobleness and pride. Like he's seeing Switzerland as the impartial mediator for worldly problems, and home of global humanitarian organizations. I get that this is part of the national identity, along with a sense of fairness."

"It looks like Schmidt sees cleaning house as the first effort in maintaining those ideals," Harry said.

"I figure any new sources of information will be useful, so it'd be good to play along. And if I accidentally have my camera with me and I'm at the same place at the same time as Buck, then why not take a photo. I promised Diana I would continue to help. She certainly has lawyers if the going gets tough and Schmidt comes down on me."

Harry stopped checking his phone for messages while he was listening and interrupted John. "The idea to join forces isn't so bad. Even if you could manage a few more shots, Mr. Buck isn't exactly a wallflower. At the last Davos World Economic Forum, he was photographed mingling with world leaders, prime ministers and top financial experts. Nobody said anything, they never do. After all, the American and Swiss governments are quite chummy in matters of commerce. There's a lot of U.S. money in this country and many multinational headquarters. And don't forget that the Swiss are the sole representative for U.S. dealings with Iran. But let's be honest, just some well-placed photos won't be enough to stir up any action."

"I've got to try everything I can."

"The average American citizen hardly cares about his own country enough to even vote, so why would they care about some miniscule country that's home to a guy who didn't pay his taxes? You've got to do something more drastic." Harry stopped speaking as Schmidt returned and sat down. He gave John an expectant look.

"I'm happy to help but this is a dangerous man, as you well know," John said. Fears of stirring up the hornets' nest even more momentarily constricted his belly.

"I must confess I dislike most Americans but I hate Buck the most," Schmidt said. It didn't make John think he was entirely off the hook even if he helped Schmidt. John accepted the well-worn business card that was offered. "I will arrange another meeting and you are free to contact me if you have any new information on Buck."

Schmidt stood up to leave, didn't offer to pay and looked down at John and Harry. "Remember, if either of you tell anyone what we have spoken about or even that we met, you will be looking at the world from the inside of a Swiss jail tomorrow." Schmidt paused and looked at each of them in turn to emphasize the real possibility of what he said. "And for your information, Buck drove off ten minutes ago with a friend who lives in the hills above here." He made his way past Harry who was sitting beside him with only a nod of acknowledgment.

What was left unsaid by Schmidt but filled in by the all-knowing Harry was the extent of the Swiss police files and secret police. "You're aware that the white police cars with orange stripes are only traffics cops. The criminal police all drive unmarked cars so there are far more observers than you imagine. Most of them look like football rowdies and beer guzzling good ol' boys in ten-year-old Opels or Fords. The latest secret files scandal only came to light recently. Earlier surveillance started right after World War Two so pro-Nazi movements could be tracked. This turned up a secret 'stay behind army' that had mutated into a rightwing organization, which was eventually disbanded. Then thirty years ago, surveillance that focused on communists and left-wing politicians became a public issue when journalists that were targeted started shouting about invasion of privacy. Now in this latest scandal, over 200,000 files were discovered. Mainly on foreigners perceived to be a threat to the country. Then to placate the irate public, an official security department was set-up under government supervision called the Federal Intelligence Service. The remit of the FIS includes taking an interest in entry and residence applications, with the power to reject nationalization applications if they're seen as a threat. And then the county and city police intelligence units partnered with the FIS. This means you're not only totally screwed but ready for being majorly fucked over, whether you step out of line or not."

ELEVEN

Küsnacht was a small village along the Zürich lake formerly known for its wine growing, that had evolved into a suburban outpost. Residents varied from Tina Turner who'd camped out in a lakeside estate to Russian oligarchs up in the hills knocking down classic villas to build ugly, over-architected monstrosities with sharp angles. There was a village center that's character was changing from a traditional collection of tradesmen and tiny shops to high-end boutiques, stratospherically priced delicatessens and the combined net worth of some Third World countries on display in the form of exotic cars parked in the towns narrow lanes. Carl Jung had founded his institute here back in the 1940's after studying nearby with Freud. Today he would've had no shortage of subjects to study for psychiatric issues, like having everything money can buy but still not being personally fulfilled. The Beach Club at the Hermitage Hotel was packed as usual on a blazing afternoon. John had cruised past the entrance and ended up near the next village before he found a place to park along the Seestrasse. The club's valet parking wouldn't have accepted his ancient car and besides, the cost would have paid for a week of groceries. Wandering through the parking lot in front of the hotel he was impressed by the flotilla of expensive foreign cars watched over by a young man in white shirt, tie and vest. Diana's Porsche was there, looking as sexy as its driver.

The octagonal, zinc-topped bar in the middle of the garden of expertly trimmed shrubs extending from the hotel to the lake was three deep with animated drinkers. It was mostly an older crowd of silver haired men in blazers and open shirts with gold chains buying white wine for blonde women of various ages. A few young businessmen were positioned around them with loosened ties and jackets slung over their shoulders. All the small tables scattered through the garden between low hedges and lush trees were crammed with a mix of painfully cool and over excited people in white or bright tropical patterns. They sported large fashion sunglasses and professional tans from not having to work too much.

John's shoes crunched on the loose gravel in the walkway as he made his way through the garden, scrutinizing every face to be sure no one knew him. He knew it wasn't likely in this upscale crowd of *nouveau riche* from another planet he never frequented. He found Diana next to an imitation Parisian gaslight, sitting alone at a table overlooking the water. She was idly toying with a large round glass of white wine and bubbly water, a spritzer.

"Good afternoon." John gave a formal nod before moving to sit down.

"John. How nice of you to join me." Diana took the lead. "What, no kiss?" John leaned over carefully to do the cheek-to-cheek greeting, enjoying the softness of her skin and the subtle perfume. He sat down on a chair on the opposite side of the table.

"How's your photography going? Tanya tells me you're always quite busy."

"It's true. I had a lot of work but now during the summer it's been a bit quiet. I'm working on my own projects, like taking pictures around the city at night. Guess you'd call it urban expressionism."

"Sounds fascinating. Do let me have any nice pictures from the ambassador's reception last month. It was quite an event, wasn't it?"

"Yes, there were a lot of interesting people. I think I have some good pictures that the paper didn't use. Not sure if I managed to get you in any." Diana made a pouting expression and John shrugged his shoulders and made an innocent expression. "There were so many guests, I didn't get a chance to photograph them all. I wasn't there too long; I don't like the consulate here in Zürich. The ambassador is too much like a college student with no experience in handling anything important. Political appointments don't always match required skills."

"I agree. You'd think an individual with a more international background would've been assigned."

"Where's Tanya? I thought she was also coming," John said.

"She'll join us soon. Running late as usual. These artists!" Diana shifted in her chair, crossing her legs so they were visible along the side of the table. Long legs: lean, tanned, waxed, soft, correctly curved, spa shaped and very feminine.

John chose a risky opening, "So what's the subject today, Switzerland on fifty francs-a-minute?"

Diana grinned. "I'm not as bad as you think. Yes, I like nice things, but I know it's a game. Look around; they're all acting like this is the ultimate reality." She motioned with her chin. "It might surprise you, but I don't take it seriously."

John peered over his shoulder at the spectacle. You could buy a Caribbean island with the money that the clothes and jewelry cost. A lot of the men looked like Hugo Boss advertisements, with shiny hair combed straight back, expensive casual wear and The Attitude. The women looked like they had just come from a logo convention with a pricey set of designer initials on their purses, belts, blouses and shoes. Covered with expensive rags but untouchable, unreachable, undesirable. John turned back. A delicate mist of sweat glistened on Diana's forehead.

"Should I move the umbrella so you're in the shade? Too much sun is not good. No ozone to protect us and all that." John stood up and rolled the circular cement base of the nearby beach umbrella through the loose stones until the table was in the shade and sat back down.

"John, I like you," Diana said surprising him. The words and deep look from her hypnotic eyes froze him in his seat. He couldn't reach for his beer – a standard defensive reflex, inoperable. She continued, "Not many people today stand up for what they believe, especially in this country. They're all too complacent and self-assured. Perhaps because you are a foreigner you have a more outspoken attitude." She paused to sip her wine.

John waited a short moment to let the compliment settle and be accepted, nodding in agreement with a slight smile. "Yes, we *Ausländers* do have a way of standing out." He made a gesture with his hand as if also offering her a compliment and she returned a toothy smile. Now that the mood was friendly, he couldn't resist saying what had been bothering him: "I'm guessing that Tanya still plans to sell Stan Buck the Basquiats."

"Oh, the famous American directness."

"No too different than the German way."

"Touché!" They both laughed. "Yes, if nobody else comes in with a better offer. He'll pay way more than a fair price, to be sure," Diana answered smiling with a naughty grin.

"What I don't understand is, who does business with a guy that killed their own brother?"

"John, not everything is as it seems. You were a naughty boy to publish that picture in the newspaper." She tilted her head and looked at him like she wanted to spank him and then they both laughed. "There are other ways to achieve our desired result. Which is why I asked for us to all meet."

"What's your plan? Hire some of your Red Army Faction friends from the old days to kidnap him?"

Diana laughed. "The idea does have some merit to it and I dare say they could use the reward money." She paused a second and looked at John with a sly smile. "It sounds like you don't mind a bit of adventure."

John wasn't sure anymore what the discussion was about. It seemed to have moved from capturing Buck to being captured by Diana. He'd forgotten for a moment that she was a natural flirt and it was also her favorite sport, so decided to play along. "This country is boring, anything to spice it up is welcome."

Diana said in a suggestive tone, "I know exactly what you mean." She leaned closer and now John couldn't help but notice how perfect her breasts were as they threatened to spill out of her low-cut top. "I also know the difference between love and fun. I think we have similar interests in mind. And perhaps there's different ways we can help each other."

John could see Diana couldn't help her flirtatious behavior and knew not to take her comments personally, enjoying the banter for what it was. "Yes, I'm sure there are many ways we could be of assistance to each other," he said with a polite smile, lifting his beer in a salute. "But before we discuss what those might be, can I just try and understand this Buck story again. Things are getting a little jumbled now regarding the art show."

"Oh – Buck. And just when this chat was getting interesting." Diana shifted in her chair as she reached for her wine and one of her legs brushed against John's. She waited to see if he would say something to rejoin the discussion but John slowly took another sip from his beer to avoid saying anything. "Alright then, if you insist. But I have to say you're starting to act like one of those boring Swiss," she said shaking her head in disapproval. "We both know about the delightful possibility of Buck acquiring those paintings. I'm like you and don't think helping this man to have a more pleasurable life is very noble. But in the interests of what we hope to accomplish…"

"But what?"

"You said the last time we met that if Mr. Buck were to be caught in a country that had extradition rules with the U.S. he could be sent back home for trial. And I believe we have a way of getting him across the Swiss border."

John was momentarily stupefied. "Really?"

"Our plan depends on getting him to agree to go for a boat ride on Lake Geneva to celebrate after we do the painting transaction. We'll see where we end up. Somewhere like France, perhaps."

"Now you want him to buy the pictures? I'm a bit lost here." When she didn't reply, making a face like the answer was obvious, he said, "Does Tanya know about this?"

"I had a meeting earlier today with Tanya. With a bit of persuasion, I came around to her perspective to allow Buck to buy the paintings. It's our only chance to get close to him and find a permanent way to get rid of him. Tanya has been concocting a plan and is slowly pulling together the loose ends. We shared some ideas and a strategy is beginning to crystalize. It wasn't an easy decision for me to agree for reasons you know well. I have to remind myself to keep the end goal in sight so I don't doubt the wisdom of this action. Besides, we have to admit the benefit the publicity from the sale will bring Tanya's gallery, helping establish her business."

"Your plan sounds a bit fanciful. Maybe you should have another glass of wine. Or maybe that's the problem."

"Thank you," Diana said taking a defiant sip from her wine.

"Sorry, but the whole plan sounds like wishful thinking."

"It was her idea. But I believe there's a way to make it work. I was only able to find out today that the Beyer family boat would be ready for sailing next week. So now I need to convince our friend that this will be a nice idea."

"I think if anyone is able to persuade him, you can."

"I appreciate your confidence in my talents." She had one of her shoes off and the bare foot was resting on top of John's shoe.

"No comment," John replied but he didn't move his foot. "And does this mean I can take some more pictures or is that plan over now?"

"I would guess that you could be in France waiting for our arrival if it didn't interfere with the ultimate goal. But there are a lot of details to organize first. Like getting the man on the boat." She made a determined expression that said she wasn't afraid of the challenge. "I almost forgot – Saturday is an opening at the Kunsthaus for Mr. Buck's collection that he's loaning them. I think you should definitely be there to keep the photo taking going because it will distract Mr. Buck. And perhaps the photos will be used for a story illustrating his capture."

"Just tell me how I can get invited and I'll be there."

"Can you ask your International Club to organize that? If you come as the guest of Hans-Peter and myself it could be suspicious. Especially after the *Blick* photos."

Tanya approached wearing a short floral print summer dress. She blew an air kiss to Diana after she sat next to John.

"Looks like you're having a good chat," Tanya said looking from one to the other. Diana gracefully took her bare foot off John's shoe and put in back in her sandal. The attentive waiter zoomed over and Tanya gave her order.

"John was suggesting we get some former German terrorists to kidnap Mr. Buck."

"They're probably a bit out practice," Tanya said trying to lighten up the serious atmosphere she walked into.

"Might help their chances to get a book deal," John said and they all laughed.

"But seriously, I've researched the famous Mr. Buck and I don't think he is as evil as people say," Tanya said.

"Easy to say when you'll earn a fat commission selling him some art," John said slipping into his angry mode. "And I guess you saw photos from his projects in Africa that were all Photoshopped to look like a happy mining activity."

"I'm not denying that he has some activities that are wrecking the planet, I'm saying you have to treat the disease and not the symptom, like Diana once said."

"Yes, Tanya's right. After the art show we'll have a good rapport with Mr. Buck. Only by engaging in dialogue can you create permanent change."

"I can't believe what I'm hearing. It's like you're both brainwashed."

Tanya accepted a wine glass from the waiter and took a sip without making cheers with anyone. The waiter stole another glance at Diana's legs. "Stan said—"

"So now it's Stan," John said.

"Yes. I had a short call with him to be professional, after his showing serious interest in the paintings. He said he's planning to diversify into real estate, which means getting out of mining. And I believe him," Tanya said.

"Just like that? I thought you were the champion of the earth, saving the wildness of the planet?"

Diana took over. "What you probably aren't aware of is, that Mr. Buck has done some serious efforts to help countries that would have otherwise fallen off the map due to severe poverty. He revived the mining in Jamaica when the government was about to collapse. By privatizing and modernizing the mines he saved the country when not even the International Monetary Fund could do anything."

"A real hero returning the local slaves to their rightful position while the politicians and commodity traders got rich."

"Timeout," Diana said making the 'T' symbol used in football with her hands. "Please let me explain the contradictory nature of our favorite friend." At her earlier meeting with Tanya she'd provided the same background to help ease any last-minute fears about the sale. Now she wanted to update John. "While I want more than anything else to avenge my brother's death, not everything is as black and white as you try to make it."

Tanya chimed in. "The only background you know until now has been your friend Harry's ranting about criminal associations and supporting dictators. Diana is well aware of this side of Buck but there are some other points she wants to make to balance the scales."

"Perhaps it's the aura of his outsized personality that's cast a spell on me. But what's more to the point, I know everyone has their good and bad sides," Diana said. "The world of big business means moral compromises and trade-offs to get what one wants as part of a master plan. I've done business in the past with companies like Buck and his subsidiaries back when I took over the family steel business. I know how Buck's commodities businesses operate. Buck's a wanted man on trumped up charges and has to constantly look over his shoulder. Not only have the U.S. government tried to apprehend him on any and every occasion they could, there're also a number of bounty hunters looking to cash in on the large reward. Added to this mix are any number of enemies from politically sensitive lands where Buck has used his influence on local politics. This means Buck lives in a constant state of controlled fear that even his world class security with former Mossad agents and an armor-plated Mercedes can only partially mitigate. So being surprised by an unknown person in a club was not just a principled argument over photo rights, but in fact an issue of personal security."

John nodded in agreement. "If the tables were turned, I'd probably have acted the same way. But if you live by the sword, you die by the sword."

"Buck was a very dedicated hard worker when he started out, becoming a star trader who went off on his own. His legal woes started when he singlehandedly started the market for spot prices that revolutionized oil trading. In the end he was too clever for his own good. He was falsely charged with tax evasion for his shrewd dealing, even though technically he was in the right. This was in spite of his efforts to support U.S. interests by secretly providing sensitive information gathered by his network. Getting whacked with a huge divorce settlement, and more importantly, unable to visit his seriously ill daughter has made Buck frustrated on a major scale. This only increased his aggressiveness on the business battlefield."

Diana paused in her storytelling and took a generous sip of wine, making a face as most of the ice had melted giving the spritzer a watered-down flavor. Tanya looked at John as if he would now be converted to a Buck sympathizer.

"This isn't only a personal fight, but part of business as usual?" John said.

"Yes, it's like a chess game and I hate to lose," Diana said.

"Not sure what else I can do to help you all. Maybe get him on the cover of *Vanity Fair* with a sweet essay about all his good deeds to pave the way for a settlement with the U.S. government. Then he would leave town. Let's not forget what this is really all about. Your own brother unjustly had his life sacrificed to protect the planet." The two women gave him an intense stare. "Look, I really don't like this Mr. Buck. That was a great story but he had me beat up, stole my camera and is forcing me out of my job. So besides wanting to honor Klaus, it's also personal." John spoke slowly for emphasis, and paused to take a sip from his beer. "If there's a way we can work together, I would like to help. But right now I'm getting the message I'm not really needed anymore." He looked at Diana, feeling frustrated.

"Of course, my heart is forever broken about losing Klaus. I desperately want justice, but I don't believe whoever was involved in his death was following direct orders from Stan. The local organizations make their own rules. He can't control everything, everywhere."

"That doesn't mean he isn't partially an accomplice for funding the operation."

Diana ignored the comment. "I wanted to meet you two because I think there's a way to achieve our goal of bringing him to some form of justice. But first there's one other thing. I had some new information from an ex-boyfriend of mine who's a top trader in Buck's organization. He confirmed out of some sort of loyalty to past love that Buck is actually involved with an attempt to take over Bank Beyer."

"What?" Tanya said in disbelief.

"He teamed up with a consortium to make a lucrative offer to the bank's executive board. And the best part is, my husband's nasty cousin is supporting the deal. He'll not only get a handsome fee to advise this group of thieves, but will see his shares in the bank hit the stratosphere. He could also secretly short the stock and make a killing when the deal was announced."

"I believe that's called insider trading. This is unreal. What are you going to do?" John asked.

"After I discuss with my husband how to sideline his cousin, I'm planning to talk with Buck when I get him onboard for our boat cruise. I'll explain that the involvement of his company in the bank takeover could easily come to light in this age of financial transparency. It would discredit the bank, rendering it a hollow shell. Act like I was giving him insider information so he doesn't waste his money."

"Sounds more like blackmail. He's not the type to scare easily. He has contacts in the government to verify any story you come up with and payoff anyone who would try to stop him. It's his style," John said.

"Yes, that's true, but at this stage I'm willing to try anything. Well, most anything." She laughed a conspiratorial, womanly laugh. "I need to get on his good side to make my plan work."

"You said you had some idea you were investigating with a boat trip," John said.

"Yes, that's the second, more important point. As you so kindly informed us the last time we met, the only way he can be arrested is if he's caught outside of this country," Diana said.

"But as we know, he's got a better network than the CIA. Also, with a security team like his, it won't be so easy," John said. There was a moment of silence, as they looked each other in the eye. John was the first to blink and averted his gaze, looking at the lake as if lost in thought.

"Would France be all right?" Diana asked swirling the ice in her drink, with the assurance of someone who already knew the answer.

"Why, is he going there sometime?" Tanya asked playing along, knowing Diana must have already pitched the idea to John.

"Perhaps," Diana said with a mischievous smile. She twisted, slightly arching her shoulders so her bust line was exaggerated. Giving a demure look she said, "I'm going to arrange something extra special. Like an enchanting celebration cruise that he can't refuse with two lovely ladies. We'll end up in

France where some gendarmes in their snappy uniforms will be waiting with handcuffs."

John could see the conversation going in circles, spiraling inward where his relevance was diminished by the two women forming their own little team. He decided to change the direction of their discussion and tell them about Schmidt. He looked at Tanya and said, "In the spirit of honesty and openness I want to share something."

It got an amused quizzical look in return. "Here we go again."

"I've been torn apart keeping some news from you. But at the present stage of the Buck project, I think it's best I shared it." He started to describe his meeting with Schmidt. When he had told Tanya earlier about chasing Buck down the lake, he merely said Buck had disappeared. Tanya tilted her head to one side with a look like 'this better be good'.

"Because of the implicit threat, I promised Schmidt not to take any more pictures. Yet at the same time I feel it's my duty to the Beyer family to make whatever effort I can to help you out." He didn't ask outright if the Beyers would have his back if the police accused him of interfering in state business, but took it for a given. "The reason I want to share this information is to let you know I have an inroad into the Swiss police that could possibly support your plan. But for that to happen you have to trust me."

"You're very kind to help. The government is possibly the weakest link in this situation," Diana said.

"Not possibly, definitely. You may have money and influence but Buck does too and he honestly doesn't care who gets in his way."

"I'll keep that in mind."

"Diana, please. We don't want any more people getting hurt. It's not worth it, even if you lose some millions," John said.

"You're very generous with my money. But I'm afraid you missed the point. It's a family matter, not one of money." She rose, pushing herself away from the table before John could say anything about her contradicting herself. "Sorry, but I must leave you both," Diana said with clipped German efficiency. "Nice talking with you. Please think about what I said and let me know if you find any more possibilities to help."

"Sooner than later. We only have a couple of days," Tanya said. John was feeling he was up against a tag team of Amazon wrestlers, without a partner to balance the odds.

Diana stepped around the table and offered her left cheek to John as he half stood trying to show some manners. She pulled back slightly, and said, "We'll see you soon. Bye." She repeated the goodbye routine with Tanya, slung her small purse over her shoulder and walked off in long, elegant strides past the restaurant building. The waiter changed his position by the serving area to take in the exit with a wistful gaze.

The sun was getting low over the mountains in the distance, past the far shore. The light made a wide path across the lake, reflected on a thousand ripples of hammered copper.

"So, what are you two up to? Sounds like you're making plans," Tanya said as she put away her phone she had been quickly scanning for messages.

"The only plan is how to get at Buck. Why else would I be here? Any of my wife's friends could walk by and I'd be busted. I don't know exactly what Diana's story is, but it's clear she's up to something."

"I think the first thing on her mind is a man, but not the one you're after. The one she's after. You. I think you're so naive sometimes, John."

"Wait a minute. I don't know, or for that matter, care—"

"Yes, I know you don't care," she interrupted. The waiter hovering nearby took an immediate interest in another table.

"That's not what I mean, let me finish. I do care what you think, but in this particular matter I think you're over-reacting. She loves Hans-Peter and is worried about his bank, but mostly she's thinking about her brother. The side of her that's a flirt is how she is, her nature. It's only a show. We all know her past – a leopard can't change its spots. And, somewhere, somehow, she has a conscience. Someplace beyond the money and pretty boys."

"So now you're a pretty boy?"

"You know what I mean. But you're right. One has to be careful with her; she's quite clever."

"And dangerous. Money is power, and she's well connected in ways you can't imagine." They both laughed. The serious spell was broken. "She already told me the plan this morning. I was just giving you a hard time."

"Thanks, I needed that. In her planning an action against Mr. Buck, she should first take some time to get a clearer idea about what the different options and possible consequences are."

"I agree."

"I think she's used to being in charge but she'll need some help. I still don't get your now being one of 'Stan's friends'."

"I know where this is going – you're still mad about the gallery show but let's look ahead now. Please." Her tone wasn't the soft soothing words of an entranced lover looking for accommodation but the sound of a cut and dry business transaction. John felt the coolness and wondered where he stood as the ground beneath them seemed to be shifting.

"Diana said I could get another chance to take some photos of Buck when he opens his collection at the Kunsthaus on Saturday, so that's not the point. I'm just wondering about the two of us. I feel really close to you and want to move beyond my reluctance to commit that I inherited from my bad marriage, so we can get to a serious relationship. But I need to know you want the same thing and will support me." He leaned over and said in a quiet voice, "By the way, did I tell you today that I—"

Tanya interrupted, "Yeah, yeah. Try me another day." She bent the other way and looked at him seriously. "I wish I could say something to reassure you but maybe I also need to have some time to understand what I really want."

John felt a jolt of pain hit his heart at the thought of losing her. John's mind spun in a thousand directions. Maybe he'd been non-committal too long and now she doubted his intentions. Or maybe she saw him as a needy person looking for security rather than really being in love. She could also see him as a guy on the rebound, having fun while working on finding his equilibrium after being separated. John wondered if he actually was in that position. He could only blame himself which added to the agony.

"No stress. We'll just take it one day at a time." Tanya nodded an OK. "Let's get out of here, I feel like I'm on a stage."

The waiter sidled over to the table hoping for another order. John asked to pay and after he was told the amount handed the waiter a twenty-franc bill and a five-franc coin. The waiter stood with an impassive expression and his hand out. John realized he mixed up the amount and *zwei und dreisig* was not twenty-three, but actually thirty-two. The backwards numbering logic of the language always fooled him. He remembered this was Switzerland and the Gold Coast, so he had to be dreaming if he thought a round of drinks would be cheap. He hoped none of the other guests noticed and thought he was struggling to pay. It was a subtle reminder that he was an outsider. He handed another ten francs to the waiter with a generous tip to cover his embarrassment. Tanya stood and started to walk out of the bar area, taking the winding stone path towards the parking lot. John followed close behind and his attention was drawn to a table ahead of them on the right, where a man and woman had been intent in conversation. The lady in a severe black dress meant to look business style but more like the summer version of a nun's habit was staring at them. It was his wife's sister, the killer lawyer. She had a sly smile like a fox eyeing a chicken on the loose and nodded a faint greeting without making eye contact. Her gaze was focused on Tanya as she lowered her phone, having taken a picture of the two of them for the record.

TWELVE

Tanya's gallery was located in a long, one-story industrial building from the 1930's. It featured floor to ceiling windows facing an interior courtyard of what used to be a local dairy. It was hidden on a side street that intersected with Langstrasse, along a block where there were some new boutiques from local label clothing stylists and obscure Swedish interior designs. Next to them were some ancient restaurants with fading facades that competed with Indian takeaways. Also catering to the diverse public were hair salons from the fifties alongside African braiding and extensions shops plus the occasional Thai massage parlor. One end of her building was the art supply shop and today the contents had been moved to a storage area to make room for all the guests attending the important art show that was just entering high gear. Her gallery had never been so full and even with valet parking, the small street looked like Times Square at rush hour.

The well to do crowd had come to see what was certainly her major coup – getting the commission to represent two Basquiats. The painter was part of the Neo-expressionism movement. He had achieved worldwide fame in the eighties with exhibits at major galleries and later fueling multimillion-dollar bidding wars at the big auction houses following his ten years of fame and tragically early death. His art was an imaginative and original mix of text and images, touching on political and social issues. Moving up from a street artist in New York, he sold his first painting to Debbie Harry from the group Blondie for $200 in 1982. Later that same year, a Zürich gallery owner, Bruno Bischofberger, became his worldwide dealer and a month later introduced Basquiat to Andy Warhol. The two artists soon became good friends and would go on to collaborate on some paintings. He lived a colorful life, often painting in expensive Armani suits and would appear in public in the same paint-splattered clothes. Over the years he was also involved with musical groups and rappers and one of his girlfriends was the yet to be discovered singer, Madonna. Basquiat had his ups and downs with drug use and had tried to clean up a few times. It was speculated the pressures of fame and the demanding nature of the commercial art scene drove him to drugs as a way of managing the stress. His use was also later compounded by the death of Warhol. At the age of twenty-seven, Basquiat died of a heroin overdose and the world lost one of its true superstars.

The prodigal son of a wealthy pharmaceutical company family had wanted to sell the paintings he inherited to finance his early retirement in Bali to be independent of his family's influence. Tanya's reputation in the local art scene as a champion of undiscovered talent had connected her with someone who knew someone and a deal was born. In addition to the Basquiats, she used the event to also showcase several talented artists whose work she represented, gathering them all under the theme Taking It From The Streets.

One serious deep-pocketed art appreciator whose modern

art collection was begging for a Basquiat or two was the avid collector, Stan Buck. His 'never take no for an answer' attitude and endless amounts of cash guaranteed he'd go home with at least one of the prizes. As John was on Buck's shit list there was no way that Tanya could allow him to show up at the exhibition, much less take pictures. That would link the two of them together and jeopardize the future initiative she'd cooked up with Diana. There was also the possibility of a general disturbance such an encounter would generate and resulting bad press it was likely to produce. It was a difficult discussion that had been postponed and sidestepped at every opportunity, so a couple of days earlier Tanya had chosen a public place to finally break the news. John had hopes that they could reach a compromise and he could get a picture of Buck, ideally next to another morally questionable businessperson. He was ignoring the warning from Schmidt, his stubborn rationalization being his loyalty was to the Beyer family. But had he been honest with himself, he would've seen it was more his pride than any loyalties that lay at the core of his motivation. His hurt ego was blinding him from looking rationally at the situation, that would have allowed him to act wisely enough to achieve his goal, while avoiding deportation.

They were sitting outside in the summer garden of Tao, an upmarket restaurant and club that had peaked in popularity six months after it opened. Now it was struggling for relevance in a city saturated with trendy restaurants and nightspots. Its main claim to fame was being a relative of the Buddha Bar in Paris from where it borrowed its exotic themed styling. It was hidden away in the maze of narrow passages and ancient buildings behind the Bahnhofstrasse. The Asian-themed restaurant had lost its Michelin star the previous year but the location kept people coming back. Their quiet table was under an ancient oak in an urban garden with Oriental landscaping that was an oasis in the middle of the city. They had worked their way through some small talk with John sharing his latest update on the office politics that were making his days there look like they were seriously numbered. Tanya was sorry to add something more to his growing list of issues but she had no choice.

"You know I'd love to have you take some photos at the gallery event but I think it'd be disruptive. Buck already knows you and it could cause some kind of an incident. Also, until the time is right, it's better he doesn't suspect Diana hired you."

"You know, it's a public exhibition and paparazzi in the parking lot are not yet illegal in Switzerland as far as I'm informed," John said.

"Sorry, but the show is by invitation only…" Tanya looked a bit demure but her eyes watching over the top of her wine glass said 'it's non-negotiable'.

"And I can't even wait outside like a cheap hack journalist hoping for a quote from some of the celebrities? Are you also going to ban the papers from covering it?"

"John, it's not about the newspapers, it's about you. You're sounding like you're on a personal crusade to harass Buck and I can't risk a scene at my show. There's a lot of old customers and friends of my family coming. My dad is very proud I'm doing this event and is telling everyone he knows about it."

"But I thought Diana wanted some more photos."

"If there were another scuffle with bodyguards tossing you into the street it would be bad publicity. There'll be other chances to take pictures, I'm sure. There's the museum opening coming up on the weekend."

"We don't have a lot of time, remember? We need to get as much ammunition against him as possible."

"Putting that picture in the *Blick* didn't really help your cause. As you know, Diana wasn't too happy about that." He started to interject but she cut him off. "And in case you forgot, we agreed the photo project probably won't be enough to help the situation on its own. Diana and I have what could be a good plan and you should also be thinking of options in case it doesn't work out."

John sighed in resignation and shifted gears to show he was a caring partner. "You know Buck's a dangerous man and I don't want you to be at any risk."

Tanya was miffed. "Diana and I are more than capable of taking care of ourselves."

"I would like to believe that," John said.

"Then believe it because I took care of myself my entire life before I met you. And Diana has been chewing up and spitting out people like Buck for lunch since she was a child."

"I bet she was."

"OK, John, we agreed to be honest with each other." She paused and John looked at her wondering what was coming, maybe something like a request for a time-out in their relationship.

"We're going forward with our plan and it involves Buck buying the paintings."

"You two are really going to do it. I wish you both a lot of luck."

"Thanks. But who knows, maybe one of my dad's rich friends will make a better offer." She said this to placate him although she knew already who would be the ultimate buyer.

"You know this guy's history with your family and you're aiming to enrich his art collection."

"We've talked about this before. If he gives me money, I will use it to bring him down a notch or two. Plus, we need to see how darling Diana will use the sale to our advantage so we can find some justice. Her boat ride idea is the best option at the moment. She knows very well how people operate at their level."

John realized he wasn't going to be able to sway Tanya. "All right, I'll leave you ladies alone to sort this out." He took a resigned swallow of beer. "But please tell Diana we should sit together again once the sale is over to see what other options there are and if I can help with whatever new plan she's hatching."

Tanya thanked him with a quick peck on the cheek which was safe given they were almost totally obscured from the other guests behind a row of ornamental bamboo. She excused herself, giving his hand a squeeze, disappearing through the exit while he waved over the waitress and ordered another beer. The logic of putting an action on hold that could ultimately bring justice was not a real option in John's eyes. And even though he grudgingly accepted the situation, he felt a wall had been erected between Tanya and him.

His doubts bubbled to the surface once more as he dared to think of life without Tanya. It was a scary proposition to even consider. It was slowly dawning on him that the stubborn attachment to his paparazzi mission might hurt his situation in more ways than one. But even while thinking about that frightening possibility, he still thought he knew better than the two women. He could prove his point by taking care of Buck with his photo expertise. He would be a hero in their eyes and Buck would be in jail.

After he was halfway through his second beer his mood mellowed out and he focused forwards and realized that as much as he wanted to have his freedom, Tanya also needed hers. Giving his partner some space seemed a wise course of action if he wanted to preserve their relationship. And having a direct channel to Buck if he bought the paintings, could lead to photo opportunities for the result they all sought. John made a call to Sean which was surprisingly answered on the second ring.

"*Hola, amigo.*"

"Yeah, whatever to you too," Sean said.

"I wanted to see if you got an invitation via Susan for the Basquiat show. Tanya just told me I was persona non grata."

"I had the same discussion yesterday, and the result was identical."

"I'm not surprised. If I'm considered a liability around Buck, you're an outright menace."

"I appreciate the compliment. On the bright side, the show at least provided an opening for me to call Susan. The outcome was her agreeing to meet for a drink."

"Excellent. I'm happy for you."

"Remember that quote by the suddenly respectable street artist Banksy. That when you go to an art gallery you're simply a tourist looking at the trophy collection of a few millionaires."

Tanya's gallery was causing chaos in Chreis Cheib. The small courtyard had been turned into a covered pavilion to house the overflow of guests from the gallery. A large white canvas awning had been put in place because during the summer in Switzerland, rain was not predictable but yet very common. The surrounding mountains created perfect conditions with inversion layers, causing storms to form quickly. There was pandemonium out on the street as cars double-parked and drivers argued with police over moving on or getting a ticket. The normal Friday night traffic of cruising drivers looking for action added to the congestion. Men of all ages and social backgrounds from out of town rubber-necked to see what the commotion was about, in hope of stumbling across a party with scantily clad Asian or Brazilian girls and cheap drinks. A pair of security guards at the entrance to the courtyard kept sightseers away so the invited guests didn't have to compete with tourists for the champagne.

Tanya and Diana were the Dream Team when it came to working a crowd, both dressed in ultra-stylish outfits. Tanya abandoning her jeans and peasant blouse for the occasion, choosing a luscious violet silk summer dress and Diana wore a low-cut white linen blouse and a little black skirt that even wowed her husband. The two women managed between them to eventually greet all the guests. They included senior citizen couples whose family fortunes and hoarded wealth made them old friends of the Beyer family. Then there were the nouveau riche who danced between Gstaad, Portofino and the Hamptons on a merry-go-round of social obligations in their Missoni dresses and Zegna suits accented with Hermes ties. There was also a sprinkling of ordinary rich people that didn't blink at the price tag in double-digit millions the Basquiats were listed for. These were the individuals like bankers and cartel running industry stalwarts with monopolies on importing high-end cars and construction projects in choice locations.

Tanya's father, Hans-Peter, mingled with the various groups trying to look like a relaxed banker, in a navy summer suit with colorful tie. He looked distinguished with the relaxed air of someone who had made it to the top, his dark hair was swept back over the jacket collar, graying on the temples. He looked visibly proud of his daughter's accomplishment and the acknowledgement wasn't lost on Tanya. She could see he was being supportive and her attitude of distancing herself from the family influence was toned down a notch. Also, the fact that a buyer would have to be someone like in his client base made her realize they were connected in some way and she didn't need to always challenge him. She smiled, thinking he was warming up the crowd to get the offers to go higher. Tanya felt happy and threw off the lingering guilt she had of denying John an invitation and as she and Diana were so energized by the hostess duties, the feeling stayed buried.

The two women had another strategy session while setting up for the show earlier that morning. Tanya detailed her plan which she was able to convince Diana would be effective in getting Buck sent to jail, even though it meant selling him the paintings. They would tell him that to avoid paying import taxes or duties, the transaction would take place in the government bonded tax-free warehouse in Geneva. It was home to one of the largest assemblies of museum quality art anywhere in the world, stored by wealthy collectors who had no more room in their mansions or simply wanted to avoid the sales tax on a purchase.

"After the transfer, we get him on our family's yacht for a celebration cruise on Lake Geneva. We sail him to the French side of the lake for lunch where a reception committee will be waiting to ship him back to the States. The French have an extradition treaty with America for crimes like his." Diana thought the plan was simplistic and had too many variables to be viable. Tanya said the beauty was in its simplicity. With a little more convincing, Diana accepted the proposal, finally surrendering the last of her reluctance to sell Buck the paintings. She offered to use her already knowing Buck as leverage to convince him to take a boat ride. The plan required a bit of acting. They would tag-team Buck, playing good-cop bad-cop to make it look like he was a clever deal maker, not a potential victim of two conspiring women.

Diana and Tanya paused in their hostess duties to have a glass of champagne in a quiet corner by the stockroom and map out their next round of personal welcomes for the newest wave of guests. Stan Buck appeared like magic in front of the two ladies with a curvaceous blonde in a body-hugging black lace dress in tow. Diana introduced the pair to Tanya, and Diana spoke some rapid-fire German with Bridgitta, as they had some mutual friends in Bavaria and couldn't resist commenting on each other's outfit.

Buck looked immaculate in an expensive black summer suit complemented by a discrete floral tie and matching pocket handkerchief. He had a radiant smile like he was the host of the party. Buck took the opportunity to sidle over next to Tanya and engage her in some art industry small talk.

"These two paintings represent the peak of Basquiat's career from 1982 to 1983 because they include the essential head, crown and the color red," Tanya said. When the conversation turned to artists they both liked, he couldn't restrain himself from talking about his collection and how his modern art section needed expanding.

Buck used the opening to reiterate the earlier offer from his art consultant of purchasing the two paintings. "I'm sure that you're well aware the amount I'm offering represents a healthy premium over the estimated price." Tanya nodded along and then turned and politely interrupted Diana's conversation.

"Excuse me," she said to Bridgitta with a sweet smile. Then looking at Diana, she said, "Mr. Buck has made a very impressive offer but I'm not sure if I can accept it on ethical grounds." Bridgitta was happy to use the pause to drift off and engage with a couple standing nearby.

"Please, call me Stan," Buck said looking at Tanya with a disarming smile. "Yes, let me explain. As you know, I'm a very dedicated supporter of the arts and collecting is my passion. I would love to fill out my contemporary wing and add a Basquiat or two to my collection. His work is original, a bit crazy and has a primal soul that speaks to all kinds of people in a timeless language."

Diana dodged the charm campaign first. "Dear Stan, this isn't like buying a coal mine, where the highest offer wins." Diana looked at him a second to let the point sink in.

"Are you saying you're going to punish me because of what you think I'm doing to the environment? Let's not be childish. And I promise not to talk about your family history." He gave Diana a wink. "Besides, didn't I drop close to a billion in your purse for some shares in some ancient steel mills? That's gotta count for something."

"That's a conversation for another time and another place between you and Diana," Tanya said.

Ignoring her, Diana went on. "Look, Stan, right now what happens in Africa stays in Africa and what happens in this gallery stays here. But you have to respect that Tanya's father comes from a well-established family. Any hint of questionable behavior can have a direct influence on the bank's reputation, as well as that of this gallery that dear Tanya is trying so hard to establish." She emphasized her point tapping her index finger on his upper arm.

"I completely respect that."

"So, what's your offer, Stan?" Diana said, sipping her champagne while putting on her cold-eyed businesswoman face.

"I'm willing to pay twenty percent more than then highest bid. Cash. No questions."

Tanya said, "That's very generous but I'm not sure that's the way I want to run my gallery. I'm trying to build up respect in art circles. If I do a show and make side deals, the other serious collectors will smell something is wrong and never trust me in the future."

"Are you doing this for art or commerce?" Buck said. "If it's because you're a kind-hearted person wanting to help a friend sell their collection, I applaud you. If you want to also make some money in addition to being a friend, I applaud you louder.

It'll mean better shows in the future and being able to help aspiring artists get a chance."

"Mr. Buck does have a point, my dear," Diana said with a bit of reluctance. "And besides, there's no rules about naming the buyer. This is the land of secrets, remember?"

"I've never done anything like this before," Tanya said sounding unsure.

"Discretion is my middle name, I assure you," Buck said with a winning smile. His phone buzzed and he took it out of his jacket pocket and excused himself while he turned to read the message. Diana took the opportunity to take Tanya aside and hold a whispered strategy session while Buck typed a reply.

Diana said, "This is the moment you let Buck buy the paintings."

"And if he doesn't go for the cruise, I'm out a couple of paintings that could have gone to a good home."

"Trust me – I'll have no problem convincing him. Men all have two brains and the smaller one between their legs has more influence. A cruise with bikinis is a hard offer to refuse. We're running out of time and I don't see any other options." Tanya gave a trusting look to Diana and nodded slowly in agreement. "You'll have a nice commission, regardless." They turned back to Buck who was just finishing typing some text. He looked up and gave them an expectant look.

Diana said, "OK, Stan, what if we make it a cash deal? And as I'm sure you're aware, the standard fee at an auction for a third-party guarantee is thirty to fifty percent of what comes in as a bid over the price that was set by the evaluator. So why don't we say thirty percent for the lovely Tanya?"

"This is criminal. Now you're the one being demanding."

"Take it or leave it."

"Ha! Of course. We have a deal." Stan smiled his megawatt smile to assure everyone they had made the right decision.

"To be sure that no one gets punished by the taxman, or even noticed for that matter, we need to do the transaction very quietly in the Geneva tax free zone," Diana said. Buck smiled broadly at the suggestion.

"Good idea, I already have quite a collection at the Freeport. Too much art, too little space to hang it."

Diana looked at Tanya whose expression was less than supportive as part of the show. "Don't be so sad. Stan isn't stingy with his art and lends it out to museums all the time. Part of his modern art collection will be opening at the Zürich Kunsthaus this weekend. This may even be the best option to let the public see the paintings rather than have them disappear into someone's home never to be seen again." Tanya nodded reluctantly.

"Great, so we really have a deal?" Stan said.

"Deal," Tanya said giving an affirmative nod. "But please don't advertise it until we complete the transaction." She knew rich collectors liked to announce their recent acquisitions or be visible victors at an auction as it was a validation of a public victory over their contemporaries and an extremely satisfying macho act.

"Excellent!" Buck was beaming and started to reach out to shake hands but stopped himself. He turned right away to a more serious tone. "Tanya, I respect you exercising caution but I also have to ask if the provenance is all documented. These days there are so many people trying to cash in on the demand for good pieces with paintings that have dubious ownership."

Diana broke into the discussion. "Stan, I appreciate your needing to know. Please understand these paintings come from one of the most established families in Switzerland. Tanya did her due diligence like any good *gallerista*."

"That's right. My friend who offered these paintings received them as an advance on his inheritance and that's also documented, so no worries. The family originally acquired them in the eighties when a Zürich gallery hosted the artist for a show. The chain of ownership is clear. And even if a forgery is suspected, the foundations representing Basquiat and other artists don't authenticate artworks or point out fakes any more for fear of being drawn into a lawsuit."

"Sorry. Didn't want to sound like I don't trust you but it is a chunk of change you're asking for here."

"It's OK, I would have asked the same question," Tanya said with a smile.

"Perfect."

Diana said, "I'll see what I can do to organize a little celebration after the deal."

"Wonderful! You can take the girl outta the party, put you can't take the party outta the girl. I remember why they called you Princess Dianamite." They both laughed. "Just let me know the timing because I'll be going to Spain soon for a little break." The two women gave each other a nervous glance, wondering if their ship had sunk before it even left the dock. Diana gave a confident wink to Tanya. "Now if you'll excuse me, I must tell Bridgitta." Buck quickly shook each ladies' hand and went to look for his Germany's Next Top Model girlfriend. As soon as his back was turned, Tanya looked to Diana with a winning smile. Diana raised her hand and they gave each other a high-five hand slap in celebration.

THIRTEEN

Herr Schmidt was exhibiting telephone paranoia and didn't want to talk to John over the phone when he called. As soon as John asked to meet, Schmidt made a gruff *'Ja'* sound and hung up. It could have meant 'yes' which would've been the literal translation or else was just another way of brushing him off. John didn't know what to do next but an hour later an email arrived from a private account he didn't recognize and on the subject line was *'Termin'* – German for appointment. Schmidt wanted to meet late that afternoon in a small bar by Langstrasse, apparently to avoid anyone spotting them. John confirmed the meeting but didn't ask how Schmidt found his email address.

John took a tram from Paradeplatz two stops east to the Stauffacher shopping area and got off in front of the large St. Jakob church with its massive needle-thin spire that looked like a gothic rocket ship. The manicured lawn in the front had a couple of homeless people laying back beside their battered shopping trollies full of their worldly belongings, staring vacantly at the sky. John walked down a side street towards Langstrasse. On every block there were two or three rundown bars and ethnic restaurants with tables outside, all full of the locals trying to find their place in the sun to girl watch. He came to Langstrasse and turned right, heading towards the train tracks. He crossed over the busy boulevard and went down a quiet side avenue. Halfway down the block on the left he found the small bar Schmidt wanted to meet at. It was called Heidi's Garten and a faded sign on the wall next to the entrance indicated the influence of the various ever-changing owners on the cuisine: bratwurst, Chinese fondue and kebabs. A couple of beat-up wooden tables outside were occupied with an equally worn-out variety of ancient customers who looked like abandoned shipwreck survivors. John was ten minutes late and looked inside to see if Schmidt was ignoring the warm evening and hiding by the bar. The interior was dimly lit and a classic curved wood bar filled half the room. There were endless rows of bottles of various shapes and sizes on shelves behind it. There were six tables spread around the room with faded red plaid plastic tablecloths. John recognized the back of Schmidt's head and ugly suit coat at the table farthest from the door. It was easy to spot him, as he was the only patron besides the few locals sitting outside.

"*Guten Tag, Herr Schmidt,*" John said as he passed Schmidt to sit on the wooden bench seat against the wall that faced the table.

Schmidt grunted an unintelligible greeting in return and took a swallow from the large beer mug that was almost empty. The bartender was studying the odd couple and John held up two fingers to signal the man to bring over two more mugs of beer.

"Nice place for a meeting. I don't think even the CIA could find you here," John said.

"I wish that were true but at least it's a precaution."

John attempted a joke. "The secret police watching you or something?" As soon as the words left John's mouth, he regretted his smart answer remembering the story from their last meeting about the investigation of the underground right-wing army that triggered the secret files scandal. Schmidt's look in return answered his question. Schmidt waited for the bartender to toss down two drink mats and put the beers on top of them and leave before responding.

"You must think you're a very intelligent man, Mr. Miller. You are in many ways like your Mr. Buck. You think you can come to this country, do as you please, get a passport with a wave of your hand and never have to pay U.S. taxes again. You do not realize what a thin thread you hang by." He picked up one of the mugs of beer and took a large swallow of the amber liquid without the customary *'prost'*. John copied the gesture and waited for the rest of Schmidt's observations, feeling the cool brew satisfy his thirst and slowly start to wash away the day's stress. The first taste of the first beer was always John's favorite moment on a hot day.

"Time is not your friend at the moment. While you play, each passing hour is slowly tightening its noose around your neck."

"What on earth are you talking about?" John said with a mix of light disdain and curiosity.

Schmidt looked at John like he was the slowest thinking person on the planet and continued. "Yes, you are correct. I am being watched. As I informed you, my supervisor noted earlier my special interest in Buck and he's now officially requested that I leave him alone. As ours is a small world where criminal records are easily found, your police report of Buck stealing your camera was forwarded to my office in relation to your citizenship application. And finally, the long arm of Buck has touched me because you seemed to have further aggravated the man by your chasing him along the lake. You should know by now he has a good security team who see everything. Congratulations on your success. The fact that I was handling your case seemed too coincidental so I'm also no longer investigating your application to be Swiss."

"My interest in Buck has nothing to do with my request for a Swiss passport. I'm guaranteed that right by marriage and years in the country."

"Nothing is final until you have a signed document. And as I understand your situation, living apart from your wife could very easily be grounds of rejecting your request. Your case has been passed to a less lenient inspector with no interest in our mutual friend. He'll be looking for any excuse to deny you the right to live here." There was a silence as the words settled in.

John still had his eyes locked on Schmidt as he swore softly, "Holy shit."

"Yes, you are in the shit, my friend."

"What can I do? There's nothing I can change about my life and I'm not going to leave Buck alone."

Schmidt shook his head. "You really do think there are no laws to which you must subscribe." He laughed, breaking the somber mood. "You wanted to speak about something. I hope you have good news about Mr. Buck, besides your girlfriend or whatever you call her selling him some nice pictures."

"You heard about that?"

"Did you get some good photos?" Schmidt was sarcastic, already knowing the answer.

"There was a bit of an issue. My girlfriend, as you call her, didn't want me there as it might have disrupted the event. She didn't want Buck to know we're friends because it seems she and her stepmother have a plan to trap Buck and it required him buying the paintings."

This time Schmidt was attentive. "Please explain."

"I'm not sure of all the details but I know the paintings Buck bought will be transferred in the Geneva tax free zone. And after the transaction is complete, the idea is to go for a boat ride to France and drop him off there so he can be deported."

Schmidt started laughing, and the laughter grew louder like he'd heard the funniest joke of the week. He saw John watching him without a smile and Schmidt started another round of laughing that evolved into a fit of coughing. He finally quieted down enough to take another swallow of beer and wipe his mouth with the back of his hand. "And who is helping – Santa Claus or the Easter Bunny?" He started chuckling and when he stopped John continued.

"As crazy as it sounds, I believe Diana Beyer, she—"

"I know who Mrs. Beyer is," Schmidt interrupted, amused that John didn't think Schmidt knew his story and connections inside out.

"I believe that if anyone can make this plan work, she can. I can't imagine Buck turning down a leisurely summer cruise with a very attractive lady."

Schmidt's serious expression returned. "And if you are not even allowed to help the situation by taking pictures in an art gallery, what assistance do you think you can provide to Mrs. Beyer?"

"That's one of the reasons I'm here today. You once said that we both have the same goal in mind."

"If I say I've been officially warned to ignore the man, what does that mean to you? This isn't a cowboy movie where we're wearing white hats, my friend."

"OK, so you can't help as a policeman but what about as a concerned citizen? You know if he's allowed to run free then it'll give other similar types the same message that this country is the playground for the corrupt and rich of this world because nobody really cares. Taking Nazi money, dictators' plunder and cash from all the Bucks of this world. Nice one, Schmidt."

"Let's say what you told me is true. Then perhaps there's

finally a way to have this man arrested and extradited. And if that is so, I'll do whatever I can behind the scenes to help."

"Thank you. That's all I'm asking." John raised his mug and he and Schmidt clinked the heavy glasses.

"When will this trip to France take place and what is the itinerary?" Schmidt asked in his official tone as he extracted a small notepad and pen from an inner pocket of his jacket.

"I honestly don't know. Sometime soon, I'm sure. Probably next week." Schmidt grunted in acknowledgement. "Actually, there was also another reason I wanted to meet. I still want to carry on with my picture taking to harass Buck. This Saturday Buck will be attending the opening party at the Kunsthaus for the collection he is loaning them."

"Ah, yes. Most interesting."

"I was hoping you wouldn't mind if I took some more pictures. Now that you're not managing my case I guess it could be OK."

"I'm still partially associated with your case as I'm in the process of handing it over. My advice is that you go to the movies instead and avoid Buck. If he was able to reach me through my superiors, my successor will also be warned. You are taking a very big risk with your citizenship efforts. And I don't think I need to tell you that you're tempting a hospital visit."

"I was hoping for your back-up. Now I'll have to take my chances because it looks like it's getting personal. Besides, Diana's brother died in Africa at one of Buck's mining operations so it goes beyond simply my being robbed." John looked at Schmidt with a serious expression. "On top of all that, I'm at serious risk of losing my job. Someone who I suspect is Buck, is having a banker buddy of his pressure my big boss to fire me."

Schmidt listened while he quickly finished the remainder of his beer. He was impatient to leave, knowing that no matter what he said, this knucklehead wasn't going to listen anyway.

His expression was tired and John could read the look that said 'good luck'. Schmidt grunted a "*Ja, gut*" that conveyed he had heard it all already. "You're only receiving the expected results of your actions. Why do you act surprised if your job is in danger?" There was a pause as they stared each other in the eye. Schmidt looked away and said, "So," the usual Swiss way of saying this party is over. He placed both hands on the edge of the table to push himself out of the chair. Schmidt managed an "*Auf Wiedersehen*" and John nodded an acknowledgement and repeated the phrase in return. He wasn't sure if the 'see you later' was Schmidt being polite or else indicating he wouldn't be surprised if John would soon be a guest in the Zürich jail.

John put a new battery in his camera, keeping one eye on the museum entrance. He was trying to look the part of a serious photographer in a black suit and white shirt with tie that was not his usual Saturday night outfit. In a city where a most revered form of culture was making money, a museum opening of a private collection seemed to John like a civic effort to show the city did give a sense of value to art in enriching a society in other ways. He was reminded of the story about the neighboring city of Basel who wanted to keep a couple of Picassos in their art museum that the family who loaned them wanted to sell. The youth of the city launched a campaign 'All you need is Pablo' and the necessary money was raised to buy them. When the artist heard about their love of his art, he donated four more of his paintings.

The somber, uniformed guards at the door collected the invitations as the guests were directed by smiling assistants down a glass walled hallway to the right of the cavernous entrance. Walking through the square transparent tube, the gray flagstone plaza of the Kunsthaus was visible on the right with the adjoining café and all the outdoor tables full of evening guests. The hallway led to a large room with an elevated stage at one end and about thirty rows of chairs. John found a seat in the back of the nearly full room of people dressed for a night out. They were chatting with the excitement of dedicated art patrons, in expectation of the presentations by the museum director and Buck who was there to discuss the collection.

A couple of minutes before the start time, Buck and his entourage were escorted in from a side door to the left of the stage and were seated in the front row. The museum director, dressed in formal attire, got up with a microphone and welcomed everybody, and then invited Buck up to the stage to have a seat. The interview covered Buck's history of art collecting and allowed Buck to elaborate on his growing up as an art appreciator. He hoped the contribution of his assorted paintings could help elevate Zürich in the world's eyes as a center for art, which earned him a loud round of applause. The short discussion ended with another explosion of clapping from the public and everyone was invited to have a drink.

Once in the reception hall, the invitees started to socialize, attended by waiters in white jackets circulating in the large room with trays of champagne, red wine, orange juice and water. John wandered around, snapping occasional pictures of couples and small groups of people, trying to find anyone from the International Club to justify their organizing his invitation. The invite came from the club's event organizer who wasn't aware of the club president's machinations. John was also being conservative to preserve the cameras battery life. The other photographer who was officially present kept to himself, more interested in posing in his tuxedo than taking pictures. No one smiled too much. Most were posturing, straining their stiff backs to look elegant.

John migrated over to a corner where a couple of musicians with a viola and violin sat upright on chairs churning out Brahms and Mozart. The man and woman were in black formal attire, concentrating on their sheet music. John was feeling nervous, wondering when Buck would appear and tried to look part of the scene by observing the musicians with the attention of a connoisseur. The museum director was a tall man with graying temples and features that looked like they were chiseled out of pink plastic. He came over to John, parading in his tuxedo accented with a cummerbund of purple satin and the matching frills on his shirt sleeves hanging out looking fashionable.

"Mr. Miller, have you taken some fine photographs?" he said in his unsure English.

"Yes, I have. Anywhere I point my camera tonight I get good pictures. Very nice people."

"Fine. Make sure you take a picture of that couple over there. He's a vice-president at U.B.S. bank, and contributes a lot to our collections."

"I think I got him already, but I'll take some more photos to be sure."

"It's quite warm tonight, isn't it?" The director's attention had drifted, and he strolled off patting John on the shoulder.

John investigated one of the long tables where the hors-d'oeuvres were laid out and then there was a ripple of activity at the entrance to the reception area. A stunning blonde in a shiny, metallic evening gown made a grand entrance smiling at everybody, anticipating all eyes to be on her. She turned her head, tossing her hair over one shoulder, leading a party of people. It was the lady from the disco and Stan Buck was her shadow, looking elegant in a black suit. John's heart beat faster, and he was sweating more. He decided on a direct approach and quickly set his small plate with unfinished snacks down on a window shelf. He was adjusting his camera as he stepped up to the group while the museum director was greeting them with loud enthusiasm.

"Smile for the camera please?" The blonde's smile stayed frozen as she adjusted her pose, always ready to have her picture taken. John's inquiry from behind his raised camera was followed with a rapid, staccato series of flashes. At six shots a second, he managed to capture twenty-four images before the subject disappeared as someone stepped in the way.

A well-dressed young man with greased back hair and the build of a professional boxer with the battered face and deformed ears to go with it had stepped between them. The man pushed forward with his shoulder as if he was clumsy in trying to pass by and drove the camera into John's face. A second assistant, a clone of the first, whispered a few hurried words to the museum director. The director took John aside from where he stood dazed for a moment, looking at the passing parade.

"This gentleman has requested not to have his picture taken. Do you mind? Besides, we already have our official photographer here. Your presence was a courtesy." The director delivered his line with the unmistakable message that John was free to go as soon as possible. John knew he would be effectively blacklisted from any more official events at this venue for a long time to come. It was another invitation for him to take a place in the unemployment line.

The other photographer had started in now and had Buck and Bridgitta posed nicely in front of a large abstract mural where they struck one of those easy poses of comfortable wealth representing the finer things in life.

"OK, sure. I was almost out of memory on the camera anyway. In fact, I think I have enough pictures. If you don't mind, I'd like to leave soon." John rubbed the bridge of his nose where it felt bent. The adrenaline had surged into his system but fight or flight wasn't on the program. The first reaction was to find the assistant alone and swing the camera by its strap, letting the weight of the brass case build up enough momentum to leave a serious dent when it connected with the man's thick skull. The thought was gratifying as John set his jaw and ground his teeth in anger. Then thinking of what the retaliation would be, made him forget the idea as quickly as it had arrived.

John felt defeated, as the desired effect wasn't fully achieved. The only photos he'd managed were a smiling blonde who thought she was going to be on a magazine cover. He'd at least let Buck know he wouldn't be forgotten but more confrontation could have made the scene newsworthy. It would've been more satisfying if there were a few direct insults and accusations traded in front of the crowd of elite society. John wished he had a shot of Buck's face when he looked so displeased at his taking photos of Bridgitta.

His moment of daydreaming was broken by the director. "Fine idea. Please, have a glass of wine first. Thank you." The director forced a grin, baring his teeth in the effort. At the drinks table, John sipped a glass of champagne, letting his heartbeat slowdown from the surge of adrenaline. The wine evaporated in three swallows. He got a refill and watched the people with a disinterested look, aware that Buck's party had cloistered themselves in a corner.

John's eyes locked on Diana slinking towards him unescorted. It was the first time he had seen her tonight. A short, white dress clung to her every contour. John wasn't the only person watching. She sauntered over to the table oblivious to him and selected a flute of champagne. She was close enough John could smell her perfume. He felt an electric charge as she brushed his elbow with hers, and as he turned towards her, she walked off in the opposite direction, joining a group of men.

John had the impression she was acknowledging his presence to give him some reassurance.

John wiped the sweat from his forehead, and then his upper lip with a napkin. His nose had stopped throbbing but he was still apprehensive. His shirt was sticking to his back under the summer jacket even though the enormous room was cool as a vault. He decided to fill the remainder of the memory card and leave.

John wandered back down the glass walled hallway to the main lobby of the museum where only a few people were lingering in the cool of the tall, wide entry area while most of the public was still intent on the free refreshments. Several couples had followed his lead and gone past him to the small exhibition hall where the Buck paintings were hanging. John also made a short token tour of the collection, pausing before a Warhol pencil drawing of Chairman Mao, studying the simple lines and recognizable style. He left the small gallery as it gradually started to fill up and inspected a narrow, marble tiled passage with open doorways on either side that led into other high-ceilinged rooms where paintings were on permanent display. He looked into the various rooms but none of them were particularly interesting. Lots of modernistic paintings and strange stone sculptures that John figured you had to be a serious student of art to appreciate the subtleties. None of the attendants were on duty, which surprised him as one of the badged students acting as an usher hadn't hesitated to caution him when he took a picture of the room where the Buck Collection was housed. On an impulse John looked over his shoulder towards the entrance of the hallway. The assistant of Buck's who had realigned his nose was treading towards him with a wary look.

The man gave a casual inspection of the various rooms but John didn't think he was an art connoisseur. He was in the middle of the hall so John's retreat was cut off. John wasn't sure where the small hallway ended but he was suddenly nervous when he realized that there were no other people in any of the rooms he had passed. It was too quiet. The music and conversation in the main exhibition hall seemed distant. John had a momentary vision of being discovered at the bottom of a fire escape in the back of the building, where he'd been tossed like a sack of garbage. He gave another glance backward and could see the second bodyguard lounging against the entrance to the hall as a lookout. John pulled out his mobile phone to look like he was calling for help but there was no signal, something his pursuer must have already noted. He strode down the hall to where it ended in a room full of large oil paintings and free-form sculptures. He had hoped to find a fire exit and opening the door would trigger alarms and a response. There were no more doorways; it was a dead-end with no standard green sign of a running person fleeing flames that indicated a way out.

John did a quick mental survey of what possible weapons were at his disposal. His camera was the only object to defend himself with and he wasn't sure how useful it'd be. John looked back and the first bodyguard was only a few doors away. Behind the man was a fire door with a lit-up EXIT sign he had hoped to find. Beside it were a fire extinguisher and alarm box but John was cut off. John looked back in the room and decided that the large metal abstract sculpture was the most defensible position. There were no chairs, flower vases or other movable objects he could use as a weapon. John had backed up to the sculpture when the bodyguard filled the doorway.

The man looked at him with a smile, as he rubbed his hands together in anticipation of using them. He purposely kept his back to the security camera mounted in a corner of the ceiling. "What's the matter, Mr. Photographer, got tired of the party? You really shouldn't be drinking so much. You might fall down and hurt yourself." He took a slow, cautious step forward. "My boss isn't very happy you took some pictures without asking. Seems to be a bad habit of yours. He asked me to teach you some manners." While he was speaking the man edged closer. His smile changed to a look that would have sent a chill down the back of a sinner in hell.

John moved around to the back of the sculpture. The bodyguard was undoing the buttons on his cuffs with deliberate care so that his arm movements wouldn't be restricted. John's heart was pounding so strong he thought he'd pass out. Buck's helper stopped, trying to anticipate John's actions. He took another step forward until they were both a foot away from the sculpture on opposite sides. The creation didn't have a lot of mass, only a six-foot-tall pile of geometric shapes balanced on a granite cube that was about a yard wide. The bodyguard was ready to spring whichever way John decided to turn. John held the camera by the body so that he could use it as a club. Out of the corner of his eye John saw a movement at the door. He thought it was the second assistant coming to join in the fun.

It was Diana. "Excuse me, does anyone know where the powder room is?" she called out in the innocent tone of a lost bimbo. The man took a look at her and stepped back from the sculpture. She hadn't moved and was batting her eyes that were opened in an exaggerated look of innocence. The man reluctantly slunk towards the door while Diana gave him a sweet smile as he passed. After she watched him make his way back down the hall she strolled into the room with her short skirt swinging with her steps.

"Are you all right?" Diana asked with a look of concern, stepping closer and studying John's face.

John smiled as best as he could, giving a slow nod. He managed, "Yes, I think so."

"What did he do to you?" John shook his head from side to

side in a gesture indicating that nothing had happened, trying not to make her worried.

"Were they after your camera again?"

"I think it was more about teaching me another lesson," John said.

"Tanya told me about your office problems with Buck pushing to get you fired. I got so angry I couldn't even greet him tonight."

"Oh my, how un-proper you've become." They both laughed as John's heartbeat returned to normal.

"You want me to tell the museum security that the donor of this collection wanted you roughed up?"

"Thanks, but there's no need for you to be any more involved than you already are. I just hope this doesn't jeopardize your plans."

"Don't worry. Buck already left and I doubt those goons are smart enough to figure out we know each other."

Diana reached over and pushed some stray hair of off John's forehead as he looked into her eyes that were green and glassy like a warm tropical sea. Diana gave him a crooked smile and excused herself saying her husband would be looking for her.

"Thanks for helping out. That was a bit stupid of me," John said.

"No problem. I got curious when I didn't see you. Then both of Mr. Buck's assistants disappeared down this hall. I didn't think they were admiring the art. Did the man say anything?"

"Only that his boss wasn't happy about my picture taking."

"Is this what you expected or wanted for a result?"

"Not exactly. I would've been happy with another unauthorized photo for your article. But it does seem to be getting on his nerves. Maybe that counts for something."

"We can talk more about that some other time. Let's get out

of here." They walked back to the main hall and as John let her go ahead of him, she disappeared into the crowd without looking back. When he joined the public in the reception room he looked around and didn't spot either of Buck's assistants anywhere. John faded into the crowd, walked down the glass hall and slipped out the door where the temperature was warm and comforting after the chill of the air-conditioning. He shuffled across the open courtyard and around the corner, following Ramistrasse down towards the lake in the direction of the parking garage where he had left his car. He stole periodic glances over his shoulder, half expecting a gorilla in a suit to be stalking him.

FOURTEEN

Diana checked her makeup in the car's rearview mirror while the tall electric gate securing the driveway to Stan Buck's mansion rattled open. There were a couple of security cameras watching her with their ever-vigilant eyes. One was mounted on the top of a fence post to observe the guests and the other was low to the ground and recorded all license plates of the cars that passed by. She drove slowly along a curved drive that embraced a vast green lawn that was so immaculate it could have been a putting green. From the curve that double-backed towards the house, the lake below looked close enough to touch, with its vivid blue water reflecting the wall of mountains on the other side. Buck stood squarely on the porch framed by the entry door with his hands on his hips studying her while she slipped her car between a new convertible Mercedes and an older model Rolls Corniche. Diana eased herself out of her low-slung autobahn terror, slowly extending one leg out followed by its lean twin as part of her conspicuous show to entice Buck for a boat ride. She was greeted with a vision of Buck as plantation owner from a banana republic, resplendent in white linen aviator shirt and matching cotton pants with navy blue espadrilles and no socks. A thick, woven chain shone through the thin material of his shirt, and a rose gold Richard Mille Chronograph that retailed at half a million dollars, reflected the midday sun.

"What an unexpected pleasure," Buck boomed from the front door. He negotiated the twisting steps down to Diana's car where they exchanged air kisses and he gave her a playful squeeze around the waist.

"Hope I'm not keeping you from your work," Diana said.

"Not at all. I welcome your kind of distraction. It's a pity Bridgitta's not here because she loves to entertain. I'm glad you called, we don't get many visitors from Zürich up here. There's a joke that if the Swiss have to drive more than twenty minutes to visit someone they think it's an overnight stay requesting a hotel. And we all know how they hate to spend even a *rappen* if they don't have to. Sorry, I mean they are frugal and watch their money. Oh, but you're not Swiss, are you?"

"No, but my husband is," Diana said with a disarming smile like they were co-conspirators.

"Yes, of course. Let's go out back and relax with a cool drink." He led her around the house to the patio, providing a tour guide's monologue elaborating the virtues of his estate. The house sat on the crest of several acres inside a gated property that rolled down towards the Lake of Lucerne known as the Lake of the Four Forested Cantons. In the distance an ancient paddlewheel steamboat chugged along, low in the water with a full load of tourists, disappearing into one of the four fingers of the lake that extended beyond a row of mountains. They sat on plush outdoor chairs under a blue and white stripped canopy by the pool, gazing out on the distant water and the jagged teeth of the Alps' north side grinning against the indigo sky. To break the ice, they started out talking about the party days in New

York where they first met. They were laughing about how crazy she was, organizing events like her now legendary Oktoberfest party where the men wore lederhosen and the women lowcut dirndl dresses in a reconstructed Bavarian beer hall that turned into a disco at midnight. Buck thought those were the good old days while Diana saw why she was glad to have moved on.

"I thought I should check up on you, Mr. Buck, while I was in the neighborhood." She exaggerated the formality as if she was a young girl. "It's been a long time since we last had a chance to really talk. Wasn't that museum opening wonderful? You've really got a most interesting collection."

"Thank you. I take pleasure in beautiful things and enjoy sharing them. I'm not like those big Japanese insurance companies who pay forty million for a Van Gogh, only for the five guys on the board of directors to look at. That's criminal. What did you think of the Monets? Nice, eh?" Diana was thinking how the art market was a lot of times an excuse for banking in public with people showing of their wealth in the flashiest way possible. It was the ultimate luxury goods shopping gone wild. She held off mentioning his announcement in the art press of buying the Basquiats, that fit this type behavior.

"Very impressive. It's wonderful to collect art like that. I prefer more modern art but Hans-Peter always fancied more conservative investments."

"These aren't necessarily investments, Diana. I buy them because I like them. If the Japs were to sell 'Sunflowers' today I doubt they would get their forty million back."

"I believe you're correct."

"After you've refreshed yourself with something to drink I'll give you a little tour of my private gallery. And if you need to do a tinkle you can see the Chagall I have hanging in the bathroom." He laughed, enjoying being able to show off his wealth and how little regard he could show a museum quality painting. "Like I said, without many visitors it's a shame more people don't see the art. I've got some Renoirs, Monets and a couple of Picassos. I think you'll be impressed."

"I'd really like to see what you've collected. Thank you." Diana was watching him and once more shifted in the chair to extend her legs. Buck smiled inwardly to himself noticing the effect he was having. "We have a few nice paintings handed down by Hans-Peter's family. Nothing exceptional. I find them too dark. I think some are by those old Dutch masters. Couldn't be sure. You'll have to come to dinner some time and give us your opinion." She paused, reaching across to place her phone on the low bamboo table in a natural movement that exaggerating her curves. A uniformed maid appeared and placed two glasses of iced tea on the table.

Buck steered the conversation in another direction to have a high-level talk about the metals market that they both had interests in. This new topic led to a discussion on how the Swiss banks like Diana's husband were getting singled out for regulation.

"I think it's outrageous the banks are getting rules imposed on them, not only from the U.S. and European Union governing bodies but now the Swiss government as well. It was triggered largely due to insider fixing of global exchange rates." Diana had to maintain a Zen-like tranquility to restrain herself from tossing her drink on Buck for his arrogance, talking like he already owned the bank. "I'm also an unfortunate victim of government meddling. It makes me angry because it interferes with being able to travel to the States to see my terminally ill daughter."

"I'm so sorry. This is truly unfair. I hope you find a resolution soon." Buck grunted in response and looked away over the lake. Diana continued, "I know what you mean about all this government pressure on the banks. The value of my husband's bank comes from its integrity and the values its held onto for many generations. But those times are over. It's a new world with new rules and transparency is increasingly important." She gave the example of private banks becoming incorporated and publicly accountable. "And if people with a dubious history or criminal motives were to become part owners because they are investors, the value of the bank would shrink to nothing." Even though she tossed out the comments while stirring her drink she could see Buck understood her point. Not only was his status as a fugitive a black mark against him, there were also accusations he'd been dealing with the Russian mafia.

He looked at her like a precocious child and said, "That's an interesting observation." She hoped playing this card would serve a double purpose of not only making him think twice about a bank takeover but also feel guilty enough to agree to a boat ride.

There was a moment of silence as each stood their ground and the weight of Diana's implied message settled in. The conversation restarted as Buck tried to balance out his sins by naming all the Israeli charities and hospitals he supported. Diana nodded in acknowledgement and moved the discussion to the art show and his purchase of the Basquiats. The conversation went full circle, talking about the summer again. Buck elaborated on his plans to visit his villa by Marbella, as Spain was one of the few countries he could visit without being extradited because he had acquired citizenship there.

"Actually, Stan, I wanted to extend another invitation to you that I mentioned at Tanya's gallery. A little celebration for adding some most amazing art to your collection. After we conclude the sale of the painting this Wednesday, I'm going for a cruise on Lake Geneva with Tanya on the family boat. I wanted to see if you would like to come along. It's the first time it's going out this year. It's a classic racing boat that was once in an America's Cup regatta and has been refitted as a pleasure cruiser. I remember how you love to sail, and thought you might want to join me."

"You? Won't Hans-Peter be there?"

"No, sad to say, he has to work. And besides, he's not that keen on boating. It was his father's boat and he didn't even like it then. He mostly uses it to entertain important clients. And if Bridgitta wants to join, we'll make you captain of an all-girl crew."

"Hmm. Sounds very good." Buck lit up at the thought of being on a classic sailing boat with some lovely ladies. "Unfortunately, Bridgitta gets seasick, even in a bath tub. But I'd be most happy to join you. Just let me know when and where you want to cast off."

"Wonderful! I'll be sure to fill the galley with champagne," Diana said saluting like sailor.

Buck was perched in a rattan armchair on the balcony murmuring into a sleek mobile phone while watching a servant in a white uniform clear the glasses off the patio table. He tapped his cigar's ashes into a large glass ashtray and waved the Havana made Cohiba like a conductor's baton to emphasize his conversation. His business manager was arguing the wisdom of going on a boat trip with Mrs. Beyer.

"Sure, it's all right. We're old friends," Buck said.

"Just because she is, doesn't mean you have to."

"You know the rule: keep your friends close and your enemies closer."

"Any indication at this point of your involvement in the bank takeover would screw things up for us."

"Yeah, I know it's a delicate matter. And if they do suspect, it's too late – we have our position locked in. Remember, the usual rules don't apply to me. I can make a million mistakes, they can't make one."

"There's always the chance something could slip out and give them an opening. Let it go, Stan. There will be other boats with other women."

"Of course I'm not going to spill the plan, no matter how drunk she gets me. Besides, the kid will be there too. Will help keep it nice and friendly. Who knows, if things go ahead as planned, it could be the beginning of a celebration of more than acquiring just some nice paintings."

The manager changed the subject. "Stan, there's one more thing. Jet Aviation asked for a bigger deposit for the charter to Spain. They're nervous about problems that could result if they have to put down somewhere like Paris in an emergency."

"Why is it that I'm always getting milked in this country for every nickel they can get their hands on? Let's discuss it later. I'll be in the office about three." He stood up and watched a black four-door Mercedes the size of half a football field with consular license plates from Geneva, swing into the top of the drive.

Ralph Owen's name flashed on the digital display of John's desk phone, as it demanded attention with an insistent ringing in an annoying ringtone John was too technically challenged to know how to change. John debated whether he should pick it up or not. Ralph wanted him in his office in half an hour.

John considered Ralph as the velvet glove with the iron fist. He was the consummate professional with a trained tone of sincerity that could charm the candy away from a toddler and ten minutes later the dress off of its mother. Having quieted down public outcry over toxic funds, tax evaders and dirty money, Ralph could bury a scandal. It was no secret Ralph's first priority was himself and the high-level job he would bounce back to in the States after his token tour of duty at headquarters. John knew he couldn't trust Ralph as the threats had been building with only one obvious conclusion in mind. When he entered Ralph's office he was surprised to see his Human Resources representative sitting at the meeting table. The alert and ever-helpful man in his late twenties had been meant to help get the mid-year review redone but had delayed it so long the review was locked down. The young man gave a sly smile like the Cheshire Cat from behind his cheap wireframe glasses. It reminded John why the abbreviation HR was said to stand for Human Remains, as their supporting employees had the same result as an undertaker. John nodded a greeting and his heart started pounding; an HR person had never been at any of his meetings with Ralph before. At this point John told himself after everything else that had happened to him, nothing would surprise him now. And if he could remember to breathe he would still be alive at the end of the meeting. He thought back to the mindfulness training he went through at a company offered stress reduction class after the many cases of burnout across the company couldn't be ignored.

"Can I get you something to drink?" Ralph asked.

"No, thanks. I'm all right."

"Mind if I get one?"

"Go ahead." John waited, flipping open his leather notepad as if reviewing some notes he wanted to discuss. Avoiding the eyes of the HR person he stared out the window at some tourists waiting for a tram in the square outside, wishing he were anywhere but in this office. The lack of respect was breathtaking.

"Shitty weather, eh?" Ralph commented on the blue skies

returning with a Diet Coke he'd grabbed out of his miniature refrigerator that had a personal Nespresso machine on top.

"I know. I hate all this sunshine."

Ralph draped himself on one of the meeting chairs and droned out a half-hearted monologue about the difference between this summer and the last and how last summer was on Tuesday and Wednesday and this year it was only on Tuesday. Finally, Ralph got to the subject he'd been avoiding.

"John, we finished planning the alignment of our organization for next year and I'm afraid nothing has changed from what I indicated earlier." John's stomach fell through the floor as the fatal words had finally been uttered. While he knew this moment in time would have happened sooner or later he had held out hope that he'd be passed over and his work on an important project repositioning the commercial department he worked for would save him. His breathing constricted and noticing it, he tried to inhale deeply to get some oxygen to his brain.

"You mean my job is being phased out," John said with his voice constricted.

"Right. I'm sorry. I warned you that this might happen. And it has." Ralph made a gesture opening his hands sideways as if to say it wasn't his choice.

"True." John was getting his breath back using some mental control and deep breathing and his voice had returned to normal.

"You've heard what other people got as their severance package? It's quite generous. Rudi has put together the standard letter." On cue Rudi slid a folder across the table.

Nice, John thought. First it was only a possibility and now Ralph had the letter already prepared without a chance to discuss options. Couldn't wait to dump him.

"Before we discuss that, what about an opportunity of

working with the Public Affairs group? Their budget was just approved for next year including one point five million for external communications and the emerging markets," John said.

"You're right. But that organization will be based in the States and any work in Europe will be contracted through our agency."

"You need experts inside the company who know the business. The funds group I've been working for will have an even greater need for help—"

Ralph cut him off. "John, do you have a problem with finding a job outside of Swiss Credit Bank?"

"No, I don't."

"Good. You have to accept that the current situation is locked in. I'm sorry." Rudi stared at John with the same professional smirk, backing up Ralph all the way.

"I just want you to understand that I'm interested to stay with this company and I think there are possibilities."

"Sure. You've been a good team player so I'll let you in on a little secret. Somebody with a lot of influence is making their desire to see you fired well known."

"What the—"

"Before you get all excited, this process has the stamp of approval from Human Resources so there is no room to move." Rudi gave a serious nod.

"Ralph, we're talking about mobbing here. That's illegal in this country."

"This isn't mobbing. Mobbing is when we give the U.S. government your name for being involved in pushing secret accounts on rich Americans by creating the presentations to market them."

There was a stunned silence and John's heart was racing a mile a minute as such an action from Ralph would have the impact of making him a fugitive. And in the current mood of the

U.S. government towards Swiss bankers helping American citizens stash their money out of sight of the taxman, a couple of years of jail time would supplement a large fine. A million thoughts swirled in his head starting with his desire for a passport as a means of security and ending with his having to leave Tanya.

"Somebody really doesn't like me, do they?"

"Let's get this formality over with and if something shows up before the end of the year, all the better. We can tear this letter up. Wouldn't be the first time." Ralph told him he had five days to sign it or not have an employment contract. The timing meant Ralph wanted the standard three months' notice to expire at the end of the year so next year's budget would show a reduction. It assured Ralph bonus points with his boss for the serious cost control efforts in addition to following orders regarding getting rid of an unwanted individual.

Once he got home, John felt confined and didn't want to be alone in his one-room apartment. The news of his layoff left him despondent and angry. He couldn't reach either Tanya or Sean by phone so he left messages. Tanya wasn't the texting type so he had to rely on her infrequently checking her messages and Sean was always a mystery when it came to responding. Working on his third vodka and tonic, John decided it'd be less depressing if he had company to get drunk with. He locked up his apartment and shuffled off towards the lake, down the small country lane with cow pastures on either side. The final leg of his expedition was the most challenging. It involved a steep walkway one block long that went straight down to the lake from the last street that ran parallel to the Seestrasse below. John knew that walking was definitely safer than driving in his current state of intoxication and pushed the thought out of his mind of what the return journey would be like.

John went to the usual summer bar attached to a grill restaurant on the lake. The seventies music blasting over the sound system challenged his ability to balance on a barstool. The motif was tropical with plastic palm trees and Hawaiian print fabric for wall hangings. If you can't be there, might as well pretend. Ease the pain of living in a country where summer only lasts six weeks.

Bertie the bartender was mixing drinks behind the bar, and shouted a greeting. John nodded an acknowledgment, pointed to a neighbor's beer bottle and turned to watch the crowd. Young professionals, or pretenders to be, in casual clothes that cost a lot to look like they didn't, and country club checkered pants, were the predominant themes.

The beer had a slight aftertaste. It had been left in the sun too long, and even refrigeration couldn't cure it. John was drunk enough that one more losing situation didn't matter. A couple of beers later John was contemplating the expedition up the hill to his apartment which was beginning to look like Reinhold Messner's solo assault on Mount Everest without oxygen. He was wrenched from his open-eyed dream by a familiar music.

"*Hoy schätz.*" It was Tanya, shadowed by Susan. "We were on our way back from town and heard your message so thought we'd stop for a nightcap. Out for your evening walk?" John's brain was working in slow motion and before he could answer Susan spoke up.

"Hello, Mr. Paparazzi. Can I help you take some snaps?" Susan laughed, edging closer.

They each gave John polite kisses on either cheek, as he looked over their shoulders as a force of habit to see if any former neighbors who knew his wife were watching. People were looking, but no one he knew. Must have been something to do with the noise level of their conversation. John smirked at them, not sure where to begin. He was spared the agony of trying to articulate something.

"Did you hear Tanya's going on a sea cruise?" Susan started, reaching over to support herself on the bar. "And we're not invited." Her tone was exaggerated, no doubt due to previous activities in town involving fermented grapes.

"Hey—" Tanya started to break in.

"...with her stepmother and some rich guy."

John gave Tanya a curious look and she said, "You won't believe who."

Susan was giggling, and waving to the bartender.

"The day after tomorrow when we complete the painting deal I'm going with Diana to Lake Geneva for a cruise on the family boat," Tanya said.

"Is it going to be like the *Titanic*?" John interrupted with his sarcastic tone barely hidden.

"No, not that big. It's a classy sailboat that's been in the family for years. We used to have big parties on board when I was little."

"I didn't mean how big it was. I was wondering if a disaster is going to transpire?"

"Why should something happen?"

"Icebergs from global warming," John said.

"Oooh, are you jealous?" Susan said, with no idea of what was going on.

"So, you don't want me to go then?" Tanya said.

"That's not the point. If it were anyone else I would say 'have a nice time, enjoy yourself' but your choice of company and timing isn't the best." John's defeated attitude was coloring his once ambitious plan to bring Buck to justice.

"And why is that?" Tanya was abrupt.

"I got news for you. You and Diana are both in dreamland if

you think you can pull a fast one on Buck." He paused to concentrate better on her face that was shifting in and out of focus. "Nobody needs enemies like him and getting on his wrong side won't be a fun ride. If you know what's good for you, I'd suggest you call Buck, say there's engine trouble and 'don't call us we'll call you' for a new date. Simple."

"At least we're taking some serious action. All you do is talk about the day the world will wake up because of your photos of him, when actually there isn't anyone out there who gives a damn about those pictures."

"Hey, you two." Susan's tone of maternal reproach slowed them down. "I'm going to call Sean. Try to act civilized until I get back." She wiggled off doing a salsa movement between the tables to find a quiet corner with a good signal to make her call. John edged closer to where Tanya sat on her barstool.

"Do you know the game Diana's up to? She's playing with fire, and ignoring the danger. You know what this guy does to people who get in his way. He's had me roughed up once and was aiming for a second time at the museum. And now he's got me fired from my job." Tanya looked startled and tried to say something but John continued. "Anybody who doesn't go out without armed bodyguards is trouble. Know what I mean?"

"He what?" Getting no response as John stared into his beer she carried on. "Look, John, we've arranged with Buck to quietly do the transaction for the Basquiats at the tax-free zone in Geneva. It's so we can both avoid a large tax bill and also because it's a cash deal."

"I'm so happy for you."

"And he agreed to go for a little celebration cruise. Dock in France for lunch and we leave him there to pay the bill from inside a French prison."

"Oh, god – and you're actually going to trust the French?" John said in exasperation. "You'll need some serious backup for an arrest if he invites his Iranian friend along. And your father, how much does he know about all this?"

"Nothing yet. He knows Buck is after the bank but we didn't want to worry him with our plan. He'd probably suggest a more conservative approach. Diana has contacted the French Consulate so they'll apprehend him at the port."

"Oh, that sounds very assuring. I still think your idea's too risky. It'd be better if there was more time to prepare." There was a silence before John grudgingly acknowledged the plan. "I guess there aren't many alternatives at this point." He sighed in resignation and took another drink from his beer while Tanya ordered some wine. Having his ego suitably humbled from the layoff news, John was now receptive to the idea of letting the ladies be the heroes with their boat plan. He realized his image of being the hot shot photographer creating a scandal was more of a fantasy than a reality. He reminded himself what the end goal was and whatever it took to achieve it was for the best.

"Darling, I appreciate your concern for our well-being." She sensed there was something bothering him and leaned closer so her lips were against his ear. "Did I tell you tonight that I love you?"

Her words were an instant elixir that reached through his depressed state and gave a feeling of hope for his future. There'd been a lingering uncertainty of her feelings his mind had been cultivating that now disappeared as her words broke open his heart, reminding him he was capable of loving and being loved.

"Actually, you forgot." They smiled at each other, feeling solid in their depth of feelings as John took ahold of her hand under the bar and gave it a squeeze, holding on for what didn't seem long enough.

Susan reappeared and before John could unload the details of his office news the two women got into an energized conversation, resuming their debate over an arthouse film they had just seen. While waiting for an opening, John leaned over the bar trying to read his future in the beer suds. The women thought he was still brooding about the boat trip, so let him be. Ten minutes later Sean made his appearance waving and yelling from the stairs that led up to the terrace wearing a rumpled Hawaiian shirt and baggy shorts.

"Now here's a fine bunch of people as any kind soul could wish for!" Sean slapped John on the back and did the routine kissing of cheeks. He put his arm around Susan's waist and they exchanged a brief but real kiss. John wasn't sure if he was hallucinating from all the drinks while Tanya gave him a knowing smile in response to his confused look. "Hey Bertie, got any beer for a parched throat?" Sean shouted in the direction of the bar. Bertie held up a Tuborg. "Nah, just bring me a *Stange*!"

"Come get it yourself!" Bertie bellowed back as she took a tall glass and started filling it for him from the beer spigot set in a large ceramic urn.

Sean lowered his voice. "Everyone all right, need a fresher-upper?" No one spoke so he retrieved his beer and sat down. Looking at John he said, "What's this, a wedding celebration or a funeral wake? Everyone looks so festive."

"In case anyone was wondering why I look so cheerful tonight it's because I got sacked today." John had processed most of the news (with the help of a few drinks that diminished the impact) so was able to explain it without getting angry. "It was fairly obvious that it was going to happen sooner or later, so now the day's finally arrived."

The others made appropriate sympathetic remarks and assured him it would all turn out for the best with something better waiting down the road. He didn't seem one hundred percent convinced but sharing the news helped lift some weight off his shoulders.

Tanya expressed her caring, taking his hand unafraid of any

prying eyes. "Everything's going to be all right," she said giving him a look that said she would be there for him, while she squeezed his hand.

The conversation shifted and when Sean was told about the planned excursion, he said, "Talk about the photo-op of the century, this sounds great."

"You're supposed to agree with me that it's not a good idea," John retorted. Both girls laughed. "I'm trying to convince Diana and Tanya to forget this idea before it backfires on them."

"What do you mean? You've got the whole Swiss Army, Navy and Marines to back you up. Or did you forget your little fat friend, the nice man from the police department?" Sean said.

"Right. I almost forgot," chimed in Tanya, playing the joker.

"Buck probably has half the people in the embassy on his payroll," John said.

"Can't you call Schmidt to back us up? He's been waiting forever for a chance like this. Besides, it'll certainly be a bit of security for us poor helpless females," Tanya said.

"Here's to poor helpless females." Sean raised his glass in a loud toast while a few tables turned to look with a mild displeasure.

"I haven't been able to reach him since the museum party. I'll try him again in a minute."

John took a sip from his beer and shuffled off to a back room inside the restaurant area where he knew there was a strong phone signal. He dug out the worn business card from his wallet and deciphered the home phone number Schmidt had scribbled on the back of it. It was just before eleven and with a few drinks to distort his sense of correctness, it seemed a socially acceptable time to ring a policeman. The call went through and John finally heard Schmidt after an interminable pause while his wife had gone to get him from the garden.

"Herr Miller, we must forget the party for now." Schmidt

was trying to speak around the actual subject in a sort of code. His natural phone paranoia kept him brief.

"Wait a minute, everything's been arranged and they're going on a boat trip the day after tomorrow and will make a stop in France. We have to act now," John said in a rush amplified by his drinks.

"I'm sorry, but I can't make any reservations as I once promised. There's been some changes in the office and all projects are on hold. Let your friends have a nice time together and we'll talk again sometime." He was abrupt, wanting to hang-up but John kept on.

"Wait. Is there anyone else I can speak to? This is serious—" The phone beeped; signaling there was no power left on the battery and John scrambled to finish the call.

"There is nothing more to discuss. Sorry, but I must go now, there are some matters I must attend to."

"Please call me back." John sounded desperate and the line went silent as Schmidt hung-up.

John waited in hopes of a return call. He leaned against the wall and time stood still while he listened to the buzz between his ears that complemented the whirring sound of the slowly rotating ceiling fan and distant music. A moment later his phone rang.

"Mr. Miller, I am calling from a pay telephone to be secure but I must be brief so listen closely. After the museum party I am suspected of meddling in other department's affairs and using secure information for my private agenda. This is because I was still transitioning from managing your case and you once again made a foolish action. I told you there were some other so called 'official interests' in this person who are watching out for him. I have been suspended, pending a full investigation. All my projects have been put on hold and I have no capacity to help.

I'm sorry." John's phone made another beeping signal indicating the power was almost used up.

"Who else can I talk to? I don't know who I can trust anymore."

"Sorry, but I can't help you." The phone made its final beep signal and the line went dead. Tomorrow's hangover was already starting with a relentless pounding behind his temples that reminded John what hell awaited.

FIFTEEN

The countryside between Zürich and Lake Geneva was the rich green of a forest covered land with all the trees in full foliage. Fields of corn and electric yellow rapeseed rolled across the countryside with occasional cows in well-manicured pastures. John and Sean drove by the outskirts of some small cities that broke up the farmland with some construction zones and slow convoys of trucks to navigate around delaying the traffic. John had cashed in some overtime hours to take the day off while Sean had shifted his schedule.

John was awake enough after a double espresso at a coffee shop to grill Sean about his relationship with Susan.

"At the time of the gallery show we organized a date to meet for a drink. It went from a prosecco at a café along the river to dinner in the beer garden behind the Reithalle restaurant. We discovered we had a lot in common and our creative interests harmonized in ways neither of us imagined. After both of us started to feel a deep, natural closeness over a long and leisurely dinner, we took a stroll along the river behind the restaurant. It's like a secluded park and there were only a couple of other people enjoying the cool location. We found a dark corner under some trees and started to make out."

"Uh-oh, getting to be too much information."

"Next thing I know, we're scrambling to find our bikes. We pedaled as fast possible to Susan's apartment." Sean said, "I was kicking myself for waiting so long to contact her. But now we see each other every day. Turns out she doesn't live too far away in Kreis 4."

"I'm so happy for you. I haven't seen you in such a good mood for ages."

Sean smiled and said, "It's such a perfect match, something I haven't felt for a long time."

After tanking up on caffeine they were back on the highway. John and Sean had passed the built-up area around the country's capital, Bern, which was the mid-point of their journey and were again into the countryside. A near empty highway allowed them to speed above the legal limit. In less than an hour they flew into the long, curved descent to Lake Geneva with the force of gravity trying to uproot them from the roadway. The banked turn deposited them onto a covered ramp slicing through the steep hillside covered with grape vines that stretched for miles along the coast. The first dizzying view of France materialized below, where it was defined by vertical granite walls on the south shore of the wide lake. Mount Blanc was visible straight ahead in the distance behind a haze crowning a range of mountains.

They took the exit for Montreux and followed the lake road towards the Rhone valley, where the river originating by Gstaad poured into the lake. Crossing the waterway, they arrived at the French border. The two of them were waved through the simple crossing of a small cabin on each side of the road and a raised barrier without showing their passports, looking like day trippers out for a drive.

Diana and Tanya had lingered over a coffee on the terrace of an elegant small boutique hotel that was tucked away in a secluded quarter of Vevey. It was a lakeside town that was Charlie Chaplin's home of many years and also Nestlé, whose ultramodern office buildings were part of the lakeshore landmarks. It was close to Lausanne where the headquarters of the Olympics were. After their late breakfast they strolled along like best friends, walking arm in arm along the broad promenade that traced the edge of the lake. They soaked up the perfect summer weather of clear skies and a mild breeze that gently ruffled the leaves of the tall trees along the walkway.

Their mutual nervousness about the upcoming cruise in a few hours made them open up to each other, almost as a form of confession before entering possible danger where hidden feelings would never again have a chance to be shared. They found a bench under a shady tree overlooking the lake, with the mountains on the other side looking close enough to touch. They sat admiring the view while the small waves gently lapped at the stone retaining wall.

"You know, during all my years running around I never really thought about family. Now being married to your father and losing my brother has made me realize how important family really is. In the end, it's our basic unit after all the friends and acquaintances fade away. I don't want to shock you, but I'm thinking about having children. Or at least one child."

"Oh my god, that's so beautiful," Tanya said.

"I'm already in my late thirties, so the window of opportunity is closing fast."

"Tell me about it. I'm already thinking about it at my age. Have you told Dad?"

"Not yet. I wanted to first share the wish with you." This

time she had put herself in the role of a big sister seeking confirmation. "It hasn't been an easy decision to reach. My free and easy life and later running a business, plus the foundation, have taken all my focus. Finally, I've been able to slow down enough to see where I stood, and my priorities have shifted. Maybe my work protecting mother earth has revived my own dormant maternal instinct."

Tanya was surprised as she had never imagined Diana thinking about this possibility. "You won't believe it but I had my own conversation with John on the exact same subject." They both laughed. "I'm not sure what to think, as it would mean me having a new half-brother or sister. And how could a child of yours be an uncle or aunt to one of my own children, who could be about the same age? OK, I'm assuming all goes well with John and he gets on board."

"This would certainly be a strange family dynamic." They could only laugh at the family construct that modern relationships created.

"I'm totally with you and I'm sure Dad would be overjoyed." Tanya was supportive as she knew Diana had a sincere wish and they leaned over and hugged each other.

They got up and started strolling which helped take the edge off the underlying tension of their upcoming plan. They talked about the morning's transaction in Geneva that had gone down with the calm efficiency of a Swiss clock, ticking off the seconds.

Both parties had met early that morning at the Geneva Free Port in an industrial neighborhood outside the city, not far from the airport. It was a compound of square gray and white buildings surrounded by train tracks and small roads. The large six-story complex could have been mistaken for a modern factory by its boxy appearance, not as glamorous a location as the name might have implied. Only the high walls with barbed wire across the top and stacks of shipping containers might have indicated its real purpose as a bonded warehouse. Conservative estimates claimed over $100 billion worth of art resided there in indefinite storage or else transiting between owners. This included over a thousand works by Picasso and museum quality paintings by the Old Masters. (It was also said to be the world's largest wine cellar.) The tax-free status meant that somebody buying a painting for $50 million in New York would have to pay a potential sales tax of $4.4 million but by shipping it to a freeport, the bill disappeared. This was a big departure from the port's earlier roots that took advantage of Swiss neutrality to distribute Red Cross parcels to prisoners of war during World War Two.

The ladies were dressed for business in power suits and Buck, his assistant and bodyguard looked more like they were ready for a polo match in blazers and open shirts. Once inside the large entry gates and after clearing a customs control, the group entered an inner courtyard that looked like a combination oriental bazaar and exotic car exposition. A couple of makeshift canvas pavilions protected stacks of carpets that traders were haggling over. The other main display was made up of antique Maseratis, Lamborghini Countachs and racing red Ferraris, while a Silver Wraith Rolls-Royce provided some understated British elegance. Buck had paused to study the cars and had his assistant make a note of the dealer's name.

Once inside the main building they assembled in a well-appointed reception area with sofas and glass topped tables. It contrasted what looked to be a large drab warehouse on the outside. The rest of the interior was a series of long, well-lit aisles with nothing but compartments on either side. Each private cubicle was identified by a nondescript white door matching the color of the walls. There were some vaults resembling luxurious galleries that art dealers maintained to support the international art markets 60 billion-dollar-a-year activities. Others were designated for storage, as even the larger museums couldn't display their entire collection at one time. Sometimes guests would be serenaded by a Stradivarius that need to be played once a month because it couldn't leave the warehouse.

The concierge had ushered them individually through a full body scanner before entering the climate-controlled area of the warehouse. It had a constant chilly temperature of 17 degrees and fifty percent humidity. They ascended on an industrial elevator to the third floor and passed through a one-foot-thick bulletproof door that looked like it belonged in a bank vault with a big wheel in the center used to release the massive bolts. The group entered an area where bundled up canvases and sculptures were stored in large rooms that appeared more like a warehouse. Their guide brought them into a small elegant showroom where the Basquiats were waiting. The room was furnished with a sofa and armchairs plus a bar cart with various bottles of liquor and glasses. Buck inspected the paintings he'd purchased where they hung on a wall, once more admiring the wild elegance of the artwork. The transaction was a formality of exchanging a document of ownership listing two numbered paintings. Like numbered bank accounts, this allowed for anonymity of ownership. The paintings were carefully wrapped after the inspection and stayed in their tax-free home, joining a collection of other paintings and figurines in a large vault rented by Buck.

After they exited the building, Buck steered the group to his large Mercedes that was in the enclosed parking lot inside the gates. His chauffeur had been waiting and activated the trunk release as they approached. Buck's assistant went over and extracted a silver metal Zero Halliburton suitcase, the large carry-on size. He set it down on its wheels and extended the handle so it was ready to roll.

Buck gestured towards the suitcase and said, "Here you go, ladies. Don't spend it all in one place."

"Wouldn't be hard in Geneva," Diana said laughing.

Tanya took the handle of the case and lifted it. "Feels like the correct amount."

"I should hope so," Buck said and everyone laughed. The ladies then confirmed the boat rendezvous details.

As Buck started towards his car Tanya said, "Thank you, Mr. Buck, it was a pleasure doing business with you."

"Likewise. Now don't get lost, we have a celebration to get started."

Tanya and Diana said their goodbyes without handshakes or air kisses and walked over to Diana's Porsche that was a few parking spaces away. The suitcase rolled along, following like an obedient dog leashed to Tanya's hand. She wiggled it into the backseat and the money was deposited in the Geneva branch of the family bank on the way to the lake.

Studying the French shore across the wide blue lake with the mountains lurking in the distance, the two women reminded each other that their simple plan was better than anything complicated. Just act natural, enjoy the nice cruise and then a stop for lunch to let the reception committee do their welcoming act. Late in the afternoon the day before, Diana finally got through to a junior ambassador at the American embassy in Paris and advised him to be prepared. He was noncommittal on how much they could deliver in the way of support. The French had sounded a little more supportive but even that wasn't reassuring as Diana knew too well the complexities of administrative bureaucracy in any dealings with embassies and public servants. She'd advised both embassies of the timetable with an estimated arrival time in the town of Petite Rive at two o'clock. She'd first tried to reach someone with authority at the FBI but they only had what they called a 'legal attaché' at different American embassies in Europe. The young man she spoke to in Bern had promised to pass along the information but she never received a call back.

The Beyer boat was docked at the public pier, a few hundred yards from their hotel. It was a sleek wooden racing yacht that had been renovated with a full cabin and motor, complementing its distant cousins, the long, elegant boats that ferried tourists around the lake. It still retained a main mast as a nod to its heritage but there was no sail attached as there wasn't much wind. The first floor above the main deck level was a dark mahogany sundeck with enclosed lounge area. Above it was the small cabin where the ancient sailor who'd been the boat's captain for as long as anyone could remember navigated.

The captain was welcoming aboard the two women when an enormous Mercedes with darkened windows and a sagging look suggesting the weight of an armor enforced body materialized at the end of the pier. Buck sprung out dressed like an admiral, all in white with a navy blazer. He gave the driver some final instructions while the man handed over a sports sack from the trunk.

"Morning, ladies," Buck roared out as he sauntered up the ramp onto the rear deck. "Perfect day to be on the water. Love this part of Switzerland. It ain't called the Swiss Riviera for nothing." He made a broad gesture to the steep vine covered hills turning golden brown and the lake ringed by mountains.

"Hello, Stan. Nice to see you ready to sail." Diana gave a seductive smile while Buck leaned over kissing her on both cheeks.

"Hello, little lady." He turned to Tanya offering his hand. "We're going to have some fun."

Tanya offered a modest 'Hi' in return while shaking his hand.

"I'm sure we will," said Diana. "This is a beautiful ship, isn't it? Hans-Peter's really kept it up well."

"You're right. One of the true classics of boating." He paused to look the yacht over, giving an admiring glance to its sleek lines, wondering if he could make an offer. He was in a deal making mood after this morning's transaction. "I bet nobody could catch this boat."

"Even the fastest boat can lose sometimes. It's all about wind, luck and who you have for a crew," Diana said.

"Indeed," Buck said with an acknowledging smile. "OK, here's my friends." A white powerboat with a large outboard motor and two sizable men packing the cockpit approached, cut the engine and drifted about ten yards away. The men were dressed in T-shirt's, jeans and baseball hats, both of them impassive behind dark sunglasses. Tanya's stomach constricted in a wave of anxiety.

"Hope you don't mind, but I never leave home without them. Such nice boys," Buck said. He waved to the two men who returned the gesture.

"What do they want?" Diana asked giving Buck an accusing look.

"They're just going along for the ride to make sure no-one bothers us. I like my privacy. Do you know your captain well?"

"He's been with the family for twenty years. I'm sure he's capable. If we get lost, your babysitters will be sure to assist," Diana said, making a joke to keep the feeling light. Buck grunted in approval. "Would you like a drink to start our celebration? The champagne is on ice." Buck gave a thumbs up signal while he scanned the boat. "Let's go to the upper deck. Come on, Tanya."

John and Sean sped along the narrow two-lane roadway skirting the lake in John's ancient Japanese car, passing small villages and wooded areas that extended to the steep mountain ridges rising up a couple of miles away. Forty minutes later they parked on a side street in Petite Rive. The miniature town had a central square dominated by an ancient Gothic church on one end. The streets were quiet except for some early morning shoppers. Most were buying bread or vegetables at market stands lining the main street that ended at the lake.

They walked to the edge of town where the public pier jutted into the water. It was an austere cement dock with broad, round mooring posts along the sides for the larger lake boats that made their rounds with tourist packed decks. It was where Tanya and Diana planned to land in a few hours with their guest of honor. A couple of small sailboats bobbed nearby against a smaller rotting pier that fronted a restaurant. It had red sun umbrellas placed at intervals along its terrace that was hanging over the water. The other boats from the village were anchored in the main harbor a few hundred yards along the shore. There was a small area of the public pier decorated with colored flags that offered pedalo boats and small motorboat rentals for the tourists. The morning haze had burned off, promising a sweltering day.

John felt the time was slipping away too fast. They sought out the police station to check on the arrangements. An aged woman bundled in a scarf, clutching a straw shopping bag with carrot tops hanging over the side gave them directions. The office occupied a portion of an ancient brick building on the main street. The dark, musty lobby echoed with the slamming of the door as they located a directory on the wall indicating they wanted the first floor.

Sean said, "Even if we find the office, it looks like the whole local government is on vacation."

"In the event the women screw up, what's Plan B?" John said.

"That's where we improvise and grab him ourselves."

"Right. You'll rent a pedalo and pedal the thing all the way downstream to the Mediterranean with Buck tied on the back. Cool idea."

They skipped up a flight of creaking wooden stairs to the first floor and found a door with frosted glass panels that had GENDARMERIE stenciled on it in gold letters. Inside was a mature looking secretary planted behind a desk with her gray hair in a bun and glasses halfway down her nose. She only looked up from her magazine when they were standing by her desk.

Sean said, "Bonjour, madam. May I speak with the captain?" in unconvincing French.

She stared at them with vacant eyes and motioned with indifference to a green vinyl sofa, the marbled pattern worn off in patches by years of use. The word 'captain' had clicked somewhere in her brain. She picked up her phone with great effort, dialed three numbers, waited a minute and mumbled something in a low voice. She dropped the phone in its cradle and resumed her reading.

Sean was fidgeting and lit a cigarette and looked around for an ashtray while John tried to sit in a comfortable position, but it was impossible. He was too restless and the springs in the sofa were shot from the many guests over the years. He diverted his attention to study the black and white photos of the town at the turn of the century that were the only decorations on the wall.

"This doesn't look like the nerve center for an operation to apprehend a world class criminal," Sean hissed, tapping his ashes over the arm of the sofa.

"This is just the local guy, the Feds are probably already surrounding the pier," John replied.

"Yeah, I'm sure the old bat with the veggies works for the CID."

The door behind the receptionist creaked open and a small, thin man in dark pants with sagging suspenders and an open white shirt appeared. He looked like he had been asleep thirty seconds earlier. The captain was in his late sixties and raked a hand through his unkempt hair in an effort to wake up. He pulled a light blue pack of Gitanes out of his shirt pocket and lit one while he studied them. Limping over, he brought an ashtray from his secretary's desk and set it in on the table, before sprawling in a beat-up armchair that matched the sofa. The man asked in French if he could be of assistance.

Sean spoke to him with his nearly forgotten university French and at one point the discussion got very lively. The man seemed to be challenging different statements in an argumentative tone. John couldn't decipher the meaning as it always sounded like the French were arguing, even in normal conversations with their best friends about love.

Sean pulled a copy of the wanted poster for Buck issued by the U.S. Marshals office out of his pants pocket that he had printed from a website. It had Buck's picture, a description of the crime and the reward – three million dollars. The Frenchman was quiet for a moment and studied it carefully, puffing on his cigarette. The ash grew long and fell on the floor unnoticed. Sean glanced at John and winked. The captain indicated he wanted to keep the poster and grunted a few more words. He nodded to Sean and they both stood and shook hands. Sean dug his dilapidated wallet out of the back pocket of his jeans and retrieved a business card that he handed to the officer. John followed along and did the same. They exchanged '*au revoirs'* and left. As soon as they were out of the office John asked what the man had said.

"He told me he wasn't sure if this was a matter that concerned him. He also said what we were involved in could be illegal."

"What the hell's going on? He should've been alerted by the embassy that this was going down."

"I told him that the American law was valid here and all that was going to happen was a wanted criminal would be deposited on his doorstep in a couple of hours. And when he saw the reward money I think it changed his mind about justice."

"Is he going to help?"

"Apparently they forgot to include him in the planning."

"That's not too encouraging."

"He's going to check with his boss and see who's around to help. If the situation is appropriate, they will 'detain' Buck for questioning. He said he'd call me in about an hour. You think we should try and claim some of the reward money?"

"Forget it. Sounds more like we're the ones who are going to end up in jail."

They were blinded by the brilliant sunshine as they commandeered a table under some dusty plane trees outside a small café, each ordering an espresso. It was only ten, but the heat was building. For the next hour Sean attempted to read a couple of French papers, nervously waiting for the call from the police. John periodically scanned his phone for office emails in-between studying the lake in the distance. Sean's phone rang and there was a short conversation in French where Sean raised his voice arguing and ending in a tone of exasperation as he clicked off.

"The police captain did his homework as promised. And after checking with the Swiss foreign police found out the liaison on the case, Herr Schmidt, had been suspended from the police force for annoying Buck. The French, in an act of official solidarity, will not provide any assistance."

"I don't fucking believe it. These useless piece of shit bureaucrats only care about a cause if they can make some money or gain some points to stay elected. Screw them all. Now we have to think of something else because the ladies are setting themselves up for a high-risk arrival." He quickly sent a text message to Tanya to advise her of the situation. He was hoping she would have a phone signal in the middle of the lake.

The Beyers' boat cruised along at a relaxed speed, the motor thumping out a quiet rhythm, with the merry making in full swing. Buck was mixing drinks for everyone. They were what he called a California Breakfast: equal parts of champagne and orange juice. All of them were in bathing suits, reclined on deckchairs. The captain had taken them about half a mile off shore, and was tracing the coastline. Thirty minutes earlier they had slipped by Montreux's hotel dotted hills and fairy tale castle. The boat had now passed the northern end of the lake opposite the twin mountain ranges boxing in the broad valley of the Valais region where vineyards carpeted the foothills. They had crossed the invisible French border with their destination slowly appearing in the distance as they sailed parallel to the French coast.

Diana started to turn the conversation toward lunch, and her most favorite restaurant. "Only in a small village can you get authentic country style cuisine like coq au vin. This restaurant's been in their family for generations. It could have a three-star Michelin rating if the owners were not so hostile towards the authorities from Paris."

"I think food is the only thing I trust the French to do right," Buck said.

"I don't know. They like to champion liberty, equality and fraternity."

"Yeah, I get the fraternity part," Buck laughed and pushed his sunglasses down his nose so he could make eye contact and give a wink.

"Their desserts are divine. I might even sin a little."

"Oh?" Buck arched his eyebrows and glanced at Diana with a devilish look, calculating how quickly he could get her bikini off.

"I just need to score a few points for good behavior first." She looked at Tanya reading a magazine and caught her eye. They both laughed. There was an irritating trilling as a cell phone rang. Buck dug into his sport sack beside the table and tapped the screen of his phone before putting it to his ear.

"Yeah, Buck here. What, slow down. Hold on a second." He pressed the mute button and turned to Diana and Tanya. "You'll excuse me, ladies, this is a private call." He extracted himself from the depths of his recliner and walked around to the bow, so he was separated by the cabin. "The hell you say. I don't believe it. What? The Marines, they want to send in the Marines?" The roar of Buck's laughter drifted back to the sunbathers. A couple of minutes later after placing a call, Buck returned.

"Ladies, can I get you another drink?" Without waiting for a reply, he poured himself a glass of straight champagne – a French Breakfast. "Are you sure you want to go to this particular restaurant? One of my personal favorites is back in Montreux at the Palace Hotel. We could go there even in these clothes. They've seen me in worse after some of the concerts at the jazz festival." He laughed again. Tanya glanced at Diana, who didn't register any emotion. Her female intuition had been alerted by something intangible and wrong in the air. The message was: the game is over.

"Whatever you like, Stan," Diana said in a quiet, hurt tone like a pouting teenager. "I just wanted you to see this place. It's so charming. If you'd rather not, we could go another time." She gave him the 'I'll break into a million pieces if you say no' look.

He smiled. "Sure, we'll take a peek. Now let's have some of that salsa music. This is supposed to be a party, ain't it?"

The two ladies were visibly restless as they neared Petite Rive. Tanya had seen John's message but couldn't show the contents to Diana with Buck sitting next to them. She hoped Diana was able to at least get some support from the U.S. embassy. She flipped endlessly through the same magazine she had been studying the past hour, unable to find an interesting article. Diana wasn't lying back basking in the scenery but sitting upright, staring down the lake.

It irritated Diana that Buck appeared amused, as if he were admiring them for having the nerve to even consider trying to trap him. He seemed to be enjoying the play. Buck folded his hands on the hairy belly hanging over the baggy bathing shorts and sat back contentedly with a happy grin and eyes invisible behind mirrored sunglasses. His escort boat had kept a discrete distance until now, but maneuvered within hailing range as the larger boat steered gradually towards the shore.

The three passengers started to pull their clothes on over their bathing suits in anticipation of docking in fifteen minutes. Buck struggled into his baggy pants, tugging them into position over his swimsuit. The two women took advantage of his momentary distraction to change into their dresses. Tanya removed her hands from inside her cotton sundress, waving a fluorescent bikini top like a magician. Buck tried to take in the maneuver and nearly fell over, as his foot wasn't all the way through the pants leg.

"Need a hand, Mr. Buck?" Diana chimed.

"No thanks, but maybe later." He gave a wink. "Could we slow this tub down? I want to work up my appetite a little."

"Don't worry," Tanya said, "we'll have a little promenade around the town and you'll be ready for a super lunch." The village came into focus, looming larger, with its church spire poking up behind the lakefront buildings. The boat chugged on a direct course for the distant flags indicating the public dock.

Buck turned from studying the shore to address the two women. "Sorry, girls, but I have to ask you to stop the boat. I'm going to leave you at this point, and let you have a nice lunch by yourselves. I phoned ahead and the restaurant doesn't take American Express." He started to laugh but he was the only one. Diana stood unmoving, leaning back with both hands on the railing.

"I'm afraid, Diana, your fun and games are over. I must admit I'm a little bit surprised by your actions, but then life is full of surprises. That's what keeps it interesting."

"What are you talking about?" Diana said.

"Looking to get me nabbed for my outstanding warrants is an original idea. Now please," he slammed a fist on the table, rattling the wine glasses, "stop this goddamn boat."

Diana wasn't intimidated and gave back as good as she got. "You're fucked, Stan. Your little party is over and you can send us some postcards from a federal penitentiary."

As if to back up her words the ancient captain appeared on the deck above them with a long pole that had a hook on the end, used to help pull the boat close to the dock. Buck laughed at the wizened old man and reached into his sports sack. He took out a small black automatic pistol and aimed it at the captain.

"Now turn this boat around or I'll blow your fucking head off." The captain looked at Diana who nodded an affirmative reply and the man dropped the boat hook and reached behind him. Without taking his eyes off Buck he turned the wheel so the boat gradually began to make a turn.

John and Sean could see from the shore something was wrong because the boat was slowing and turning away from the shore. They strained their eyes to see any action onboard and could just make out everyone standing around on the back deck but couldn't tell what was happening. Instinctively, the two of them ran over to the public dock they'd been exploring earlier. Sean flashed credit cards and cash to the rental person, jabbering about needing a boat immediately. John went to where the small boats were tied up and commandeered something advertised on a sign as an Aqua Quad. It looked like a jet ski with a wide, flat hull, roll-bar and small outboard motor in place of a water jet. It was designed for tourists, as no license was required to pilot it.

John started the motor while the young man in charge of rentals dashed from his booth over towards the boat. John had already untied the rope tethering the Quad to the dock and was off. He swung the small craft away from the dock in a wide arc as it picked up speed. The motor had the power of a lawn-mower, so while sounding strong, was only as fast as if he'd been swimming. He steered wide, trying to angle his approach to arrive at the Beyer's boat from the back. The speedboat with Buck's men spotted the quad buzzing like an angry mosquito aimed at the large boat and gunned their motor to intercept him. The two boats' collective noise distracted the people on the Beyer ship. As everyone looked off the side of the boat to watch the action, Tanya used the distraction to quickly mount the steps to the cabin. She turned off the motor and took the keys from the ignition. Buck turned to face Tanya with the gun pointed at her but not before Tanya had time to position herself at the edge of the cabin platform and dangle the keys over the water.

"Now what the fuck?" Buck was exasperated, looking at Tanya not sure what he should do. Before he could say anything the sound of an approaching boat with a large motor coming up quickly from behind them caused everyone to turn and look in that direction. It was a black sea police cruiser with official markings that bore down on them in a straight line from the back of the boat away from where they were facing. The boat altered its approach to arrive from the side and started flashing its blue lights mounted on the roof. Several men in white shirts carrying rifles were visible on deck.

Buck's escort boat swerved away from its mission to cut off John and one of the men on the police boat had a megaphone, shouting out something in French. Buck stood looking at the boat dumbfounded. The wiry captain quickly reached down and retrieved his boat hook. He raised it and leaning over, snapped the metal pole against Buck's hand, knocking the gun to the deck. Buck hesitated to retrieve it, as the hook was dangerously close to his face and by then the police were alongside.

Another high-powered police motor launch was visible now, skimming towards them from the along the French shore. "What the hell...?" Buck said. He waved frantically to his escort craft but the second police boat closed in on the bodyguards. Seeing all the flurry of police activity, John turned his Aqua Quad around and headed back to shore. He hadn't made much progress so was soon back at the dock. Meanwhile, the French sea police had secured their boat to the Beyers' and had boarded. A tall man with the physique of a bodybuilder and a wide belt with a holstered pistol approached Buck and took hold of his upper arm. Stan stood defiantly as if waiting for a play to end and the actors to disappear offstage. A second officer retrieved the fallen gun and handed it to the officer in charge who commented about illegal possession of firearms.

"You don't think two unescorted ladies would sail into uncharted waters without a little back-up, do you?" Diana stated, demurely glaring at Buck. Buck's jaw had dropped. "Come inside, Tanya. I hate to see a grown man cry," Diana said.

"OK, I'll play along. But this is only round one," Buck shouted after her as he turned his back on them. Buck was guided over to a gap in the railing and down the ladder with the policeman following him. Buck gripped it like he wanted to rip it off the boat. He watched his two assistants being handcuffed without any resistance and their weapons confiscated. A towing line was secured to Buck's escort boat from the police cruiser which then set-off to the main dock in Petite Rive. The police departed with Buck after some exchanges in French between the officer in charge and Diana. The larger patrol boat also made its way to the shore where a couple of police cars and a dark blue van with blacked-out windows were now visible by the dock.

The cruiser that had gone to Petite Rive with the two bodyguards had exchanged passengers after securing the speedboat and was now pulling up alongside the Beyers' boat with John and Sean onboard. One of the crew held the mooring rope so the two young men could climb aboard and then it took off back to the shore. The Beyers' captain returned to the cabin firing the motors and steering again along the lake. As soon as they were alone Diana and Tanya alternately gave the two men big hugs, smothering them in kisses.

"Hey, slow down, it's not all my doing." John playfully swatted Tanya away as she tried to strangle him with a hug. She had straddled the recliner behind where he had sat down and was hanging on his back.

"But you were so brave to try and come to our rescue."

"More like crazy. I think there's someone else to thank," John said turning to look at Diana.

Diana spoke up with a big smile from where she was sitting on a chair by the drinks table, while Sean examined the contents of the bar cart. "Yes, I did manage to pull a few strings," she said trying to look modest. "The French embassy ultimately didn't seem to give a damn. They gave me a big runaround and wouldn't commit. Said their orders came from Paris. And the U.S. embassy was equally useless. They told me I would have to call the president or some such nonsense. In the end, it's always about who you know. It seems coming from a noble family still means something. Yesterday I called one of the Bourbon dukes I know in Paris who's done business with my family over the years. He's also part of the Monaco mafia I party with every summer. Like all good French businessmen, he's got a good connection with the current prime minister so he contacted the right authorities and – voilà!"

"Vive la France!" Tanya said raising her fist in a salute. They all started laughing.

"It's a pity we weren't allowed any pictures," Sean said regretfully. "The police kept us at a distance so we'll have to find some other way to document this momentous event. Maybe at the arraignment."

"Can I twist your arm to join us in a little celebration drink?" Not waiting for an answer Diana popped the cork on a champagne bottle with a professional flair, and the cork sailed overboard. She gave a shy smile as the champagne flowed out over her hand where she gripped the bottleneck around the neck. The captain headed the boat towards the middle of the lake.

"I hope you don't mind, but I told him to take the scenic

route before we finally have the celebration lunch I promised," Diana said as she handed out glasses of champagne.

SIXTEEN

With the natural elements to induce sleep, bent head and blurred vision from trying to focus on meaningless overhead slides in a semi-dark room, John had no trouble closing his eyes and embracing a quiet, black void. His elbow slipped on the table knocking some papers to the floor. The commotion and arm movement woke him.

Ralph, sitting beside him, looked over and, satisfied that John had only dropped something, turned back to face the two large screen televisions at the end of the room. One broadcast the image of their room so they could see how the other participants in the videoconference viewed them. The picture was zoomed back enough to make John's falling asleep unnoticeable. The second screen was filled with talking heads from the U.S. headquarters. The video image traveled with a three second delay from the audio, which made it look like a poorly dubbed foreign movie. John was a passive observer, there to bolster his boss's position and reinforce the lonely stand against the unblinking red eye on top of the television.

There was a constant stream of standard phrases like: 'the message is to...', 'did you think of...', 'how about trying...', 'what I would suggest...' mixed with corporate responsibility for stockholders, employees first and community engagement. Then the personal touch came in with: focus leads to teamwork and team building that brings unity and harmony but unity is not uniformity. It is not sameness; it is complementariness, building a complimentary team synergy. Everybody needs to sharpen his or her saw to maintain a personal production capability. Plus, a couple of 'repositions', 'paradigm shifts' and 'value marketing' were thrown in to meet the buzzword quota. To justify the meeting the managers agreed on a project for the sake of keeping face although it was clear to John that it didn't bring any value and only assured him a lot of running around during his last days of groveling for his payout. In three months, it would be forgotten with no one able to remember why the decision was made.

After the ordeal in the lower worlds of purgatory, John crossed the sweltering parking lot to a second building in the bank complex. He was going to meet the departmental vice president he reported to functionally as part of the unfathomable dual reporting line matrix structure the company adopted. Ralph was only his administrative boss but the work John did was on behalf of the commercial department. The secretary wasn't in her cubicle so John knocked softly on the V-P's door and entered when he heard a noise from the other side.

The vice president turned from his desk with a hand over the phone. "Hello, John, can I get you a coffee?"

John shook his head.

"I'll just be a second. Have a seat." The executive turned his back while John sat at a small conference table. John glanced from the back of the man's bald head to the computer screen sitting on the curved desk that was flashing an error message in a hypnotic pulse.

"Sorry, but I need to finish some games for the squash

league. I've fallen behind. Is it all right? Yes. I'll be home about eight. I know what I promised. Thanks. Bye." He carefully parked the phone and turned to John with a satisfied expression as though he had concluded a deal for tens of millions in new deposits instead of negotiating with his wife. "How are you, alright?" The man's British accent made the words sound more cheerful than their business-like tone.

John said, "Fine, thanks." He nodded affirmatively indicating he was ready to listen. The vice president got up and closed the door, then dragged a chair over to the table.

"I thought I'd let you in on some news before it's announced. This is confidential but I thought it was important to tell you in person as soon as possible. Ralph will probably fill you in on his half later today as your administrative boss – we haven't informed him yet."

"Thanks for the consideration."

"As you know, your current job's being rolled up into one global marketing position which will cover several commercial departments. But you would need a few more years' experience to be appointed to that position." He paused a split second to see if there was a reaction. He went on in a quiet tone, "I recommended you for a position that's coming up in our community relations department, doing the communications work. It's a very new and fast developing area. You should do well there."

John was surprised and paused a second before replying with a smile. "Thanks so much. That sounds really good. I thought I'd been given my marching orders. But of course, this is much better. When will I be offered it 'officially'?"

"Ralph will give you the exact details sometime soon. I just wanted you to know I appreciate your contribution. Ralph wasn't too supportive for some reason but I know you'd be the right person. I hope you don't mind." John felt good knowing Ralph would never counter a senior manager in the commercial department for fear of jeopardizing his position. Those departments brought in the money that paid the salary of the support organizations like marketing.

"No, of course not. I guess I owe you a beer."

"Just do your job and I'll be happy. You'll still be responsible for the open projects until the handover in October. But I'm sure we'll be seeing more of you over here. The policy board is making engagement in local community actions one of the key goals for Europe next year, so you should get some high-level exposure."

An hour later Sean sauntered through the door of John's office waving a manila envelope. "Bad news."

"You're always bad news. What's the rest of it?"

"You're not going to like it." Sean kicked the door closed and flopped in a chair. "Your friend is not where you think he is." He accented the statement with a grimace.

"What's that supposed to mean?"

"He never went to jail. Nice, eh? That's what I call Swiss justice."

John cut him off. "Wait a minute. You mean French justice. Buck was grabbed in France, wasn't he?"

"*Jah*, OK, you're right but now he's back home. You see, with enough money you can do anything you want and get away with it. He's no doubt relaxing in his little hacienda in Zug guzzling champagne. Probably borrowed a few Swiss Guards from the Vatican to be extra secure."

"I've been trying to reach Schmidt to see what the status is. He's not answering or else went on vacation. You're sure of this?"

"Heard it from a buddy at one of the papers. And this guy

doesn't joke around. They just haven't published it yet until their lawyers OK it."

"Somehow I can believe it. But I want to hear the official story straight from the horse's mouth."

"I'll let you know as soon as I get any more details."

"After all the efforts everyone made this is unbelievable."

"Shameful."

"Want to hear something funny? I just got asked to make the bank look like a local hero instead of a legal robber and wrecker of economies."

"What?" Sean exclaimed slapping his knee and making an exaggerated open-mouthed grin, frozen in place to emphasize his shock.

"Yeah. I would be doing the communications to make local communities see our good side. Not how we're helping the super wealthy 'point zero one percent' dodge taxes while supporting oil companies and big industry ruining the planet. It's either that or else join the unemployed."

"Well at least that's some good news. I'll buy you lunch in honor of your new job. We can eat dolphin steaks on plates made from tropical hardwood with a pesticide coated salad grown in acid rain and some endangered herbs uprooted from the rainforest sprinkled on top. We'll go to that place where we can look down on the lake."

"Sounds good. I could do with a free meal. But I'm not so sure about accepting the position. It would just be spreading more lies."

"You don't want to try and change the status quo from the inside?"

"I'm looking for something with a little moral integrity."

"There's time for that. I think you should take the job 'cause it will give you some breathing room and let you pay off your lawyer."

John sighed and looked away for a second. "Actually, I was thinking the same thing." He turned to Sean with a big smile. "I hate to admit it, but you're right." Sean let out a victorious 'ha' while raising his fist. "More important, it would also mean I can stay in the country and be with Tanya."

"Choosing love over pride? There's still hope for you yet, you lowlife dirt bag."

"Ain't too old to learn it seems. It also means I can't take you up on your Miami agency offer."

"No worries. It's taking longer to pull together than I hoped. You're making the right choice."

"Anything new with you?"

"I just got a job from one of the big German weekly magazines. They want me to do a spread on Langstrasse and how it's changing."

"It's really sad when I remember back just a few years to what it was like. Free and crazy."

The phone rang.

"See you at twelve, I'll still buy you lunch." Sean waved on the way out as John picked up the phone.

"Miller."

"Hey Mr. Snapshot, how's it going?" Harry was shouting over the traffic noise in the background.

"Not too bad all things considered."

"So when can I visit your buddy in lockup? Ha, ha! You got the bastard, eh?"

"You might want to save the laughs. I just heard the guy never went to jail. I need to confirm it with our good friend at the police department. There was nothing in the papers. Even the efficient system to suppress bad news couldn't hide that story unless there was some big weight behind it."

"Are you serious? After all the arrangements and Buck heading into the sunset in handcuffs? I find it hard to believe.

But there's not much that would surprise me these days. Listen, I've got a tip for you. Another rotten apple in the barrel. This time it's a German businessman based in Switzerland brokering deals for nuclear bomb parts."

"Hold on a second. Before you get started, I want to cool it a bit. I was lucky so far and don't want to push it. I'm going to retire from the paparazzi business. In fact, you'll have to find another photographer for your newsletter unless you start paying."

"Wait. Let me tell you about this guy, it's real interesting," Harry bulldozed over John. "His company was caught at the French border with centrifuge endcaps used in making a nuclear bomb. They were on their way to Iran. When the police raided the factory, they found out what they intercepted was the last shipment. As the parts could also be used for university research, the shipments were approved by Swiss customs."

"Great stuff, Harry, but I'm not interested. I'm serious. Let's talk later. I'll give you a call as soon as I find out what happened to Buck. Bye."

John lay entangled with Tanya in a giant multicolored woven hammock. They were swaying in the last rays of the afternoon sun, suspended on her balcony. John shifted his weight to get comfortable, making a latticework out of their legs. "I spoke to Schmidt this afternoon. Buck's back home. The French police were either threatened, bought off or both but either way he never saw the inside of a French jail. Apparently, a car with other bodyguards that was following the action intervened."

"Somehow it was to be expected. Anyway, he can't retaliate against Diana. After the arrest in France, the board at the bank decided to turn down the offer from the potential buyer and in the process voted that slimy lawyer uncle of mine off the board. He was reprimanded and put on a short leash. And now it looks like a friendly merger is finally going to be worked out with another family bank based in Geneva. It's either merge or die these days."

"That's excellent. Schmidt also told me Buck's decided on a more low-profile life and organized a management buyout of his company. Schmidt thinks his ex-wife motivated it by saying she could organize a political pardon right from the top. And each day the fines for tax evasion are compounding into the hundreds of millions which means he'll have a serious bill to pay if he can't find intervention in his case."

"That bastard so deserves to be in jail. If nothing else for what he's doing to the environment. Not to mention what happened to Klaus. I wish the police hadn't let him go so easily," Tanya said.

"I'm sure there wasn't much of a choice. With all his lawyers he can keep them dancing for years. Anyway, the U.S. government just raised the reward for his capture to four million dollars so perhaps the idea of making him more noticeable worked. Apparently, Buck is talking about a move to Israel, as they also don't have an extradition treaty for tax exiles. Maybe the climate there is better for his health."

"I wish him well. You know, a little bit of compassion. Speaking of which, our dear Diana seems to have found religion. She's started attending a Tibetan Buddhist center along the lake and has given up drinking and smoking. She is diving into it with her usual laser beam intensity, meditating daily and wearing a mala necklace – of course from a designer boutique in Küsnacht. Now she's helping organize a visit by the Dalai Lama. His view of the planet includes an environmental outlook that harmonizes with her foundation's goals."

"Good for her. Never too late to find yourself. I hope it helps her to achieve some balance in her life."

"Have you heard anything from your wife yet?"

"Her lawyer called my lawyer and explained that they agree to let the divorce proceedings wait until I have my citizenship papers."

"That's wonderful!"

"Yeah. My lawyer thinks she was advised that this could be dragged out and made into a long battle that nobody wins. Sean thinks it's more because she found another guy. Said he saw her in a café getting cozy with some skinny hipster dude with a man-bun and scraggly beard."

"See, I told you that an artist look is attractive." John shook his head with an expression that said 'you never give up'. "And after all that sneaking around you had to do to be correct. She should be ashamed."

"It doesn't matter anymore. All's well that ends well, I say. Besides, whatever was going to happen, I was ready to tell her about you and to deal with it."

"Darling. You're so sweet. But what's the matter, *schätz*, you look so serious?" She slid alongside him to put her arm behind his shoulders so they wouldn't fall off the hammock. "You tired? We can go inside and take a nap." She giggled and made a playful face.

"I am tired but that's not the problem. It's just that I want to be honest with you and everyone else, especially myself. I don't want to have to sneak around in my life anymore."

"You don't have to. You just said your wife will let you go," Tanya said.

"It's not only my marriage. I've been living in a foreign land working for an equally foreign company and having to live a lie with the person I was with. I want to be truthful in what I say and do and not compromised by what other people or society think is 'right'."

"You're not thinking of leaving Switzerland, are you?" She sounded concerned.

"Are you crazy. I have one really good reason to stay here for a very long time." She pulled him closer and rested her head on his shoulder. John whispered in her ear. "Did I tell you today that I love you?" She laughed and hugged him again, twisting over to plant a quick kiss on his mouth.

Tanya rose up on an elbow and spoke to him playfully. "It's good you're sticking around, because I've cooked up a little surprise with my artist friend Miror."

Buck stood in the long, sparsely furnished room under his mansion that was built into the hillside like a bunker. It housed his art collection and the thick steel shutters were rolled back to let in some sunlight through the gauze curtains that protected the artwork from discoloring. The white walls had paintings by Van Gogh, Picasso and Miró scattered around in small groups. Buck stood in the center of the room admiring the Basquiats while his art advisor, an older man in a charcoal gray suit and thinning hair was closely examining the pictures.

"Mr. Buck, I'm afraid I have some bad news." The man spoke with assurance edged with some hesitancy as if he might lose the possibility of collecting a commission on future acquisitions.

"What is it?" Buck barked, moving closer to the paintings.

The man took of his spectacles and looked at Buck a second before replying. "These are two remarkably good fakes."

Buck started shouting. "What the fuck. Are you sure?" He

knew he didn't need to ask the question given his advisor's impeccable credentials but had to say something. He turned and strode off without another word, shaking his head. He stomped up the stairs to go to his office and make a call. On the way down the hall his assistant Elmore came bustling along waving a newspaper.

"Boss, boss, you gotta read this—"

"What is it?" Buck said, angrily cutting him off.

"The paper says you just donated 25 million to some environmental group called the Earth Goddess Foundation."

"You're shitting me. That's about what I just paid for some fake paintings. Those two bitches fucked me over. I'm calling my lawyer and going to tear them to shreds."

"Stan,' Elmore paused to take a mini breath while he was hyperventilating from fear of being the messenger who gets shot. "You can't make a scene. It was a cash deal. And because you didn't report it, the Swiss will accuse you of tax fraud which is illegal, compared to tax evasion which isn't." There was a pause as Buck looked at Elmore as the implications sank in. Breaking the reverie, there was a loud clanging of the doorbell reverberating through the house that signaled they had a visitor at the front door.

"Now what? I'm not scheduled to meet anyone am I?"

"Not that I know of."

"Goddam Jehovah's Witnesses trying to push Bibles and redemption."

Elmore headed to the front door and Buck followed, curious about who could be visiting. Opening the door, they saw Schmidt standing on the porch in a rumpled suit and ancient tie holding a document in one hand. He was flanked by two uniformed policemen with a couple of police cars angled on the drive. He spoke slowly and clearly in his best Cambridge English imitation. "Is there a Mister Stanley Buck in residence here who owns a black Porsche with license plate ZG 39043?"

Buck pushed Elmore aside. "What the hell is this about? Yes, I own a turbo fucking Carrera."

"It seems you have an unpaid parking ticket from last year and it's gone past the time limit for settlement. We sent it to America where they have worked with us to issue a warrant. I'm afraid you're under arrest."

Buck stared at Schmidt a second, too stunned to respond. He turned and started shouting over his shoulder, "Bridgitta." He was sure she had borrowed the car and gotten the ticket, tossing it in the trash as a minor annoyance in her busy life.

Before Buck could react further, one of the two policemen stepped forward saying, "You'll have to come with us," and took Buck's upper arm in a firm grip.

Forced to walk off with the two policemen, Buck managed to shout orders to his assistant to call his lawyers, the police chief and the ambassador. Then the back door of the second police car opened and John jumped out with a camera in one hand and immediately started taking pictures. He paused while quickly checking his screen to see if the images were framed correctly. He called out to Buck, "I remember you – I never forget a face!"

ACKNOWLEDGMENTS

I want to thank the many people who helped me bring this book to life. Your support has been invaluable.

The story took shape and was refined with the generous feedback from my prereaders,

Donnalane Nelson, Susanne Mueller Zantop, Mouna Blila and Kathy Miller. The super-agent and talented writer Paula Munier provided expert guidance to help fine-tune the first chapter. My long-time friend and 'agent', Philip Guerdat, generously gave me detailed feedback, and we spent a most enjoyable afternoon on his terrace in southern Spain, talking through the story for many hours. My good friend and bestselling writer Anna Kupka provided a lot of valuable feedback on the story and encouragement to the finish line.

A special thanks to JJ Marsh, another superstar writer, for her inspiration and guidance in story-telling, marketing, and navigating the publishing world (with the generous support of her husband, Florian).

My research was almost as much fun as writing the book. I'm most grateful for the insights into the workings of the Swiss banking universe from an insider — you know who you are! Besides all the people in the international business and art world who shared their wisdom, I also wanted to say a big thank you to the journalist Daniel Ammann. He's the author of *The King of Oil* about the fugitive billionaire Marc Rich, who spent most of his life safely in Switzerland, where tax evasion is not a crime. We had a most wonderful lunch meeting with some intriguing behind-the-scenes stories about the book's subject. Still waiting for the movie!

A big thank you to Enrica Rossi, the cover designer at E-Django Designs, who created a captivating cover that perfectly captured the essence of the story.

I had some expert help with the editing from Anne Gillion, development assistance from Debi Alper, and Helen Baggot proofreading and sharing useful feedback.

The book would not be what it is today without Joseph Olshan, a most talented novelist and editor at Harper Collins whose expert advice over a couple of years, line-by-line editing, and instructive conference calls transformed the first draft into a polished final version.

ABOUT THE AUTHOR

Chris Corbett was born in the UK and grew up in Northern California. After attending university, he moved to Los Angeles, where he worked for Playboy Magazine, Walt Disney, and on an Academy Award-winning film. For eight years, he ran a publishing business with a unique connection to music history – his business partner was a brother-in-law of one of The Beatles.

Now based in Switzerland, Corbett has worked as a corporate storyteller for CEOs at various global headquarters, crafting narratives that shape finance and pharmaceutical empires. This gift for storytelling runs deep in his blood—his grandfather not only penned bestsellers in London's literary heyday but was also the BBC's first Artistic Director.

In his debut novel "Nirvana Blues," Corbett reimagines literature's greatest love story against the backdrop of Silicon Valley's dawn, where ambition and innovation collide with matters of the heart. His latest venture, the "Double Trouble" series, introduces readers to an irresistible mother-daughter duo who prove that wit and charm can be the perfect weapons for justice. These women don't just solve problems – they do it with style.

www.chriscorbett.com

A SPECIAL GIFT

A special gift for you!
To receive exclusive behind-the-scenes news about real-life art crime, international intrigue, antics at jet-set playgrounds, and background details of the colorful people who inspire some of the characters, please sign up for Chris's monthly newsletter below.

A SNEAK PREVIEW OF

DANGEROUS DAUGHTERS

BY

**CHRIS
CORBETT**

Featuring the Double Trouble duo, Diana and Tanya

Available as an E-book from amazon.

DANGEROUS DAUGHTERS

The Metamorph Gallery had just closed for the day, and Tanya Beyer and her stepmother Diana were sitting outside at a small café table where Tanya could smoke. The inner courtyard of the building, circled by some other small creative enterprises, was still radiating a soft warmth from the afternoon sun that made them want to linger. Tanya's gallery was in Zürich's Kreis 4, gradually transforming from a red-light district to a gentrified quarter. Her casual look of an elegant white blouse and faded jeans matched the neighborhood dynamic. The two women were a contrast in styles. Diana, as befitting her privileged background, went the designer route of a light blue Chanel jacket and skirt with the traditional woven square pattern.

Tanya took a final puff, exhaling a plume of smoke overhead. Diana waved a hand in front of her face to avoid secondhand smoke, making an exaggerated, unhappy face. Tanya quickly stubbed out her cigarette and said, "Sorry," shrugging her shoulders at the guilty pleasure. After their polite small talk, it was time to get down to business. "Thanks again for stopping by on short notice. You want to hear something wild?"

"The wilder, the better." Diana leaned forward, not wanting to miss anything.

"The national art police in Italy contacted me, and I have no idea what it's about. They sent me a totally random email, inviting me to join a Zoom call in half an hour."

"Is this related to the bogus Basquiats you sold last year?" Diana was immediately on alert as she had also been part of the scheme to bring a criminal to justice.

"The mail didn't say anything about them. I'm hoping those paintings are history." Tanya sounded mildly worried but not enough to dwell on the possible issue.

"You should've told them you can only do a face-to-face and got a free ticket to Rome."

"I like it," Tanya said, laughing. "But seriously, this is an Italian policeman asking for help with an art crime. If you know what I mean."

They paused and looked each other in the eye. "Did you say Mafia?" Diana asked, breaking the momentary silence. The unspoken was now articulated, with a feeling of dread similar to seeing a shark's fin at the beach where people were swimming. "So, you need some moral support?" Diana said, more of a statement than a question. She sat up straight, put on her *power-frau* face, and understood the seriousness.

"Absolutely." Tanya sighed in relief and explained that the Italian police had requested the meeting because the two of them had helped bring an international fugitive to justice. They'd tricked him in an art deal, as the paintings Tanya represented were irresistible bait for the fugitive billionaire collector. Diana's connections from her jet-set society background had made the trap complete. Getting the man to unwittingly donate many millions to Diana's environmental foundation from his buying two fake Basquiats was a bonus. While the forgeries were kept out of the press, the police knew about them, and Tanya was nervous that she might be in trouble.

Thirty minutes later, Tanya sat motionless behind a glass-topped chrome desk in her office at the back of the gallery. She was transfixed by an Adonis that had popped up in a Zoom window on her computer. Diana was sitting next to her, watching the young man from Rome with dark curly hair and intense mesmerizing eyes atop a 30-year-old rugged body, visible through his immaculate white shirt. The label underneath the image said his name was Piero Missoni. Tanya expected the policeman to be an ancient pencil pusher with a double chin and receding hairline or an Italian version of Inspector Clouseau. Now, she wished she'd spent more time on her make-up and done something to her hair, which was pulled back into a rough braid.

"*Buongiorno*. My name is Piero. I'm with the *Carabinieri del Nucleo Tutela Patrimonio Culturale*. The Division for the Protection of Cultural Heritage." Both women were momentarily speechless looking at the young God, enchanted by his charming accent. Tanya found her voice first.

"Hi, I'm Tanya, and this is my stepmother, Diana," Tanya said, briefly turning towards Diana. "I asked her to join us because she has a broad knowledge of art. And as you know, we're also partners in different projects."

"*Perfecto*." Tanya nodded an okay for Piero to continue. "Our squad was established in 1969 due to the theft of a famous painting. We're the largest art crime team in the world, with over 300 agents. Our job is important because thousands of artworks are reported stolen each year, just in Italy. I am new to this organization and head a team looking at open, unsolved crimes. What you call cold cases." The women stared, hanging on every word as Piero gestured to emphasize his speech. "I'm sure you're wondering how I found you." Obvious question, Tanya thought. "I am part of a European-wide group of police involved in stolen antiquities and art, including representatives from Switzerland. One of the Swiss members suggested your name as someone with many connections in the Zürich art world. Also, you two were extremely helpful once already to the police. Your bringing a big criminal to justice with some paintings is a legend."

"I'm not so sure we're exactly legendary," Diana said with a crooked grin.

"Don't worry, your secret is safe with me." Piero gave a disarming smile and a wink. "Only the brotherhood of cops knows the true story."

"I'd feel a whole lot safer if the police didn't have such big mouths," Diana said as a joke, but behind it was a legitimate concern.

"That is anyway now an ancient story – dead and buried. I have another reason I wanted to talk with you. It's a much older situation, but still very much alive. As an art expert, I'm sure you've heard of Caravaggio's *Nativity with Saint Francis and Saint Lawrence,* stolen over 50 years ago."

Tanya said, "Yes, I remember seeing it in the news. A new claim is made about its latest whereabouts every couple of years."

Tanya looked at Diana, who nodded and said, "I know about it. It's still missing."

"Good. I can be brief. As you know, the painting was stolen out of a small church in Palermo long before the art business became so lucrative. It ended up in the hands of the *Cicero,* Palermo's number one crime boss. He was eventually put in jail for his role in the 'Pizza Connection' where tons of heroin were shipped to America. He died in a US prison about twenty years ago. Before he was captured, he wanted to sell the painting and contacted an art dealer in Zürich who flew to Sicily. The dealer was already quite old when he bought it and has since passed away. And that's the last known status. Of course, as all this information came from a *pentito,* it could be fiction. These informers often tell us a story to get consideration for a lighter jail sentence." He looked into the screen to ensure they were following his heavily accented English. Seeing their rapt faces, he gave a dazzling smile and continued. "This painting is still on the FBI Top Ten Art Crimes list and is an embarrassment for our law enforcement efforts to be lost for so long."

"Thanks for the background. You think we can help somehow just because we live in Zürich?" Tanya said.

"We need all the help we can get. Your local police are not very interested in the matter. And I'm sure you appreciate that this is an Italian national treasure."

"I totally respect the provenance of this painting and wish nothing more than for it to be restored to its rightful owners," Tanya said hesitantly, leaning back from the screen.

"But?"

"You said the 'M' word. I'm not comfortable risking my personal well-being to find a lost painting associated with the Mafia." She shrugged her shoulders, imitating Piero's gestures, and made a sorry face.

"I am only looking for information." He translated his request into Italian by lifting his hands in an open motion. "No action will be required on your part. You will be in no danger. Only my assistant and I will know you are helping."

"The problem is the Mafia are everywhere," Tanya said, defending her reluctance to help.

"It is the world we live in. The mafia is both legal and illegal." The words legal and illegal came out as an accented rhyme.

"I'm really not so sure I can help." Tanya shook her head

apologetically. "Sorry, but I'll need time to think about it." She raised an empty hand, giving him back a little of the same body language. "I'll send you an email when I decide what to do. Please don't get your hopes up." She had wished to be able to make more of a connection but knew anything to do with the Mafia carried a risk.

"Just your giving consideration to my invite for a talk is good news." He flashed his alluring smile, and his eyes crinkled with an engaging effect.

"I'll talk it over with Tanya because we're a team. She'll give you our answer," Diana said, playing mediator. Subconsciously primping her already immaculate hair, she gave a promising look.

"You two ladies have been most kind to spare some of your precious time. I will look forward to your response." The last word was drawn out casually to show there was no pressure.

"And thank you for thinking of me. I'm honored that you asked for my help," Tanya said.

"Totally my pleasure."

The lazy Italian accent was killing Tanya. "Your work is so important, especially these days with so much art crime. I hope we can help somehow, someday." She didn't know what else to say to prolong the call and hoped for future contact.

"Me too. Thanks again." He raised his hand in a goodbye gesture and said '*arrivederci*' before his window went blank, with only the gray icon of a head and shoulders representing his profile picture positioned next to theirs. Tanya closed the Zoom program and let out a big exhale. She pushed on her desk and rolled her chair backward, rotating it to face Diana.

"What do you think?" Tanya said. She rested her elbows on the arms of the chair, with her chin on her folded hands.

"What a hunk," Diana said with a naughty grin.

"Come on. Don't always be such a flirt." It was Diana's turn to shrug her shoulders.

"On one hand, it could be a noble pursuit. He makes it sound harmless. But we're talking about the Mafia," Diana said. She turned to face Tanya fully and gave her a serious look.

"Right? They're scary people. I'm thinking about you and me. If we make inquiries and the Mafia hears about it, we could get into trouble." Her voice had a worried tone.

"I'm not so sure about that. If the informer wasn't lying, the Mafia chief got rid of the painting years ago. There would be no reason for them to want it back. We're talking about a fifty-year-old event. Gangsters are more interested in NFTs these days. A portable way to store their cash by using digital art," Diana said.

"And what if the Swiss dealer story is fake? We're sticking our necks out and stirring up a wasp nest for nothing."

"Like I said, this is an old story, so there's no risk for us. This cop is only trying to close out a case because his team is ashamed it's been unsolved for so long. And think about your reputation. Even though the Basquiats were mostly kept out of the press, there were a lot of not-so-pleasant rumors circulating in the art world. And in this business, one's name is everything."

"I know." Tanya agreed, and her resistance slowly started to melt. "And we both know that Switzerland is like a small town, full of gossip. Negative talk could impact new clients wanting me to represent their collections. They would go somewhere else if they had any doubts about my integrity. The flow of work coming my way has already started to slow down since the Big Bang with the Basquiat's."

"You'll be ok because this country is very forgiving if you show good intent. What could be better for your reputation than helping the Italian art police find a lost treasure?"

"Would also help put me on track for the big league," Tanya said, pondering the possibility.

"And come on – maybe we can unravel the mystery. Could use a challenge in these boring times." They both laughed.

Tanya paused and looked out the window briefly, weighing the options. She turned back to Diana and said, "Okay, I give up. I'll send a message to Piero that we're on board and to email us any details. Then we can start investigating."

"Great. And I hope we can have another Zoom call with that gorgeous man."

"I do too, but don't forget you're a married woman."

"No worries, I haven't forgotten." Diana laughed, "But maybe something for you?" She stood up to leave and started towards the door.

"Long-distance romances aren't realistic. Look at me and John. A flight to Miami is only six hours long, but it might as well be on another planet."

"Have some fun. Italians know how to enjoy life. And Rome is only a two-hour flight." Diana went out the door, tossing a "*Ciao*" over her shoulder.

Tanya sent a short email to Piero confirming her support for his inquiry, and he replied with a '*Grazie mille.*' His response included the name of the Swiss dealer and some dates, plus the technical details of the painting, with a '*buona fortuna*' at the end. Tanya did a quick online search and found the dealer, Thomas Hildebrand, who once owned a small gallery in the Neumunster area of Zürich's old town. There were a lot of small galleries dotted around the same quarter, some new, some old. The gallery had closed after his death, and now it was a showroom for a local designer of women's clothes. Hildebrand had no children, and his wife had passed away about ten years earlier. His private collection had been listed in his will and was gifted to the Zürich Kunsthaus. She would ask Diana to go to the museum and talk to an administrator she knew there. They were always chasing Diana to show her family's collection, so the women had some leverage. The search was on.

To read the rest of the story, click below to order a copy.

www.ingramcontent.com/pod-product-compliance
Lightning Source LLC
LaVergne TN
LVHW032008070526
838202LV00059B/6343